The Mundane Work of Vengeance

Clayton Lindemuth

Hardgrave Enterprises
SAINT CHARLES, MISSOURI

THE MUNDANE WORK OF VENGEANCE

Baer Creighton 2

CLAYTON LINDEMUTH
HARDGRAVE ENTERPRISES
SAINT CHARLES, MISSOURI

FOR JULIE.

Rights is bullshit. You got no right in the natural world.

Just what you defend.

—*Baer Creighton*

Chapter 1

Put all that nonsense behind me. There's two buckets of gold in the bed of the truck. I'm heading to see Mae and give her one. Thought occurs I could strike a deer, roll the truck, and all that gold would spread over the macadam road. Folks would stop at the smoking wreck, look past my face shredded in glass, and fix on the glitter.

"Me lying dead in the cab, I'd miss all the red. Wouldn't that be sorry?"

Stinky Joe looks at me.

"Use your words," I say.

Thought you wasn't going to call me Stinky.

"Well, puppydog need a bath."

Joe sniffs. Licks his jowl, and that reminds him his nuts need it too.

"You and me need cheddar cheese and cabbage. That's the truth."

I drive and a thought floats like a mile-high bird—slow and easy, you can't tell it's moving. Haven't yet committed. Mae doesn't know about the gold, and the odds of her finding a worthwhile man are the same as me finding a woman. And speak of the devil, by now Ruth's halfway back to Mars Hill.

Suppose I knocked on her door. She'd open it, sure. She'd pull me inside and we'll be fornicating in no time. After twenty-eight years in one sleeping bag or another, snuggled next to a dog crate, I'd relish a woman's round rump.

After all these years, Ruth finally gave me the invitation. I get chubby at the thought of swinging by Mars Hill for about six minutes. Then venturing west.

But I'm not a man for entanglements.

Spot glowing eyes, roadside; belong to a rabbit most likely.

In no time, I rap Mae's door. Stinky Joe sleeps in the truck cab. Just be a short visit. The lights are off and Gleason is silent, save a way-off dog or two. I start soft on the door but after a minute get to beating it. Standing in the dark I wonder if after all that's gone on, maybe I'd best wait for daylight. Mae doesn't yet know about Cory or Larry. Doesn't know the man she called Daddy all these years is dead as disco, and he wasn't but her uncle anyway. Soon as I back to the edge of the rotted porch the light blinks on and a curtain moves.

Mae opens the door and her eyes are sleepy slits.

"Got news," I say.

She pushes open the screen with her naked toe and shiny leg. Shifts sideways to clear the path and I see silver in her hand.

"What's that?"

"What?"

"I'm proud. Let me see." I take the revolver. She gives it up too easy. Got to tell her about that. It's a forty-five. Rare. "You know what to do with this?"

"Point. Shoot. What brings you out? I'm in bed."

"Touch more to it than that." I spin the cylinder and slap it. "Fits the hand real nice. You shoot anybody yet?"

"What time is it?" She scoots over as I walk in. Closes the door.

"Why you get a gun?"

"Didn't you want me to? I heard on the news about that girl. They say a cop took her."

"What girl?"

"That sixteen-year-old. I saw it on the news but I guess it happened almost a week ago. She disappeared. Abducted."

"Yeah. Heard about that. Well, I won't be the one to save her."

Silence.

"I'm sleeping. I'm happy to see you but, why you here, Uncle Baer?"

"Corey's dead. I rigged a trap with some barbed wire and he bled out his crotch. Larry's dead too—though I didn't shoot him like I wanted. The wood alcohol got him, even after I said not to drink it. But it was my honest fault—Oh, and he was your uncle, not your daddy. And I got a couple hundred thousand dollars in gold I'm going to give you. Maybe a million. I don't know. We'll talk about it. They're Canadian Maple Leafs, and other coins too. Then I'm heading west."

Mae stares at the ceiling. Blinks. Looks like a cat eating a turd off a wire brush.

"Oh. And I'm your father. Did I say that? I was with Ruth first and when I kicked your daddy—uncle—Larry in the nuts when we was kids, I made him a mule. Sterile. That's why he was such a prick his whole life."

Mae slumps to the sofa that eats people. Slides over the armrest and sprawls back with her legs a little indecent with the pink undies.

"So anyhow I come to give you the good news and some advice. When you want to hear it."

Mae grabs the edge of her t-shirt nightgown and pushes it down. Looks hard left and then hard right and won't bring her eyes to me. She shakes, and her cheeks pull back like she's fish-hooked out each side of her mouth. She shudders and bawls. Now I've done it again—you'd think a person would want the facts with no varnish, but no, not a woman.

She folds her arms and legs up small and tight and curls her shoulders. Her face gets shiny with tears, and fast as the storm comes it goes, and she wipes her cheeks.

"Is Ruth dead too?"

"No. I talked to her a little bit ago."

"Oh."

"Yeah. She was good and all."

"You said west?"

Chapter 2

Josiah Swain was born to Norman Swain. His uncle Ernest raised him. Josiah murdered Ernest with an M100 firecracker.

He used a firecracker for his next two targets, then other methods.

The quirky inevitability of Josiah's life began with his grandfather.

Sanford McSwain was born and raised in Jamestown, New York. He returned from a stint in the Army reconstructing Germany in 1947. He stood guard over George S Patton III at the hospital where he died. Post-war Germany ignited his youthful brio.

While he was away, Jamestown became more conservative. Sanford became more lawless.

After a night of drinking, he drove a friend's father's Ford Deluxe Coupe through a sewing parlor window. The next day, sensing his hometown's unwelcome, Sanford sought his fortunes westward.

The farther he traveled, the less welcome he found, which he attributed to his Scots-Irish name. He dropped the Mc, stopped drinking and started going to Sunday Mass at the nearest parish. He even broke bread with Episcopalians if no Catholic church was handy. He landed in Buena Vista, Tennessee, the town with the heaviest Italian population in the state.

Choosing this town was like dropping a fair-sized boulder a couple feet from the edge of a placid pond. The ripples rolled outward. The final ramification would hit the opposite bank in 2008, with his thirty-eight-year-old grandson staring at two buckets of gold.

Sanford Swain answered a newspaper ad and found a job as an auto insurance claims adjuster. He met his future bride—the victim of a nasty T-bone car accident—on his second day on the job. Hilda rode in a Chevrolet Series DJ Stylemaster driven by her father, an insured of Sanford's employer. Sanford interviewed her as part of his investigation.

He visited her in her hospital room only hours after she roused from a short duration coma. A metal frame suspended both of her plaster-casted legs, and Sanford fell immediately in love.

Sanford concluded his interview. He returned three hours later with a bouquet of black eyed Susans and daises. He dated Hilda while she recovered in the hospital. They married in June, and she gave birth to Ernest eight months later, during January 1948.

Within months of delivering firstborn Ernest, Hilda conceived Josiah's father Norman. She gave birth in January 1949.

Ernest and Norman were best friend brothers, each ever at the other's defense. Their freckles, fair skin and hair stood out. They often brawled with the Buffa, Antonuccio, and Romano brothers.

One day the Swain brothers walked home from school. Tony Romano and his brothers Dominic and Gio jumped from behind a parked car, ready for battle. Each stretched a pair of fat rubber bands between thumb and index finger. They used a wad of folded cardboard covered in a narrow strip of tin. They always aimed for the face. The tin doubled the weight of the projectile and, unlike cardboard alone, left a nasty cut and bruise. The boys liked to say it increased the projectile's knockdown power.

The Romanos released the missiles then rushed. The Swain brothers drove them back with Scots-Irish glee, using surgical strikes from fists and feet. Although outnumbered, Gio Romano was a runt. His brothers permitted him to rabble-rouse with them only due to his accurate rubber band. After the initial assault, Gio was useless.

The Romanos retreated before the fury of the Swain defense.

Ernest and Norman picked up their books and returned to their walk home. Ernest noticed Norman's eye was bleeding. The tin-covered projectile had punctured the orb.

Norman hadn't noticed. He'd thought he was crying in rage, and although he wasn't, he was too ashamed to mention the pain in his eye.

After a few days, his eye had not improved. Sanford took his son to the doctor. Norman lost sight in his right eye—which prevented him from going to Vietnam.

The United States Government drafted Ernest in 1967. Although he considered burning his card and listening to the Doors instead, he wanted the GI Bill.

Ernest thought a lot about money.

Ernest served a relatively safe tour in Vietnam as a member of the REMFs (rear echelon mother ****ers). He also learned something interesting about himself. He strangled a prostitute and afterward, looking at her, felt nothing. This surprised him. He left unseen, rotated stateside the next day, and was never connected to the murdered woman.

After Ernest returned to the United States, he and Norman took a drinking holiday. They wound up in Benton, Tennessee, which would host the famous fireworks disaster on May 27, 1983. The disaster did not take Ernest's life. But it did figure in his death.

That was many cheerful years to come.

First, at the county fair Ernest met a pretty girl, Emma Nelson. He married her that week. It was 1970 and Ernest was twenty-four.

Unlike his father's instant attraction to his mother's raised legs, for Ernest, it wasn't love at first sight. Instead, Emma said her father was owner of the Polk-Benton Savings and Loan.

If you want money, Ernest thought, you need to work at a money factory.

Chapter 3

Sophia Ellen Whitcombe was sixteen. At the age of twelve she'd realized her body was developing faster than her peers at school. Her period had started at nine, long before her mother got around to warning her. If not for the helpful folks on the internet, she would have thought she was about to die.

Her bust swelled at twelve and grew plump by fifteen. Her hips remained small, but they rounded where they were supposed to. In five years Sophia metamorphosed from a spindle-legged frog into certified jailbait.

Named for Sophia Loren, her look was closer to Raquel Welsh.

Men no longer got their fill by turning their heads. They stopped and rotated their whole bodies. Forgot themselves. Sophia could count the men who walked into lamp posts, trees, walls. Her mother said it would only get worse.

The attention made her self-conscious and shy. She sensed jealousy in some of her friends. She was more developed. They seemed to assume that jocks flirting with her meant she was giving them what they wanted. The prettier and womanlier she became, the fewer were her friends.

Sophia was close to a couple of girls in marching band. Twin sisters who played the clarinet and saxophone. Sophia played the xylophone because her real interest was piano. She remained in band because of her friends and because she liked how the uniform blunted her curves. In the classes they shared, the girls sat together. At sixteen, the twins' only curves were their knees and elbows, but they didn't envy Sophia. All three were shy about their bodies.

During her sophomore year, Sophia dated a senior. When he became possessive, she ended the relationship. She accepted a movie date invitation from a guy who had graduated the year before. He came home from college on weekends. That was better.

She understood he had other girlfriends at college. Her parents knew his parents from work at the hospital. They trusted him despite his age. It was simple and good. The college guy was more relaxed than high school boys. Seeing him only on the weekends helped keep the relationship cool.

The last thing Sophia wanted was to get tangled up with a serious boyfriend.

Her parents were both medical doctors. From the time she could talk, they helped her understand her destiny.

Perfect grades. Scholarships to Ivy League schools—preferably Yale, like mom—and then med school. Sophia could choose any medical specialty she liked.

Things were going well for Sophia.

Her father, a former Navy SEAL, tried to instill self-reliance in her. Between the ages six and fourteen, he taught her wilderness survival. How to escape an active shooter situation. General self defense. His lessons were the coolest thing in her world.

At fifteen, Sophia's adoration for her father remained perfect. But her focus on academics overshadowed her interest in survival.

Chapter 4

"No. You aren't going west." I drop into the sofa too close to the middle. Try to scooch to the other edge but it's like sitting in pudding. Once you drop there's no sideways going on. Either stand up and try again or stay put. I work to my feet and plant myself farther from Mae.

Car headlamps flash against the window; someone makes the turn at the edge of the block.

Mae punches my shoulder. "What do you mean, no? You come here and drop all that on me and think you're going to run away?"

"Mae, I can't hardly get my mind around it. You don't know but part of what's gone on."

"West is a long way. You'll have time to tell me."

"What do you want that's out west?"

"You. Dumbass." She sucks in her sniffles and jumps from the couch. In the kitchen, she spits snot in the sink. Swigs root beer from a two liter in the fridge. Clears her throat.

Outside, Stinky Joe lets out a short, clipped woof.

I wrestle the couch. On my feet, I stoop low as old bones allow. Scoot to the kitchen. "There's someone outside. Probably looking for me."

There's dead people everywhere… in the trees by now.

Boots on the steps. Two sets. The porch. Rapping at the door.

I got Mae's forty-five in one hand and put Smith in the other.

Mae's eyes bug wide.

Beating on the door.

Two hours ago I stood in the wood, death all around. Saw the dreamland men strung up in trees, flopping on the ground, spitting and gasping. Blind and going dead. I wanted free of it forever. Wanted to disappear from all mankind's lying and treacherous ways. But the two archangels from the FBI had second thoughts.

"Mae, I've done enough killing for one day and maybe two. So if you can get them to clear out with just your words that'd be fine as water."

Mae blinks herself coherent. Nods. I lean against the wall, rest my skull back comfortable. Got a broke down hutch to my right, and beyond, the kitchen entrance. I don't get seen unless they come inside the kitchen. That happens, I got the drop.

"Who's there?" Mae says, door still closed.

"Open the door. FBI."

"How do I know?"

"We have our ID's out."

"I can't see them."

"Open the door."

"Yeah, *right.*"

Mae flips on the porch light and in the kitchen stands at an angle to the window. She pads back to the door. The handle clicks and the hinges croak.

"Let me see. Put your identification badges up close. And I got a gun pointed at you through the door."

Quick bootsteps on the porch.

"Miss, we're with the Federal Bureau of Investigation. The truck in your driveway belongs to a homicide suspect. He's armed and dangerous. Let us in."

"No."

"Ma'am, we have probable cause to enter the house."

"No you don't. Just because some asshole parks his truck out there doesn't mean you can come in here. 'Sides. That's Baer's truck. He's in town drinking."

That's right Mae, come clean. They'll bite.

"Ever since Joe Stipe burned his house and still, Baer drinks in town. He's down at the Town Pump, most likely."

"Still, we'd like to check the house."

"Fact is, he's about worthless and you ought to haul him in. You know that old pervert tried to kiss me? My own uncle. Lock him up, is what I say. I got babies around."

"Ma'am, step aside."

"Didn't you hear me? I got babies upstairs. And you need a warrant."

"Ma'am, the suspect's truck is in your driveway. That satisfies for exigent circumstances. Let us in. We do a quick sweep, and we're on our way to the Town Pump."

"No." The door clicks.

I could slip out the back. But the bigger problem is the truck in the driveway and two buckets of gold they'll see as soon as they look. They'll grab my life's work, truck, and dog, and I'll be sneaking into McDonalds dumpsters for food.

No I wouldn't, but it's the principle.

Got to meet these two head on. I don't want to. But the problem with killing one guy is he ends up being two, and sooner or later twenty. Then the lawmen they send after. It never ends. I don't want these men's souls on my conscience. Near as I can tell, they aren't pure evil like the others. But it's looking like I die, they die, or I go to jail, and out of three choices, only one preserves me, my dog and my truck.

Fact is, they could have this place swimming in red and blues in ten minutes, if they call the Gleason police. My choices slip from slim to none at that point.

Mae returns to the kitchen window. She whispers, "They're talking to themselves. What do I do?"

"I'm going to slip to the basement and unscrew the bulb. You open the door before they bust in. Then get them down to the Town Pump."

Walking easy on the sides of my feet, rolling slow, I make it to the downstairs door at the stairwell. Reach to the switch but think better. There's a twelve-inch window, top of the foundation. I descend the steps in the dark. Feel along next to the stone foundation where the steps are less likely to creak. At the cement floor, I probe out one toe at a time, arms waving, blind, trying to recollect what Mae's got piled in my way.

Footsteps above. Shoes with heels. Voices.

I reach up, find the joists, follow to the center I-beam, then toward the basement middle. I keep one leg out, probing, and one arm above my head until I find the bulb. Twist until it's about to fall, then wait. Pull Smith and rest my thumb on the hammer, sort of stroke it while my mind wanders on about Ruth and Mae.

And all those bodies in the dream, hanging from trees. Could be right and good that these FBI boys haul me in. Bring me to account.

Should I give myself up? Has my whole life been upside down, and it's me the crazy one? All the world's lying and stealing from one another is the way things are supposed to be?

I can't get my brain around the thought these people's rules have anything to do with me.

Nah. I'm not going to rot in a jail. Not so these liars and thieves can pretend to other liars and thieves they're all good and righteous. I don't enjoy shooting a deer or even throttling a chicken, unless I'm hungry. But I do it to eat, when I got to. These people think they have the right to bluster because they gave themselves badges?

Righteous man has no friends and needs fewer.

I'll kill what needs killed.

Worked up for whatever comes, I reach, find the bulb. Twist it back in.

FBI ventures down here, I'll take out their legs, then heads as they fall.

Boards groan above. One lawman's in the kitchen and the other's at the stairwell to the kids' rooms upstairs. Basement door swings open and a shaft of light gives the lay. I glide five steps to cover behind the oil tank. But Smith is in my right hand, against the wall with the oil tank in front. I'm not worth anything shooting lefty. Would've been better in the middle of the basement, with some flexibility. But I'm here, so I wait.

One step. His leg rests, like he put it out to prompt a bullet. Then the light flashes on and he's descended six steps. Has his gun arm level and pistol ready to preach. He swings his arm back and forth. Whatever he sees already has a bead on it, but the basement light is a yellow forty-watter and his eyes squint.

I could ease Smith over the oil tank and drop him if I wanted.

My nuts roll over and my stomach cinches. I don't breathe while he looks left and right. His partner calls from somewhere above.

He lowers his arm and climbs the stairs.

Chapter 5

Josiah Swain was ten when his parents died in a car accident in 1980.

Before they died, Josiah had a nightmare... or a daymare, since he hadn't been asleep. He knew his parents would die. Not in an abstract, someday sense, but a literal, near sense. Their fates were cast. His knowledge was certain. The darkness of the thought corrupted anything that entered his awareness. Everywhere he looked, he felt his parents' death.

Shortly after, as he walked to school, Josiah experienced a compulsion. A remedy to the certainty of his parent's impending doom.

IF YOU TOUCH THIS SIGN, YOUR PARENTS WILL LIVE.

Even at ten years of age, Josiah knew his mind lied; the world didn't work that way. He'd heard about people who moved objects with their thoughts. They showed it on horror movies he saw when he snuck downstairs after midnight.

He'd tried to move objects with his mind, and it didn't work.

IF YOU TOUCH THIS SIGN, YOUR PARENTS WILL LIVE.

Josiah stared at the yield sign he passed every day walking to and from school. He hadn't realized he had passed the intersection and walked another thirty feet, before turning back to the sign. As if whatever mysterious force informed on his parents' demise also guided his steps. Twisted him, lifted his head and whispered the words into his thoughts.

Josiah stepped toward the sign and stretched out his arm. He unfurled his finger.

But he didn't close the final inch.

"It doesn't make sense."

Josiah put down his arm.

Grounded by his failed experiments with telekinesis, Josiah possessed an instinctive self-awareness. He rejected the metaphysical power of his thoughts. He couldn't have articulated the concept. But he sensed thoughts cause people to do things, but they do not cause things to do things. His parents both dying—it was a vagrant thought, searching for an agent with the power to shift stones. He could reject it.

That afternoon, returning from school, Josiah saw the sign a quarter mile away. He remembered his parents would die if he didn't touch it. He walked past. Didn't look up to read it, didn't heed its warning.

The next day…

IF YOU TOUCH THIS SIGN, YOUR PARENTS WILL LIVE.

He continued to school.

On the walk home, Josiah was less certain. The idea was persistent. Several times during school, he'd revisited the connection between his failing to touch the sign and his parents dying. One of his teachers reprimanded for daydreaming. When he saw the sign a long way off, his steps slowed. He considered crossing the road.

Arriving at the sign, he stopped and stared up at it.

YEILD.

His mother had said it was a complicated way of saying STOP. More like, STOP AND LET OTHER PEOPLE GO FIRST.

The sign demanded politeness.

"Want a ride the rest of the way, son?"

Josiah spun, startled. His father had pulled to the side of the road.

"Sure!"

Josiah opened the back door.

"No, up front. Your mother's not here. Sit next to me."

"Whoa. Cool."

Josiah sat with his bookbag on his lap. It was only another quarter mile home, but it was with Dad.

"How come you're early?"

"I had an appointment near the house. I've made my quota of sales for the week, so I'm coming home to surprise your mother."

"Surprise her with what?"

"With me! We're going on a date tonight. Sally will be over to look after you and your cousin Mary."

"Mary?"

"We're going out with Uncle Ernest and Aunt Emma. Going to see a movie."

"Which movie?"

"It's called *Any Which Way You Can*."

"Why don't you take us?"

"Because you're too young."

"Why don't they make it so young people can see it?"

"Because young people don't have any money."

"Why can't young people—"

"Josiah."

"What?"

"Why were you staring at the sign when I pulled up? You didn't even hear me. That's dangerous."

"I didn't mean to be dangerous."

"Why were you staring up at the sign?"

"Because the sign told me I had to touch it."

"What?"

Josiah hesitated. "I thought if I didn't touch the sign, you and Mom would die."

"Oh, I see." Dad pulled into the driveway. Turned off the engine and pulled the parking break out of habit—to keep it exercised, he once said. "What gave you that idea?"

"I don't know. I thought it."

"Is this the first time you've had this thought?"

"No."

"When did you first have it?"

"Yesterday."

"Did you touch the sign?"

"No. I was going to but I didn't. It didn't make any sense. But I kept thinking about it all day."

"Did you touch the sign today?"

"No."

"Josiah."

"No. I didn't."

"And your mother and I are okay, right?"

"Uh-huh."

"Does that teach you anything about those kinds of thoughts?"

"Uh-huh."

"That's right. Next time something doesn't make sense, but you think someone might be in danger, tell me about it, okay?"

"Okay."

"But don't worry about your mother and me. We're not going to die. Not anytime soon."

Later, after supper and before his mother and father left for their date, Josiah's father sat beside him on the sofa. He lifted the Zenith's remote and muted Happy Days.

"Son, I want to have a talk with you. A serious talk."

"Okay."

"Stop looking at the television."

Josiah looked at his father.

"Nothing is going to happen to your mother and me."

"I know."

"But if something did happen to us, I want you to know that you'll be okay. Do you know what I do for a living? Where I go to work all day?"

"Your new job?"

"That's right."

"You sell stuff."

"I sell life insurance."

"Uh-huh."

"Do you know what that is?"

Josiah shook his head, no.

"Life insurance is money. If someone dies and they own life insurance, the life insurance pays money."

"Who gets the money?"

"The people who depend on the person who died. So if I died, your mother would get a lot of money. A lot of money, and she'd be able to take care of herself and you, just like I was still here."

"How much money?"

"Five hundred thousand dollars."

"Whoa."

"That's right. It sounds like a huge amount. But it would have to last the rest of her life, so she could take care of you."

"But what if you both die?"

"Well, in that case, the money would go to Uncle Ernest, and you'd go live with him."

"I don't like Uncle Ernest."

"Well, you don't know him like I do. At any rate, I wanted you to know everything would be okay. That's all. Nothing more to think about."

"Okay."

His father handed him the remote and Josiah restored sound to Arthur Fonzarelli.

That night, driving home after the movie, Josiah's father and mother died. A man swerved his F-150 truck into the oncoming lane. Josiah's mother and father smashed through the windshield. Neither were alive when first responders arrived.

Most people who suffer odd compulsions never have them verified by future events. The compulsions must adapt to reality.

For Josiah, the opposite occurred. His parents died, confirming the compulsion. The episode ended there. He had no special clairvoyance. The premonition didn't transform into another premonition about the next to die. After moving in with Ernest and Emma, he no longer walked by the sign. In the tumult of his changing life, he was never at a loss of other things to think about.

By uncanny coincidence, Ernest Swain was not surprised by his brother's death.

He'd spoken to his brother days before the accident. "You know, I've read those rice burners—yours in particular—have horrible safety ratings. Especially for head-on crashes. There's no metal there."

"Too bad they wrote the article after I bought the car."

"So you won't be getting rid of it?"

"How can I? Oh, by the way. I wanted to talk to you about life insurance."

"Not in the budget."

"No, that's not what I meant. I was talking about mine."

"Yeah?"

"I made you my contingent beneficiary. In case something happens to me and Sue. I should have asked you first."

"No, no. I'm happy taking your money."

Norman laughed. "Sure. What I meant was the money's to take care of Josiah. If anything happens to both of us, Sue and I want you to take Josiah and raise him right, you know? Would you do that?"

"Yeah, of course, brother. Of course. As if he was my own son. Heck of a kid."

"It's only until he's eighteen. After that, I'll change the beneficiary to him. You know."

"Yeah, sure." Ernest was thoughtful. "You don't mind me asking, how much is the policy? I mean, you got me thinking about how much life insurance I have, and I—"

"A half million."

"Holy—uh, wow."

"Well, you have to think about how much income your family will miss if you aren't there to make it."

The conversation devolved into the mechanics of life insurance.

After Norman and Sue died, Ernest stepped up. Josiah moved into the spare room and made it his own.

Chapter 6

Mae's at the window. I'm hunkered at the stairwell, with the bottom of the door cracked open an inch.

"They gone?"

"One of them left. The other's in a car next to your truck. He's waiting to see if you come back for it."

Time for a jailbreak.

I drop back, turn on the basement light. Take the steps sidey-footed. Downstairs, fetch a fifty-foot extension cord I saw when the archangel flipped on the light.

Back upstairs.

"Mae, we got but one shot to make a break for it. Right now, while his partner's away. I want you to go out there—hold on." I grab a mug, fill it to the rim with water, and sit it on a saucer. "Carry this to him. Once you get to the window, play a little coy."

"What'll he want with a mug of water?"

"He'll think it's coffee. I want you to walk like you got to balance it. He won't know whether to watch the saucer wiggle or what's behind it."

She looks at the extension cord. "What are you going to do with that?"

"Whatever needs done."

I slip out the back door, ease around the left side of the house where the shadows are darker than the rest of the night.

I wait at the front corner. Mae pushes rear-first out the door, t-shirt long enough to cover the top of her backside but not the bottom. She walks slow and balanced, careful the water doesn't spill, and the archangel studies her close. His frown levels off as she descends the steps. God made a woman's jiggles for man—I can see him think it.

I set out perpendicular from the house. Find cover in a line of trees off the side lawn. I stoop and scoot. Stop thirty feet from the rear of the car, straight behind. Got the orange fifty-foot extension cord coiled in hand.

"I was rude to you," Mae says. She reaches to put the mug and saucer on the car roof. Pulls her t-shirt to the Union and leaves the Confederacy undefended. She puts her face in the window. "I thought you might want something to help you stay awake."

I stand straight. Lean backward until vertebra crack, then do my best glide to the right side of the archangel's car. See his profile through the rear window, head pointed square at Mae's mams.

I rap Smith on the side glass. "Hands on the wheel, Mister FBI."

"Better do it," Mae says.

"Step aside, Mae, so I can shoot him when I want."

"Ho-hold on now," the archangel says. "No need for that. Let's think about this a little."

"You going to do something stupid?"

He places his hands on the steering wheel. "No. I'm not."

His eyes are dark in the shadows, no red. And no juice on my arms. "I know. I'll also know when you change your mind. Then I'll shoot you. Get out of the vehicle. Hands up."

He places one hand on the door latch. The dome light goes on. He steps out.

"Turn around. Face me."

He does.

"Hands on the roof. Keep them there."

I level Smith at his head. "Mae, stand back toward the house ten feet so I can shoot his head and not get you wet."

Barrel pointed for his noggin, I shift around the hood, then on the same side of the car. "Now get on your knees."

"Please, mister. I got a wife—"

"Hands high. Get on your knees. Going to tie you, is all."

He drops.

"Mae, come back here now. All right, Mister FBI. Put your head on the car door and lean against it."

He does.

"You so much as twitch, I'm going to paint your car and put a hole in it too."

Mae stands beside me. I give back her forty-five. "Keep this barrel on his noggin. Now he's trained to push back against the barrel, to locate it, then spin and knock it away. So you feel him start to move around at all, pull the trigger. He'll catch on the first time. Promise."

I holster Smith. This man won't run, won't do anything without I'll feel the juice when he thinks it. Extension cord's plugged into itself. I uncouple the boy and girl and spill out ten feet of cord. Tie the archangel's right wrist snug enough I can't get a finger under. Same for the other. Then wrap the whole mess a few loops.

I have forty extra feet; I'll use it on his legs in the house.

"Get up." I lift by his elbows and he wriggles and bounces until he hops to his feet. "Look at me." I spin him. "Your buddy. He was going to the Town Pump. What else?"

Archangel's eyes glow red.

"He was going to check the other bar in town, then out to Swannanoa, maybe all the way to Asheville. Most likely be a couple hours. I was going to wait in the car to see if you'd come back for the truck."

His partner will be back soon as he's done at the Pump. Five minutes there, five to poke around, and five to get back. We already used half.

"Thanks. And next time you lie like just now, I cave in your head. Like this, but harder."

I strike the butt to his head, halfhearted.

"Two things you need to know about Baer Creighton," Mae says. "He doesn't lie. And he knows every single time you do."

I push him toward the house. "Move. Do what I say, you'll see your wife again. Vex me, you're one more corpse I'll hang from a tree."

Mae squints. Catches herself.

That's right. Daddy Baer's a different man than Uncle Baer. Killing half a town will do that. The archangel's seen the whole mess of bodies at Stipe's fight circle and knows I didn't want to kill them but I did. So he ought to know one more stiff won't change my fate.

Archangel steps toward the house and Mae keeps the gun handy his head. "Let me get that back, Mae. You take the cord."

I pocket her forty-five and push Smith into his neck. "Just so's you know, this is a Smith 'n Wesson Model 629, a forty-four magnum. You know enough to be impressed?"

"Yes."

"I shoot you anywhere at all, it'll be a humane death. Climb the steps."

Mae gets in front, opens the screen, holds it. We pass inside. "Sit on the sofa, in front of the window. Mae, you got twenty seconds to run upstairs and get some drawers. Not a second longer."

She hurries. Wasn't right to see them pink undies as her uncle. Damn sin as her daddy.

"No, I said in front of the window. Move to your right."

He squirms. "I can't. This sofa—"

"I know. I was dicking with you." I reach, lift him part by his shirt front and shift him. He's square in the window.

Mae rumbles down the steps with sweat pants in one hand, socks and sneakers in the other. She steps into the sweats and jumps them on.

"Mae, I want you on the chair, opposite Mister FBI. Keep the forty-five along your leg, finger in the trigger guard, ready to pull. Keep that barrel on him all the time, and if he does anything at all, if he sneezes, you kill him."

"O-okay."

I tie his feet so even if he works his hands free, she'll see him bend over for his legs.

"If he says anything at all, you're allowed to shoot him."

I step to the kitchen.

"Where you going?" Mae says.

Through the kitchen, I exit the back door like before and circle, this time to the right. Hiding at the front porch, I have a clean view of the drive and road toward the Town Pump. I can also step back to the kitchen window with a clear line of sight to the archangel on the sofa. He's got no red, no juice; I expect he's content to let things unfold the way they will.

I exhale long and slow. Close my eyes. Lean my noggin against the wood siding. Didn't realize until now but I'm ready to stretch out and snooze. Legs feel ready to buckle. Adrenaline works until it doesn't. Then all that saved up haggardness reaches up like a rope about the ankles to drag you under.

Ruth.

She sounded like you remember a girl. Her voice is like a scratched record and the last I saw her face, it was like a mile of bad road. But I recall her at nineteen.

I thought she would be mine.

Chapter 7

Ernest Swain went to college, earned a bachelor's in business in three and a half years. Married Emma and joined Stanley Nelson in the Saving and Loan business. Procreated, the output being Mary Swain—cousin of Josiah.

Stanley Nelson was second generation. Bankers learn as children from their parents that banks fail in the third generation.

The first generation grows up in the wild. They're street fighters with a dream. Hungry. Willing to risk everything to build the life they imagine.

The second generation walks a tightrope. They remember times in their childhood when the family business wasn't doing so well. They remember bean and onion soup. Dad saying, if you're hungry, have another slice of bread. But as young adults they see their parents' success. They rub elbows with their parents' moneyed peers. They see lifestyles beyond theirs, but within determined reach. The second generation sees momentum and projects itself into the wealthy class.

The third generation grows up emancipated from hardship. They learn their genetic and social superiority. Their class empowers them to be anything they dare dream. They never suffer hunger. Never fear ruin. They dream not of overcoming hardship, but of enjoying the fruits of their entitlements. They dream of attaining a still higher expression of leisure.

Emma was third-generation-soft. A doctor told her mother that bearing another child would kill her. She had her fallopian tubes tied. There were no other heirs.

Stanley Nelson knew he needed to breed a wild strain into the ownership bloodline of the Polk Benton S&L.

In the early 1800's, banks did not lend money for home purchases. Pennsylvania saw the first savings and loan created in 1831. The new business model fulfilled the nation's need for home financing. The concept was simple. Men would pool their money to build a house, and when the loan was repaid, build another. By 1980, half of all mortgages in the United States originated in a savings and loan.

S&L's were smaller than banks. They suffered differently from Federal Reserve mismanagement of interest rates and money supply.

Stanley Nelson had been aggressive with loans and had a higher than normal default rate. Town had shifted over the years. His middle-class location had devolved. By the time of the crisis, Stanley was adept with a high-pressure washer. He used it to clean graffiti from his bricks and glass.

Illiquid, hand tied, and surrounded by thugs, Stanley Nelson died of a stroke. He left a trust in place that siphoned his salary and company stock dividend to his wife. The trust required Ernest to run the S&L. If he did so, ownership would someday pass in equal shares to Ernest and Emma.

To keep Stanley's salary and dividend flowing to his mother in law, Ernest froze his own. When profitability fell, the difference came from his paycheck.

With Stanley Nelson's death, Ernest became a slave to Stanley's estate. He kept on though, because if the S&L survived, he would someday own half.

If.

By 1983, many thrifts were insolvent, and Polk Benton Savings and Loan led the charge. Regulators tried to figure out how to cover twenty-five billion dollars of liabilities with six billion in reserves.

The regulatory stance eventually shifted to forbearance. Insolvent S&Ls stayed open because regulators couldn't afford to shut them down. Many S&Ls adopted a go-for-broke strategy. They approved loans to riskier borrowers, hoping the payoff would make them solvent.

Ernest was in shock from the loss of his father-in-law. Reeling under the weight of running the company unprepared. Panicking at the prospect of bankruptcy, as soon as the regulators shut off his liquidity.

Ernest had an account in his name with a $500,000 check from Columbus Life.

The transaction took minutes. A couple forms. A couple entries.

He bought half a million dollars' worth of stock in the Polk Benton S&L.

Two weeks later, the regulatory forbearance policy began.

After the money was in, there was no way to get it out. Debt trumps equity. Even with the infusion of cash, Ernest was unable to manage the thrift back to profitability.

The Polk-Benton S&L folded May 7 of 1983, and the fireworks plant blew up three weeks later.

Chapter 8

Footsteps on the porch. Open my eyes with a half snore in my throat. Dry swallow a couple times. It's the other archangel. He walks slow, hand floats over his hip. I step out, swing Smith level.

"Stop there."

He halts. Twists his head. Eyes glow red before he says a word. Got deceit in his soul.

"You make one sudden move and I kill you, then go kill your partner. He's got a wife and kid."

"I got a wife, too."

Still red.

"No you don't. Your partner's bound up, hand to foot. With a gun pointed at his belly, in case he tries something. Put your gun on the porch and all this'll turn out fine. I'll leave both you here; long as I get a couple hours' head start I'm happy. You done me right at the fight circle and I'll do you right. That good with you?"

He nods. "I'm placing my pistol on the floor." He squats low.

"Fingers."

He lifts a block-looking plastic gun by thumb and forefinger, rests it on the porch. Stands.

"Wait."

I circle the porch. Behind him, say, "Go inside."

"You know there's a reckoning coming," he says. "You can't kill men like you did and think the Federal Bureau of Investigation won't find you, someday."

"You want this reckoning right now, with my gun in your back? Or how's say we kick the can down the road a ways. Your choice."

"Down the road."

"I thought. Inside the house."

He opens the screen. Pushes open the front door. I let him clear both, sure to have the front sight center mass before following inside. Mae lifts her forty-five from beside her leg, shifting it toward his belly. The barrel crosses over me. I want to cuss her, but it's my fault for not schooling her.

"Lay on the floor. Arms over your head."

He shifts to his knees, then the pushup position. "Even better. Hold that."

I take the leftover extension cord from Archangel One, pull Leatherman from my hip and cut the cord. Tie Archangel Two's legs. First, snug on the thinnest spot of his left ankle, then the other, separate. Then a couple loops around both for good measure. Doesn't take sixty seconds, but his shoulders shake.

"On your belly."

He lowers himself. I pull his wrists and tie them like his ankles.

"All right. This is what's going to unfold. You boys could have shot me a couple hours ago and you didn't. Now I can shoot you but I won't. Long as you don't force me. Understand boys, I feel for you. Trying to uphold law and order. But that's all I'm doing, too."

I stoop over Archangel Two. Grab his shoulders and slide him forward a foot. Tuck his head between sofa corner and end table, his body stretched diagonal.

"You, get on the floor." I point a pathway on the same diagonal. "Your head up to the wall, in the corner."

Archangel Two twists and bounces on the couch.

I pull him by the shoulders. He carries through on the thrust. I step aside and instead of taking me down, he bounces his face from the wall. He's on his side, sneezing blood and coughing. His nose drips to the floor.

"The carpet," Mae says.

"Leave him be. It'll stop on its own."

I take Mae to the kitchen. Hush. "You got involved in all this without knowing the full extent. So if you want out, I understand. I got to fetch another vehicle, since they know the truck. But you got to decide before I do.

"I tracked down the boys that stole Fred and fought him. Same boys as burned my house, burned Brown's house with me in it, and tried to shoot me in the woods on two occasion. I murdered every one of them. These two lawmen was there. They take me in… North Carolina still has the death penalty. Though we haven't used it in years, I bet they'd make a good case for me. No bunch of liars and thieves has the right to put me down. I won't stand for it."

"Don't say that."

"Well, I won't."

"That's not what I mean. Don't talk like that. We can get away right now. I'll gather the kids; we'll be ready in five minutes. Leave with the clothes on our backs. It won't do to take anything. We'll never be the same people again. Might as well go."

"But you think on it. You take up with me, your whole life'll be on the run. You'll be part of it. You helping me get away, they'll say is the same as you killing those men yourself."

"I'm already in it. And I just now got you as my father; I'm not willing to give that up. Let's go, right now. Be done with it."

I don't trust her to sit and watch the two archangels without them trying to cut a deal with her. Though her mind seems strong, on principle, I don't trust her to not to change it.

"Here's what's going to happen. They know my truck and your car, and I know where I can grab transportation they won't know to look for. Buy us a couple days. You sit where you was before. If either of them starts moving around, shoot him. Being nice is a luxury and you ain't rich. Yet."

Mae sits in her chair, forty-five on her lap.

"I'll be back in thirty second."

I leave the door open and as the screen door closes behind me I hear one the kids upstairs let out a wail. Turn around. Back inside.

"Run up and handle him."

Mae's on her feet. She takes two steps, stops, and looks at the forty-five in her hand. "Can I—"

"Give it here." I take it. She turns. I sit where she sat. "Get Morgan to look after him."

Her footsteps thump up the stairs and the boy goes quiet.

"Hey." I nudge Archangel One with my boot. "What'd you boys do with all them dogs? Back the fight circle?"

"They're still there."

"In the crates?"

"Uh-huh."

"You call in the police on the circle, yet?"

"No. The Gleason department's compromised. We set up a triage and tried to ferry some of your victims to the hospital, but they all died before we got there. The rest were all dead. We left them to come after you, on a hunch you might visit your niece. So no one's seen to the dogs yet."

No tingle, no red.

"Shoulda looked after the dogs."

Upstairs, Mae walks on her heels and anything in the kitchen not bolted to the floor rattles. Goes from one room to another and I suspect Morgan's the most levelheaded in the house. Put her in charge.

"You boys got to know I didn't want none of this. I tried to put a stop to it."

Archangel Two huffs.

"What? Say it."

"You wanted every bit of it. You distilled wood alcohol. That's not temporary insanity. You wanted to murder those men, and you stoked that desire long enough to turn wood into poison."

"They provoked me."

"No choice at all."

"What else could I have done? Sit and take it? Let them do what they want to my life's work? Steal. Cheat. Lie. Take my sole friend and give him a miserable death. All the while, I step back and step back. But each time I let up, Stipe and his boys edge closer. That's the way with evil. You can't give any slack, ever. Evil man'll use your good against you. Want to treat people right and fair and suppose the best, but the evil man will get away with it because the good man won't give what he gets. Isn't civil. Doesn't have the belly for it. Well, I found the belly."

"You're a mass murderer. There's no way you get out of this."

"Guess I keep hoping you law enforcement types will get fed up with the evil too."

Footstomps descend the stairs. Mae comes in.

"This one likes to jaw." I kick FBI Two's foot. "Don't let him. I'll be back in a second."

I return Mae's forty-five and head outside to the truck. Pull a roll of duct tape from the glove box. Something's off—can't place it. I close the door and puzzle it. Rest my hand on the door handle, let my eyes adjust to the dark.

Flat tire.

Sometimes a man wonders who exactly he pissed off.

Take the tape inside.

"Now Mae, these boys are liable to tell you anything to make you untie them. They'll scare you any way they can. So don't take this tape off no matter what. You hear?"

Mae nods.

I grab a rag from the kitchen, lift Archangel One's face and wipe the blood from his nose. Stretch a piece of silver tape across his mouth. "You can breathe, right?"

He exhales a clump of blood through his nose. Grunts. That means yes.

Pull Archangel Two back a little, get his head from between the sofa and end table. Tape his mouth shut, too. Then tape his arms, snugging them together over the electric cable at the wrists. Then as far up the arms as I can get them together.

I finish the roll doing the same to Archangel One.

"You want either of these boys to behave, just pinch his nose shut."

Mae nods.

I take Mae to the porch. "You keep a gun on them at all times. They wriggle, whatever, you got to shut them down. They see weakness, they'll work it."

"I understand."

"They're men, not puppies. They'll screw you if they can. Okay. Need your keys. My tire's flat."

Mae goes inside and returns. Places keys in my hand. "I love you," she says. "Dad."

I hug her, quick. "Love y'all. All right. Take care them fools. I be right back."

Chapter 9

Josiah Swain didn't know other people struggled to recognize faces. For him, it was second nature. He called them to mind when he wanted. Identified people even if they changed attributes, such as new facial hair, since he had last seen them.

A few days after his parents died in a car accident, he sat on Ernest Swain's sofa watching The Dukes of Hazard. Boss Hogg protested that Bo and Luke selling marijuana for any amount of money was reprehensible.

The front door of the Swain house erupted to a pounding fist.

"Who the?"

Ernest sat in the kitchen reading the newspaper. Chair legs barked on linoleum, and Ernest stomped in stockinged feet to the door. "Go to the other room," Ernest said.

New in the house and grateful for instruction, Josiah obeyed. He sat in the kitchen where Ernest had read the newspaper, and his gaze fell upon a photo of a horrific car accident.

Josiah recognized the car, a Honda Prelude. Though the photo was black and white, he knew it was his parents' car. It had a sticker that said REAGAN, located on the driver's side of the front bumper.

The sticker had survived. The impact smashed the front end of the car into the passenger compartment. He saw spider web cracks in the glass, discolored with blood. His mother's head must have caused the delicate imprint. He stared at the image.

When the conversation between Ernest and the man at the door grew heated, Josiah listened.

He shifted so he could see into the living room. In the doorway stood a gruff man with a defiant glare.

"You can't come here!" Ernest said.

"I am here, and I want what's mine before I go to prison."

"I don't have it yet. I won't get it for a few days. Don't come back." Ernest slammed the door.

The conversation didn't make sense. Josiah assumed the man was a customer. Ernest was angry because the S&L is where you go to get the money, not Ernest's house. It was strange the man came at night and was angry.

But, as with most things he didn't understand over the last few weeks, Ernest deferred thinking about it. His mind was sharp, but untrustworthy. It led him to believe things that didn't mesh with what others told him.

Josiah sat back down at the newspaper. As Ernest stomped back to the kitchen, Josiah saw another photo on the same page. A man with a beard stood in front of a cement block wall.

"Is that the man who killed my mother and father?" Josiah said.

"What? How did you—what—oh, the newspaper. Yes. You shouldn't be looking at that. But that's the photo they took at the jail of the man who drove into your parent's car."

"How did he get out of jail?"

"It's called bail. What do you mean, how did he get out?"

"Why did he come here?"

"When did he come here?"

Josiah wrinkled his brow. Tried to understand Ernest's trick. "Just now."

"That was a different man. The man just now was a guy who wanted a loan. I didn't give it to him at the S&L, and he got angry. The man tonight didn't have a beard."

Josiah was silent.

His father, Norman, had never lied to him. As far as Josiah knew, telling lies was exclusively in the domain of bad children. Seeing Ernest lie with ease jarred Josiah into questioning his senses. He'd seen the man at the door—it was the exact man as in the newspaper.

Perhaps Ernest hadn't seen the man in the newspaper?

"Look at him," Josiah said. "That was him."

"That man has a beard. The man at the door didn't."

Josiah spaced out as the fabric of his world accommodated a new truth.

Adults lie.

If he couldn't believe an adult—and adults were the ones who knew and controlled everything—his situation was precarious.

To Ernest, three pieces of a solution fell together with Norman's surprise pronouncement about his life insurance.

First, his brother drove a car known to have poor front impact safety.

Second, Ernest had nothing to do with Norman naming him contingent beneficiary.

Third, a sorry fellow named "Gay May" Maynard Reynolds had problems with a shark in Chattanooga. He begged Ernest to give him a second mortgage, so he could repay the loan with home equity. Without twenty big ones, his next dwelling would be six feet deep in a corn field. Gay May was pulling out the stops.

When Gay May arrived to complete the loan application, Ernest completed the questionnaire to avoid a scene. Everyone knew Gay May associated with the wrong people. Gay May *was* the wrong people. He wore a lot of leather and rode a motorcycle. He didn't shave as often as most men and seemed to have taken a stand against hygiene in general. Last, and what mattered most: he had no job.

But as the wheels had turned in Ernest's mind, he saw possibility. A few days of musing concluded when he realized, without a massive infusion of cash, the S&L would fold within months. Five hundred thousand dollars would buy serious time. Maybe years. Long enough for the economy to recover.

Ernest telephoned Gay May and spoke to Gay's wife. He'd be at the Hitching Post at seven if Maynard wanted to discuss a couple of items.

Maynard showed.

Two and a half weeks later, Josiah's parents were dead.

Gay May went to prison for a year for involuntary manslaughter, but he kept his life. After Ernest received the life insurance money, he gave twenty thousand dollars to Gay's wife. She repaid the Chattanooga shark.

Everyone was happy.

Chapter 10

In the fall of 2008, Sophia Whitcombe started her junior year of high school. Her parents had secured her admission into honors classes. Some of her test scores indicated they were not appropriate for her cognitive skills. She struggled. Compromised on sleep. To stay awake during the day, she filled up on colas and iced teas.

She walked home in a haze, dreading her homework. To prove her worth to Yale, she had to maintain perfect grades. Plus take part in extracurricular activities. Theater. Cross country—with boobs. Mock trial team. Meanwhile, the instant attention from every male got to her. She felt like she was carrying around a plastic bag of a million dollars. Everyone could see, and many would take it by force if given the chance.

She was thankful her father had taught her some skills. But she also wished he hadn't made her fear every shadow. She neared the park on her walk home from school.

The chilly temperature kept people indoors. No one was near.

Sophia didn't notice the police car as it approached her from behind. Not until it was next to her and the driver's window rolled down.

She jumped.

"Sophia? Miss, are you Sophia Whitcombe?"

"Uh, yeah." She looked at the pained face of the thirty-something police officer inside.

"Miss, I'm sorry to surprise you, but I'm afraid I have very bad news. It's your mother."

"What!"

"I'm afraid there's been an accident. She asked for you. We don't have much time."

"Oh my God!"

"You want to get in the car? I can get you there as fast as possible."

"Where?"

"Miss, we have to hurry. She's in bad shape. We've got to go all the way to Sylva."

Sylva was close to an hour away. Sophia's heart jumped in her throat. She raced around the back of the car and opened the front passenger door.

"I'm sorry, Sophie. Could you hop in the back? The department has a policy about letting anyone in the front. I'm sorry."

Sophia hesitated. "Yes, of course." She opened the back door and jumped in. As she closed the door she realized she was in a Gleason police car, not an Asheville or Sylva police car.

"What happened to my mother?"

The policeman pressed the gas and the acceleration pushed her into the seat. He didn't put on the siren.

"She was in a car accident."

"What was she doing in Sylva?"

"A conference."

"What conference? I know about her conferences. I go to some of them. What happened? Did you say a car accident?"

"That's right. I guess she was driving there. I don't know if the conference was in Sylva or someplace else. Knoxville. I don't know. But she's at the Sylva hospital, and they're not going to fly her to Asheville. Said she wouldn't survive the flight. I'm real sorry but she's not supposed to make it."

"Oh my God."

Sophia looked through the window with eyes full of tears. They were already on the highway speeding west.

"Does my father know? Where is he?"

"He's already on the way there. He's the one who called and asked us to pick you up and bring you. He stopped by the school and couldn't find you."

That didn't make any sense. She walked the same route every day. Her father knew the route—they'd reviewed it as part of their safety plan for the household. Her father knew where she was, always. It's why she had a cell phone.

Sophie cleared her mind. The panic receded. She would call and find out everything was okay. Her mother would be fine.

Sophia dug in her purse and pulled out her phone.

"Don't be stupid," the police officer said.

She looked up. He held a gun up for her to see and, in an instant, Sophia understood. Her mother had not been in an accident. Her father was not speeding to Sylva.

Sophia looked out the window. They passed a car with a female driver. She made eye contact, and the woman looked away before Sophie could think of how to communicate.

"All right. That's all. I want you to push your cell phone through the opening here. Do it now."

Sophie held onto her phone.

"I can stop the car, come back there and beat you senseless before you can place a call."

She pushed the phone through the slot.

"Good girl. Now I want you to lie down across the back of the seat. If you don't do what I tell you, I'm going to pull over up here and knock you out. Understand? You do what I say, you'll get through this all right."

She looked for a door handle. None. Nothing to control the window. She tried to think it through. She tried to calm herself.

"Where are you taking me?"

"I already told you. Sylva."

"Who are you?"

"Police."

"What do you want with me?"

"I want to take some pictures of you for a scrapbook I keep. After that, I'll take you back home. That's it. I promise."

"I don't want you to take my picture."

"LAY DOWN ACROSS THE SEAT!"

In the rearview mirror, Sophia saw the nothingness behind his eyes. He didn't want her photograph. She lay across the seat and tried to think of how she was going to survive.

Chapter 11

Unlock the Tercel and sit, get her started. Wish the truck tire wasn't flat. Be easier to take, but soon as I ponder the problem I ken the solution.

That's Baer Creighton; yessir.

Tercel engine running, I step out, leave the door hang.

At the truck, I study the gold buckets in the bed. Tempted to hide them in the cab, as my westward plans are delayed. But the truck's in a shadow. Someone would have to be right there squinting to see three hundred pounds of gold.

I calculate the math. Sixteen ounces times a hundred pounds is sixteen hundred ounces. Times three is forty-eight hundred ounces. Times eight hundred dollars per, is—uh—round up to fifty times eight is almost four million?

Four million dollars in coin, ready for the stealing. Who would have thought that if you don't trust government fiat paper, you actually have something to show for a life's work.

Has any man in history ever left as much money to chance? But it'd take fifteen minute to move it, and who knows what sort of trouble might arise?

Headlights flash to the trees out front. I hunker between the FBI car and my truck. A Cordoba rolls in, dust floating in the beams. Door opens and dome light—

Ruth.

Double-thought myself on Ruth. Saw her. Ran. Wanted to see her again. Now she's here and I want to run.

"Baer? That you over there?"

"Just clearing out."

Open the truck door. Cab smells like the dog has a rotten gut. "Come on Stinky Joe; out the truck. Puppydog got to poop. Lessgo."

Ruth leaves her door open, lights on. "Baer! Don't go. I was hoping you'd be here."

Tercel sits running, lights on. I gander out, can't guess who all these headlights are waking up. But if I tell her we ought to turn them off, I'm stuck talking to her.

Don't want to poke her; damn sure don't want to talk to her.

"Thought I said what I had to say."

"You wrote me all those letters. You wrote me more than two thousand letters, Baer."

"Now I decide to leave, you want to talk?"

"I want another chance. I want one chance at honesty and something new. The world is so corrupt and I'm terrible for being a part of it, and being awful to you. But we're born bad and taught bad, and none of us is ever taught good. So it's no wonder we turn out bad. And the curse of it is we want to be good but can't. No sooner than we promise to turn a new leaf, and we're right back doing bad again."

"You finally read some of my letters."

I kill the Tercel and take the keys. Leave Ruth mumbling. Go to the house. Mae sits where I left her, gun in hand like it's glued to her palm. Not a bad idea. "Put on coffee, Mae, we're going to be up a long time." I kick Archangel One. "Which of you has the keys to that Wrangler outside?"

Archangel Two grunts. I fetch keys from his pocket. "I'm borrowing your vehicle. Bring it right back. Maybe."

I'm at the door.

"You want coffee or not?" Mae says.

"You drink it now. I'll have it later. Shortly. Remember, kill either one of these men that move."

Outside. October chill drove the bugs to the bark. Or is it November?

Ruth sits on her car hood.

"Baer, I love you. I always have, but I've never had the courage to face everything else in my life. You can't just change things. Our whole lives are intertwined and going back to you after all these years ..."

"Gimme peace."

"But you have to still love me."

"Woman!"

Unlock the Wrangler—a long boxy one—and swing open the back gate with the spare tire and happy face. Expect a couple gun cases; instead get a radio, lights and wires. Probably a tracking device hidden in here somewhere. But they've no reason to suspect it's me and not an archangel driving around.

Commotion. I turn. Ruth grabs me. Arms around, forehead square in my chest. She shakes. "Take me with you, Baer. Please. Forgive me."

I get her shoulders in my hands and pry her loose. "Damn. Is all."

At the Wrangler passenger door, I call Stinky Joe. "C'mon, up in the truck."

It's good to drive a Wrangler. Cut the wheel, burp the tire.

Not as much power as I'd hoped but maybe enough for the job at hand.

Was good to leave Ruth before I put a knot on her head like a calf could suck on. Woman ignores two thousand letters and the day I'm ready for quits, she's mad in love. Don't know what to make of it.

Love a girl two years. Spend the next thirty trying to remember exactly what was so compelling about the first two. Ass? Well, yeah, but... What's left after all that? I'm not sure I existed, thirty years ago. Let alone love.

Now Ruth's concerned about the evil world?

Go west her own damn self. She got wheels.

Clock says 1:13.

Should have stayed at Mae's for coffee. Feel along the center cup holder. Lift. Sniff. Gag. Copenhagen spit. Find the dome light and the window power. Get the glass down and toss the cup of mouth sewage. Nasty. Power up the window. Dome light off. Careful, I sniff the second cup. Coffee—black. I sip it. Cold, not bad. I drink the what's left.

Deer eyes glow off the road, back a couple dozen feet in the field. Late enough in the fall they're starting to worry about spotters and poachers. Wouldn't mind a venison steak—

Haven't had a gulp of shine in so long I can't think of it. Ought to be in the sleeping bag. But staying out of the electric chair requires an all-nighter and maybe an all-dayer after.

Up on the right is Farmer Brown's burned down house and across the road is my burned down house. I drive by slow, then three point turn on the road and park in the drive.

Stinky Joe sniffs. Look from the window to me.

What are the odds Mae's already let them archangels loose and they stole your gold?

"That's a lie." I rub behind his ears. "Don't talk stupid like that. Mae's got a good head on her shoulders. And loyal."

If she was a dog, she'd be a—

"Ha! But I seen it coming."

Jeep Headlights reflect off the back window of Burly Worley's black Suburban, nose down over the bank. See it beyond my burned down house. I kill the Wrangler engine but leave the headlamps on. Only thing left of my entire stilling empire is the tool shed. I swing the door open and delight to see nobody's stolen so much as a bent nail.

Inside, a sealed fifty caliber ammo box sits on the dirt in back under a walnut sap board—high class shelving. I drag it out into the headlamps' glow. Pop the latch and bust the seal. Dump out CGU-1B straps, coiled tight and bound with rotten rubber bands. Bust the bands, stretch the strap, work the lever a couple times to recall how it operates. Proceed to the Suburban.

Lift a tank with these straps, if a fella had the back for it.

Burly Worley liked to haul a boat to the river and the Suburban has a hitch. I wrap the strap behind the knob and affix the karabiner-style hook on the nylon strap. Stretch the straps full out, twenty feet.

Drive the Wrangler so the front end is over the strap, get out and fix it to the hook on the left and ratchet things taut. Put the Wrangler in reverse and get some real tension.

Now the question: Did anyone take the keys out of the Suburban since I left it?

The Chevy's run over a bank covered in blackberry briar and nosed against a nest of quaking asp. Any luck, the front end'll look fine, if I can get it out. I walk side-footed and press briars over at the base. Follow where others have already struck a path. Open the door, lift my right leg with two hands and get it to the footwell. Then climb the door and the steering wheel until I can swing into the seat.

Hindsight says I was a dumbass to drive Burley's truck over a bank and through a mess of briars. But I'm in a silver lining mood, and delight I had the sense to kill the engine and leave the keys.

Sometimes it's a marvel to find out today you wasn't a fool yesterday.

I press the brake, give the key a twist. Engine starts. With the inside lights on, I find a button left of the steering wheel with 2 and 4 on it, up and down arrows. I press but it doesn't move. Search the whole dash and nothing looks to control four-wheel drive. I press the button again. Nothing. Pull it. Nothing.

Damn thing a knob?

It turns. Four-wheel drive controlled by a knob, not a stick. Feels like communism. Twist again so the 4 with the down arrow is on top, hope that's low range. Shift to reverse and tap the gas. Vehicle settles in the briars but doesn't move rearward.

I leave it running in reverse. The engine idles and the wheels are still. At the burnt house, I grab a patio stone. Back at the vehicle, I put the paver to the pedal so the tires chug. Slope is too much, but maybe the Wrangler won't have to do all the work.

Back the Jeep, I turn on the dome light and look for the four-wheel drive. Ah! Got a lever. Boys know how to build a truck. Shifter to neutral and lever to four low. Now the shifter to reverse. Release the parking brake and press the gas.

Giddyup.

Occurs to me I got the rock on the wrong gas pedal. Soon as the Suburban's free I'll need to hop inside while it's moving. With the open door coming at me. While if I'd put the block on the Jeep gas pedal, I could let it pull me up in the Suburban, and stop it with the brake. The Jeep would stop, being lighter.

But soon as the thought reveals itself the Suburban shifts and the treads grab. I stop the Wrangler and the Suburban keeps coming. Jump out the Jeep, but the Chevy picks up speed, headed straight for the tool shed. Not willing to sacrifice my tools.

They aren't many—just all that says I ever lived here.

I bound back inside the Wrangler and put it in first gear and gas it hard. Cut the wheel and cut again so as I'm straight in the Suburban's path—now it comes for the door. I'm a damn fool and know it. Reverse. Cut hard again, and the Suburban chugs into the Jeep. There's a split second of peace, then the Suburban pushes the Jeep toward the shed. I lock the brake. The Jeep still moves, but slow enough I leap out. Circle the Suburban, come up on the driver side door and hop in. Toss the cement paver out the door and hit the brake.

Got me a truck.

Yessir.

Get Stinky Joe in the Suburban.

Nice wheels. I'd have kept the gold.

Chapter 12

On his drive to the Polk Benton S&L Ernest Swain turned on the radio. Instead of news, he twisted the knob and caught the last half of the New York Philharmonic's rendering of *Fanfare for the Common Man.*

Ernest wept.

When the masterpiece concluded, he turned off the radio. He attempted to recapture the melody in his mind. The main tune carried by the brass—what, trumpets? —was easy enough. But the other instruments—here, Ernest failed.

There was something in the music. *Fanfare for the Common Man.* Ernest was common—and there was something noble in him that deserved a fanfare. Something. Even in all his sweat and toil and frustration. His aching shoulders at the end of a tense day. The constant fear of failure. The dread of losing everything he'd worked for. The miserable thought that he might let down his wife. Daughter, adopted son, mother-in-law, employees, and the entire town. Everyone depended on the Polk Benton S&L.

In a strange way, he didn't want to have killed his brother in vain.

Ernest was a regular man doing anything for success. While the world pulverized him. There was something so noble in him, Aaron Copeland wrote a masterpiece to celebrate him.

Tears rolled over his cheeks. His collar wetted.

The common man.

Ernest pulled over. He couldn't see for the tears. He sobbed and in between gasps, as the snot ran from his nose, he bellowed the tuba's part, BWAH BWAH BWAHHHHHHH!!! Then the trumpets BAH, BAH, BAH, Buh BAHHHHH!

A truck passed at speed. The wind rocked Ernest's car. He rolled down the window. Collected all the snot and mucous he could gather in the back of his throat and spat it to the road.

He released the air in his lungs slowly. His heart juddered and his eyes burned from the high-pressure cry. But as his pulse slowed he could almost feel the tension floating away. When he pulled onto the road five minutes later, Ernest Swain was empty, and okay with that.

Ernest sat at his desk at the Polk Benton S&L. He looked at his clock. After Aaron Copeland's Fanfare, he'd put on sunglasses and stopped at a McDonald's to buy a cup of ice drizzled in Coca Cola. At the office, he alternated placing the cup against each eye. It didn't seem to reduce the red and swelling.

He had a nine o'clock appointment with a regulator from the FSLIC. The Federal Savings and Loan Insurance Corporation. The regulator demanded access to all files, books, the works.

Ernest didn't understand why it had taken this long. The Polk Benton had closed its doors three weeks earlier.

First there were lines outside. Then pickets and chanting. That night he received two death-threat phone calls to the house. Ernest started carrying a firearm, displayed on his hip, always. Even at home. And when he went to bed, he slept with the handgun within arm's reach on his night table.

Ernest had made his best effort over the last three years to welcome his dead brother's son into his family. He tried to remain mindful of the tragedy through the eyes of Josiah, losing his mother and father. But there had to be a line. Bed wetting? The kid was thirteen years old.

One more frustration. Josiah overheard Ernest telling his wife the regulators might close the Polk Benton. They would lose everything.

All the selfish little bed pisser could think about was himself.

"Is my money there?"

"It's not your money. It never was your money. Your father named me his beneficiary, so I would take care of you. I have. You eat. You wear good clothes. You have a bedroom."

"He told me the money was for my future."

"Fine. Sure. It doesn't matter. I put it in the S&L and it's gone. Like everything else."

"How is it gone? You put it in. Take it out."

"Equity doesn't work like that. It's late. Go to bed."

That night Josiah wet the bed, all over. Like he was rolling around and taking a three-minute leak at the same time.

There was no other place for the kid to go, so they were stuck with one another. Ernest would do his absolute best by his dead brother's son. He felt a pesky, niggling responsibility. But sometimes he hoped the boy would grow up and have a family. Someday he'd have people depending on him. There's be a challenge. Something huge, a catastrophe so big it threatened his entire self-concept as a provider. With luck, just then, someone he loved would swing a pipe wrench into his nuts. So he could see what it felt like.

If there was such a thing as justice.

The S&L was empty. Ernest had told staff not to come in any more. There was nothing to do until the regulator took over and started making people whole. Or not.

He looked at the clock. Eight forty-five.

Should he put on a pot of coffee? Would he be here long enough to drink it? Would the regulator want a cup? Could he afford a pot of coffee?

Like he needed more caffeine to steady his nerves.

He would lose everything.

At five minutes of the hour Ernest walked to the glass doors, knelt and unlocked the one on the left. While on his knees, a shadow crossed over him. Ernest looked up and beheld a man in a white suit fringed in sunlight. Close-cropped hair and a face hidden by the glare of his sunny corona. Ernest stood. Pushed open the door.

"Morning, Swain," the man said.

"You're Mart Fairweather?"

A nod. The man produced a laminated card with small type and the FSLIC emblem.

"So, what happens now?"

"Now you let me in."

Ernest stepped aside. "I guess it's a good thing you're here. I did my best. And if it wasn't for the old man dying—"

"First things first. Coffee? Then show me to your office." He looked around. "And where is your staff?"

"I didn't put on any coffee. And everyone's at home. There's no need to have them here. We can't conduct business."

"I see. One, put on a pot of coffee. Two, give me your keys. Three, call in your staff. Four, go home and wait."

"What's going to happen?"

Fairweather cocked his head. "Four items. You might recall."

"I mean, what happens with the S&L? Receivership?"

"I will examine your numbers, top to bottom. If there's anything worthwhile in this place, we'll look for a stronger institution to absorb you. If not, receivership. Either way, I'll give you the kindness of being direct. It will take a little while. You have a couple moves left, but they won't help. You're out."

"But ownership? I still have that."

"Coffee, Mister Swain. Actually, give me your key ring first."

Three weeks had passed since the Federal Home Loan Bank refused to lend funds to the Polk Benton.

The day before, Ernest had tried to clear his mind.

Sometimes encouragement came from strange places. He'd picked up a copy of Rolling Stone magazine stashed in his desk drawer. In it he saw an ad for a modern feat of technology that would give him the gentle nudge he needed. A mini cassette player. He'd bootstrap himself back to success. Turn around his entire life.

In yesterday's lethargy of failure, he'd procrastinated.

But this was today. Something in Fairweather's forthrightness inspired Ernest. Maybe divine good fortune gave him the *Fanfare for the Common Man* experience to put him in the right frame of mind. Queue his ambition so the no-nonsense Fairweather could kick start it. Shake the nonsense out of him.

After forfeiting his keys and making coffee, Ernest sat at the phone. He made a few dials and recalled the staff, telling each he would not be there when they returned later in the day. Each conversation was a confession of failure.

"The regulator is here. He needs you back. You'll be reporting to him and doing what he says."

After the last call, Fairweather said, "You may leave now."

Ernest remembered yesterday's inspiration—the technological marvel advertised in Rolling Stone. If he didn't act now, if he didn't do something dramatic, his entire life would stall. He'd never recover.

He had two possible options. He could go to a bar and see how much alcohol it would take to knock him out. Or he could stand resolute against the tyranny of personal failure. He could seek a path of growth and perseverance that would one day lead him to financial success.

He stepped into his office and approached. Fairweather sat at his desk. Ernest swung around the side. Relished how the white-clad, pale man shrank from him. Ernest pulled open the top desk drawer.

Fairweather lifted his leg and lowered his hand as if to shield himself from a feral animal.

"Swain! Wait!"

Ernest smiled. Fairweather must have thought he was going for a gun.

Ernest extracted the copy of Rolling Stone he'd been reading the day before. Displayed the cover. "Personal property."

Ernest sat in his Volvo 240 DL Wagon, a bright red little tank of a car. He reclined the seat a little and flipped through Rolling Stone until he found the page.

It was an advertisement by the Japanese company Sony. The device had been around for several years--on the west coast. As with all new technology, it took years to travel inland to places like Benton, Tennessee.

Ernest read the ad again.

SONY TURNS EENSY INTO EENSY-WEENSY.

This is an actual-size photo of the eensiest, teensiest, weensiest cassette player ever made- the new Sony Super Walkman. The only thing that isn't teeny-weeny is the sound.

Ernest placed his hand over the photo and imagined what salvation would feel like. He imagined walking through the woods. Thumbing play on a cassette recording of *Fanfare for the Common Man*. Having the sounds transport his soul, right there in the woods.

And that was only the start. Everyone was talking about subliminal messaging. You play cassettes while you sleep, and the information soaks into your subconscious mind. You could buy tapes for all sorts of things. Building confidence, improving memory, or learning Spanish.

Ernest left the S&L in the capable hands of the Federal Savings and Loan Insurance Corporation. He rolled down the windows on both sides and drove forty-seven miles to the Sears in Chattanooga. Driving to the big city ensured his best chance of having a reasonable selection to choose from.

He talked to a one-armed salesman named Jim. Showed him the ad he'd ripped from the Rolling Stone. "That's what I want."

The Chattanooga Sears didn't have it. But Jim showed him another model, not quite so eensy weensy, but certain to produce big sound. Ernest paid cold cash. He asked the man where he could buy cassettes. Looked down the giant hallway when Jim pointed to Camelot Music.

"Walk a quarter mile past the food court and hang a left."

At Camelot he picked up cassettes of Aaron Copeland. He also grabbed an interesting-looking tape of some touchy-feely self-help hippy. His wife had mentioned the guy. Wayne Dyer. His cassette would teach Earnest how to have inner resolve and motivation.

Last, he couldn't resist John Cougar's *American Fool*. He dug that little ditty about Jack and Diane.

He bought several packs of batteries and played *Fanfare for the Common Man* on the trip home. He rewound and listened to the complete song seven more times. He drove the last miles in windblown silence, dehydrated from unloading buckets of tears. At home, without changing clothes, he climbed into the backyard hammock. Placed Wayne Dyer in the cassette player.

The touchy-feely guy made a lot of sense.

It was as if Aaron Copeland's timpani crashed open his defenses. Battered his self-doubt into submission.

Ernest was ready to heal.

On the hammock with his eyes closed, he didn't see his dead brother's son Josiah walk out on the back porch, creep to within fifteen feet, and study the Sony on Ernest's chest.

Chapter 13

I read *Call of the Wild* as a boy. Only book I ever finished. It had a dog turn into a wolf. As a boy, I puzzled on why a dog would leave its easy life with people and prefer the angry ways of the wood.

I was young, I thought the book was full of nonsense.

Dogs like men because men feed them and keep them out the cold. A dog'll walk alongside a man, and defend him, like to a higher cause.

Early on, I was picking berries in a briar patch. It was in town. Grew between houses we passed taking a shortcut on the walk home after school. Over time we stomped a path through the thicket. We'd come back every day, steal more berries, and push the path deeper into the briar patch.

One day I busted through the other side. Fell into some fella's backyard. He had a German shepherd chained to a stake in the ground next to a mossy wood doghouse.

Time I saw the dog he was an airborne bucket of teeth. I was maybe ten and we didn't have a dog. Mother wore the skin off her knees feeding me and Larry, couldn't hardly afford food for an animal. So my introduction to the mighty canine was a German shepherd in flight.

Chain caught him short, flipped him over. He rested on a dirt flat, dizzy like a bird that flew into the picture window. I come up to him because his eyes didn't mean no harm and loved on him. Turned out he wasn't quite the mankiller he let on. Tie an animal outside and leave him all day and night, only natural he's quick to rage.

And so it was with the dog in that book I read. Dogs are good people but can take only so much abuse before they turn to the woods. Take their chances with the natural world, instead of the certain misery of civilization. Leave the lying and deceitful ways to human beings, who do it better.

Nothing like a dog snoozing next to the fire. Nothing like his trust.

There's a bunch of dogs in crates that never got to snooze next to the fire. Maybe they started out showing trust. But after landing in the fight circle, they learned it risked their lives to give it.

When I get to the fighting dogs the archangels left in their crates, I'll cut them loose and let them live free.

Last I was at the fight circle, it was a cathedral of death, built by Joe Stipe so his boys could bend a knee at the altar of misery and blood. I turn from the dirt road to the sludgy tracks cut along a soybean field, withered and dead and ready for harvest. The single track is smooth in the mud but in a quarter mile cuts into the wood. I vibrate over rocks and ruts and weave between trees as the trail cuts left and winds around a dome. Opposite where I entered the wood, down in the flat, the fight circle glows orange from a mess of lanterns. The archangels didn't think to drop the wicks. I see the light and cut off the Suburban's headlamps, but I can't see and turn them back on.

Come on the place slow. Glass from headlights and windshields flash reflections of my lights back at me. Couple trucks got doors open and dome lights on. Eyeballs glow in the fight pit and behind wood pallet slats. See a couple more in the back of a truck with the tailgate down, maybe the dog they'd have fought next—if I hadn't murdered them.

Drop the windows and breathe dank forest air. Can't tell if it's rich earth or death. Moths flutter at the lanterns and I search the trees for hanging corpses like in my dream. Soon enough I see dead men, scattered on the ground. Clawing for hope, dead where they lay on poison I stilled to bring them low.

I spend a minute in quiet then put the Suburban in park and kill the lights. Occurs to me that I sit in a comfortable seat. Got warm feet and the aches in my back and hip kind of dissolve into the backrest. Feel the knots, but the pain is good like an itch. I drop my head against the rest and close my eyes a minute. Got the coffee sparking my brain but I'm weary. Want to drop the seat back and take a snooze but Mae's waiting with the kids. FBI boys are trying to work her any way they can.

And who knows what trouble Ruth'll be?

Joe's curled on the front seat. I bet Burley Worley'd mess himself, he saw a dog on his leather seats.

Should have made Ruth piss off for good.

"Joe, I've had a lotta dogs but none with such a coarse mouth as you."

Shit.

Outside, a dog growls. I open my eyes, shift in the seat and check the side mirrors. It's dark behind me. Other dogs whine. One looses a clipped bark.

Joe perks up. Looks out the front window and sees the pit. He shudders like it's a thunderstorm out, fidgets like he can't sit where he is but can't go anywhere else. He crawls down into the footwell, and I bend over and talk at him. Rub behind the ears, down the shoulder.

"Joe, you got to understand every last one of those men that had anything to do with that fight pit is dead. They swim the fiery lakes of hell, this minute. I did that."

Joe studies me, like he's unsure if he can take the word of an animal that walks on two feet.

I step out of the Suburban. Drift to the pit, taking in the death and dark. Behind the pallet walls sit two pit bulls, both bleeding. They've been locked up together for the last few hours. If they loved fighting as much as the dogfighters say, there'd be one of them dead.

Maybe these animals don't want to murder one another after all.

"C'mere, puppydog."

I lean over the pallet. Reach in. The pit bull is black. Has a slice above the eye and down his muzzle. His snout twitches and he gives me a tickle of electric on my arms. Detect a tiny red glow in his gaze.

"C'mon you sorry brute. Baer loves you."

The other—a black nose pit the color of old red bricks—growls. I recognize his voice. He's the one that spoke up when I was in the Suburban.

"Hey you, c'mere." I turn to him and the first one growls. "Lighten up. You want your freedom or not? You—yeah you. C'mere. I'm trying to love on you."

I wave him forward, small motions. He moves like I swung a shovel at him. He lowers like a compressed spring. If he wants, he can close with me in a half second. His growl goes high pitch and works out into a tremble. He stands. Shakes, not knowing if I'm the one he ought to kill, or if I'll beat him back like all the other men he's ever known.

Now the black one growls. Steps away from me and closer to the red brick pit, like to signal they're in it together.

I pull Smith. Still got the marks on my neck from Achilles trying to rip out my throat. These pits are wonderful if you love on them all their lives, but maybe some you can't love late.

Pit bulls and other dogs are wily animals. Sometimes you love on them, but they growl. The growl gets sharp, even as they lift a paw so you can scratch their belly. Sometimes they get confused and want the love, but also want to kill. You suspend them between with the belly rubs.

Blackie's eyes turn redder. My arms tickle. Almost hear electric like radio static. Feel the hair shift on my arms, and I look to the red brick pit. His eyes are bright like his brain shines evil.

Other growls join in. The pit bull in the crate next to the fight circle—in the truck ready to go next—he's angry, too. Eyes red. Static on my arm starts to pulse like I grabbed an electric fence.

Maybe it's the late night sober and maybe it's all these animals ready to trick me any way they can.

I see red eyes scattered around the trucks parked with tailgates facing the pit. Must be twenty crated dogs, and if it they wasn't confined I'd be in a mess of trouble. Hard to think with the shocks coming every two seconds. I blink. Shock. Scratch my ass.

Shock.

Spit.

Shock.

Still have my arm reached out offering love. I back off a hair... That's all the uncertainty Blackie can take. He leaps.

I clear an inch. He clamps my arm in his teeth. Redbrick leaps. I'm part away, twisted. He hits the pallet, bends the pickets back three inches. Another go, and he'll have a gap he can get through. Blackie grinds teeth in my arm. I get the electric. It hits his face. He goes nuts.

He thrashes. Jerks me into the fence where the other can get at me. All their lives men've put suffering into these dogs and they

aim to empty it all on me. Inside the pit or out, one working each
side. Redbrick charges again, hits the pallet with his shoulder.
Knocks it all but loose.

Blackie's heavy. He pulls my arm into the pit all the way to my
shoulder. I lose my feet a second; all my weight is on my armpit.
Redbrick lunges through the gap, get his hind paw stuck in the
narrowing slot between pallets. He drops face-first to the dirt. But
his paw pulls free and he spins.

Now he's on the outside.

I got you, Baer; I got you!

I twist back. Stinky Joe's half climbed out the Suburban
window. I look at Redbrick. Never thought it would come to this.

Stinky Joe flops to the ground and charges.

I pull Smith, swing my arm to Redbrick not two feet off.
Squeeze the trigger. Blackie yanks and another shot of electric
frazzles my head.

Redbrick doesn't know a chunk of lead passed him. He
hesitates with the muzzle blast. Now I got all the juice I can stand,
constant volts coursing my muscles, keeping them tight. All I can
do to think. Blackie jerks again, but I'm next to the vertical pallet
so at least he won't get me in the pit. But Redbrick leaps for my
head and I shove Smith in his belly and squeeze another chunk of
lead out the tube. Like a giant belly fart, all the noise and gas and
flash go right up in him. Redbrick grunts. Drops from my side.

Before he can loose a whimper, Stinky Joe shoulder butts him
into the pallet. Redbrick drops dead.

Joe looks down at him. He looks up at me. I shrug best I can.

"You got him."

Blackie busts up the romance and jerks my forearm like to rip
it off.

I get my feet under me, collect my thoughts. Stand up, bring
Blackie along. Place Smith to his neck and pull the trigger. Half

his neck disappears in a mist, but his teeth still clench my arm. His eyes dim as the blood drains from his head. Shake my arm but he's clenched tight.

I put the barrel so close I feel my backside pucker. Shoot once more; Blackie drops inside the ring, and now I got powder burns.

My lungs heave and I bend at the belly, chest resting on the pallet so my brain can reconnect and make sense. "I wanted to save you!"

The electric chills off mostly but, soon as I get my wits and know what I got to do, the juice comes back. It's all the other dogs, all the eyes in the crates wishing evil on me. Like they're laying with their bellies up for scratching, while in secret they wait for a chance to rip out my throat. Break for the woods.

I look at Stinky Joe. "You trust these fellas?"

Joe frowns. *You got to do it.*

I rub my arm where Blackie tore it up, and I'll need some Mercurochrome for sure. A tin of Bag Balm.

"I was going to let you pricks go free! I got hamburg hid!"

That's the problem with evil. Each of us carries some and if it's our lot to live with evil people, we nurse ours to match. You take an animal that could go either way, like a dog. A noble animal. Put him with the likes of Joe Stipe and he nurtures his darkness because without it he'll die. Seems every one of us, dog or man, will choose evil over death. And if I wasn't cursed with electric insight, I'd be no different. Happy in my evil.

And now these dogs got to end.

I look over the dead men still stretched on the ground. There—a holster with a gun in it. That's Lucky Jim Graves, the card player. I nudge his shoulder and he's stiff like a slab of hemlock. Bend and grab his gun. Why looky, looky. It's one of those square plastic-looking guns. Glock. Supposed to shoot clean or dirty. Underwater. With a fist of sand in the slide.

I check the chamber. Loaded. I pick a path through the dead men to the first truck with a crate in the back. The pit bull growls and his eyes are red.

"I don't hate you. But if I cut you loose, you'll be wild. All your pups'll be a pack and you'll sneak up on a kid someday and think he's a sammich. You brute. I'm sorry."

I put the Glock to the crate, line it with his head, and end his torment.

There's eleven more to go. I'll need another gun. I wish there was a way to save them. The Almighty might forgive me butchering men. But it's going to be harder to explain shooting these dogs.

I have to do it.

On my way to the next truck. Stipe's flat on his back, wearing a death face. A snarl drawn across a tub of Crisco.

He's why all these dogs are here. I kick his head, then do what I have to do.

I want to throw up.

When I'm done I gather six gun belts and three more loose pistols. Plus three jugs of my own shine I swapped out earlier with the poison.

Got a feeling I'll want them, I ever get out of this godawful town.

Chapter 14

On May 27, 1983, at 9:15AM, Ernest Swain sat on a patio lawn chair with his earphones on. His new morning process was working miracles on his self-esteem and ambition. It had only been two days since the FSLIC had taken over the Polk Benton S&L.

In that time, he'd listened to *Fanfare for the Common Man* seventy-three times. He'd started his second listening of the seven-cassette program by Doctor Wayne Dyer.

Ernest no longer perceived Dyer as a touchy feely hippy. He was the Einstein of human self-actualization.

Ernest could finally relax. Let go. He realized he was making the pressure, not society. Society didn't even exist. It was just people out there. They couldn't make him feel anything. Only he, Ernest Swain, could make Ernest Swain feel something. That's where the responsibility lay. And that's where the power rested.

He kept a notebook at his side with a pen tucked in the spiral for recording such insights. He pulled out the pen and wrote:

Only Ernest Swain can make Ernest Swain feel something.

Ernest filled his lungs slowly, allowing them to expand wide. He savored the cool, sweet morning air.

The aluminum and nylon lawn chair vibrated. He pulled off his ear phones.

"What the—"

It felt like a soundless earthquake. Then it was gone. Ernest reached over and put his hand on the patio. Nothing. A tiny ant crawled on his finger. Ernest looked at the ant a moment, then crushed it.

A shockwave arrived like a physical wall of sound and air. He felt the boom and rumble in his chest. It was like walking in front of a marching band drum section, but ten thousand times more concussing. An audible convulsion, more than a sound. He shrank in his chair and looked to the sky to see what might be falling on him. He twisted toward the forest, half expecting to see whole trees hurtling toward him.

Somewhere nearby, someone had dropped a bomb.

Ernest looked at his tan shorts. He'd peed a little.

He rolled sideways and the cassette player fell to the patio. Ernest picked it up, glanced at the marred corner. Pressed play and heard the tinny sound from the earpieces. Clicked it off.

He got in his car and before he drove a quarter mile saw the smoke, high above the trees, wide at top and skinny below.

A mushroom.

Ernest went to the scene of the blast and returned home by noon for lunch. He turned on the television news. Channel 12 had a reporter at the scene, standing in front of the smoking remains of the barn. That's where he had been, minutes ago. When Ernest was there, firecrackers exploded here and there, like small sticks of dynamite. Each time, bystanders jumped. He saw it again on the news.

The Benton Fireworks Disaster took place at a hidden fireworks plant. The only locals who knew about the factory worked there. People heard the explosion twenty miles away.

Local law enforcement learned about the fireworks plant when it became a fireball.

The enterprise had started in December 1982. Dan Lee Webb, owner of Webb's Bait Farm, joined with Howard Bramblett and David Parks. Bramblett had the connections to get the components to build M80 and M100 fireworks. He understood how to assemble them, and taught Webb and Parks.

They worked inside a metal dairy barn on Webb's property. The group started mass production by hiring family and friends at five dollars an hour.

In six months of operation, they sold more than 1.5 million M-series firecrackers. They distributed to twelve surrounding states.

The local sheriff and ATF had gotten wind of a sizable illegal operation, but had no idea of its location. A fact that changed on May 27, 1983 at 9:15 AM, when all involved cocked an ear.

Eleven workers were inside the barn when it exploded. Tommy Webb, cousin of Dan Lee, was mowing the grass. Tommy flew seventy yards. The blast leveled trees a hundred yards away. Bodies of the eleven workers—many decapitated and stripped of their clothes by the shock wave—flew up to five hundred feet. Witnesses said the cloud rose eight hundred feet.

No one knew what caused the explosion. A spark from an electric drill, static from the floor, or the lighting of a cigarette. No one knew.

Regardless of the cause, the disaster rained thousands of M-Series fireworks on the woods surrounding Webb's Bait Farm.

Deaths accrued.

Chapter 15

Sophia Whitcombe thought, if any girl ought to be prepared...

The car speed increased. She rocked forward. As the car took a long curve, centrifugal force pulled her toward the right. She rolled forward as the driver braked. *He's exiting the highway.* She tried to remember being on Interstate 40 but didn't know the road. She had no idea where she was, and asking would do no good.

"You're doing real well back there. Just lay low, and it'll all be fine."

"Who are you?"

The man hesitated. "Can I tell you my real name?"

Sophia thought about that. She recognized the ingratiating tone. Did he want her to like him? Or was he trying to pacify her with a friendship that would disappear when the car ride ended? She knew what her father would say.

"You better not."

"Yeah. I don't want you to slip up and tell somebody. After the photo shoot."

Sophia's mother half-jokingly called her father Mister Safety. He worried about his wife and daughter and did all he could to ensure they would never be easy victims. He'd trained Sophia how to dismantle and assemble several popular handguns, a Glock, SIG, and Ruger. She, like her mother, had learned how to shoot and maintain her skill. Sophia knew from age twelve she would certify for a concealed carry license when she came of age.

Her father bought books written by survivalists. How to make bombs and incendiaries. Man-trapping techniques. Escape and evasion. What to eat in the woods. Her mother called him the most prepared man in Tennessee.

Her father had made her watch *The Silence of the Lambs*. He told her that getting the killer to use the victim's name, to humanize her, was total Hollywood crap.

"He knew she was a woman. He wanted to make a suit out of her skin. See, killers don't have a problem seeing their victims as human. They don't care. Normal people worry about being nice, and think if a killer could just get real with you, he'd feel empathy. He wouldn't be able to hurt you. But killers operate in a different mental dimension. They already know what you are. It's like— hey, see that ant on the sidewalk?"

"Yes."

"Here's twenty bucks. Step on the ant."

Sophia jumped on the ant.

He gave her the bill. "You knew what the ant was. You knew it was alive. But you didn't put yourself in its place, and imagine a giant foot crushing your exoskeleton. You saw the money and did what you did."

"But it was just an ant."

"Yeah, and to a killer, you're just a beautiful girl. A perfect match for who he wants to kill."

"But if the ant had said, 'Hey, my name is John,' I wouldn't have killed it."

"Right. *You* wouldn't have. But a killer would say, 'Even better.' You ever get into a real-world situation, don't kid yourself. You can't make a killer forget his reward. You have to escape, kill him, or die. No hero will come save you. The world doesn't work that way."

Sophia's father insisted she memorize the five rules of survival. She thought he made them up, but his commitment to her safety made her want to know them.

The first rule was to trust no one. She'd already butchered that one.

The second was to survive. Always live another minute. When things get desperate, another moment means another chance to think of a solution.

The third rule: Know your surroundings. Every environment contains hidden resources.

The fourth rule: Your mind is your best weapon. Protect it by feeing your hope.

The fifth rule: Choose your moment. Resistance all the time requires you to have more strength than your adversary. It is futile. But resistance at the right moment allows you to conserve energy. You unleash your power at the right opportunity.

Thinking of her father inspired her. It was unlikely he would track her down and destroy her captor. But he had already given her what she needed. He'd taught self reliance.

She would use her wits, wiles, and even her charms to survive. Sophia would do what she had to do. Every environment had resources. She was a walking environment. She had resources. She would fight. Kill. Gouge his eyes and bash his brain.

Thinking of the lengths she would fight encouraged her toward action. She felt along the underside of the front seat, hoping to find a car jack or a wrench or something. Even a nail or screw would be useful. The space was empty. She looked around the rest of the back-seat compartment. Bare features. Nothing removable.

She remembered she had several bobby pins in her hair. She removed one and placed it over the waist of her jeans, under her belt.

The car slowed. Turned. The suspension rattled and the road noise increased.

A dirt road?

Sophia tried to remember every single word her father had told her about survival.

If he is tying you up, your chances of survival are decreasing. It is almost always better to try to escape—even taking great risk to do so. But if you can't escape, inflate yourself while he binds you. Inhale deep. Flatten your hands. Don't allow yourself to be pressed against a rigid structure like a board, a pipe, or a chair, without slack in your form. You need to be able to create motion to escape.

What else did he say?

The farther you are from other people, the more risk. So don't let him take you from the first crime scene to the second. The first is risky for him. The second is deadly for you.

Great job with that.

Sophia reversed the self criticism. There was no place for that, now. She could have been more careful, but the outcome would depend on her positive state of mind.

She thought about what her father had said about escaping from a zip tie. What else? How to break free of duct tape.

Unfortunately, her father never said anything about escaping a police car. But she knew there would be an opportunity. Eventually her kidnapper would stop the car and get her out of it. The longer she waited, the more difficult escape would be.

When the car door opened, she would make her move.

Chapter 16

I'm unsettled by what you did.

"Leaping lizards, Joe! I got issues with it too. But you was in it."

I know, but those dogs was my people.

"Mine, too."

It just doesn't feel good.

"Listen. Joe, you've not been in this world long as I have, but here's what I learned. Conscience doesn't remember the moment, so nothing ever feels right after you do it. That's the curse of being one of the upper animals. Dogs and Men."

Stinky Joe licks his jowls, already on to the next thought. A crafty thinker, Joe.

I bet they took the gold. Hey, why park here?

"Those archangels don't know this Suburban."

I park a quarter mile away so they don't have a chance to see the vehicle. A few night stockers' cars sit parked next to an Ingles grocery. They're in the skinny lot alongside the building. I swing next to a rusted Civic. The Suburban is shiny black, but I don't guess it'll draw the eye of someone looking for a beat-up pickup. I park the back next to the building so when it comes time to swap the gold out of the truck, I'll be part hid.

Got to think clever, like a dog.

Come on Mae's house by foot and get the tingle in my arms. Got a fierce two in the morning sober pinching my brain, and it's a powerful help to the electric curse. There's deception ahead. I know it.

Left side of the house, trees stretch from woods to road, but thinner and thinner as you go. I sneak along and once I get within fifty yards I low crawl. After five feet of roughing my knees, I walk at a hunch. The dog that wanted to chew off my arm wrenched my back. I stand all the way up and hope the sober will help me pay more attention.

Through the side window I see no one, which is good because they're tied on the floor. Still, I don't trust Mae to keep her head and don't trust Ruth to have one. No matter what a man does, a woman can turn it sideways.

If all unfolds like I imagine, nobody need get shot. I'll leave the FBI archangels on the floor and call the cops from a phone booth a few hour down the road.

I'll take Mae and we'll start over. Me the fool daddy, and fool grampa. Teach her how to shoot a gun and maybe use my curse to help her spot an honest man.

I can almost see us in the breeze, picnic table covered in burgers and beans. She's found a decent man who can talk guns and World War Two. The kids are off pitching water balloons and climbing trees and falling on their heads. Good summer fun. Can almost see it through the North Carolina two o'clock dark. I'd be happy; she'd be set right. I'd visit—and for the most part, live somewhere else. Retire. Talk to no liars.

"Halt!"

I do. Turn my head. See nothing but black night.

"I said halt. Don't move!"

"Awful particular. Who you?"

"Same one you threw in the wall. Now we're going back into the house. Don't make any sudden moves. I'll shoot you this time. I swear to Christ."

"You should read up if you think that would impress him. Where are you?"

A form resolves from shadows at my feet. He was crouched in the bushes. But why can't I see his eyes?

I turn part way around and, holster hid, make a slow reach for it.

"Don't do it! I said I'd shoot you."

"What?"

"Your gun. Don't go for it. I got you center mass and before that forty-four clears three inches you'll be dead."

"It's pitch black. How you—?"

"NVGs."

"What?"

"Night vision goggles."

"Cheater."

"Uh-huh. Hold your arms in the air, like to reach the stars."

I Feel Smith leave my hip. Get lonely quick.

"Walk."

"Aright. Aright."

But I'm not ready for prison. Spent three days in jail and it made me understand no group of thugs has a right over me. Make laws against murder—without *good reason*—and I'll go along. But some of these other laws—like I got to let Stipe and his boys burn me down and kill my dog—these laws don't apply to me. No cabal of liars and thieves has the authority over me. Law is gang force.

Rights is bullshit. You got no right in the natural world. Just what you defend.

I'll defend my freedom and property against all. If it means I shoot an archangel here on the lawn and another inside, they chose their fate.

I cut to the house. Long as I don't feel the juice, I don't worry about a bullet in my back. Climb the steps. "You want me to go on in? Your partner won't shoot me out of surprise?"

"Not from surprise."

"Maybe we ought to call out."

"Frank, this is Jeb. I got him. We're coming in. He doesn't want you to shoot him."

"Jeb? Your name Jeb?" I open the door. "How you like that?"

I go inside. Mae and Ruth are sunk in the sofa, hands on their laps, cuffed. Mae's cheeks are red and shiny. Upstairs, little Joseph wails. Frank nods at Mae and she tries to stand but without her arms to push off, she can't clear the sofa. She rolls sideways, uses her cuffed hands to push off, gets to her feet.

"I can't tend him with handcuffs on."

Frank takes a key from his pocket. Unfixes her hands.

"Stand here. Don't move. You—" He turns to me. "Hands behind the back."

"Okay, but I need to use the bathroom."

"Use the one upstairs," Mae says. "The lower one's clogged. Was meaning to ask you to fix it."

"You're not using either."

Joseph wails again. Mae winces and her eyes get narrow. "Can I please tend to my son?"

Frank reaches to put cuffs on me. Mae heaves up the steps two at a time.

"You can't—" Jeb says. "Frank. Put the cuffs on Baer and get up there with her."

I put my hands out front. "This way I can wipe my own ass, you finally let me relieve my bowels."

Frank slaps the metal to my arms and cinches them tight. Follows Mae upstairs.

Ruth looks straight ahead, and I get a sizzle on my arms though her eyes are blank. I never did have the full power with her. On account her deceit coming so natural—twisted ass woman eats nails and squats screws. Ruth had something to do with this.

"Say, Jeb."

"Yeah, Baer?"

"I need to squat."

"Wait until Frank comes back."

"He takes too long, I'll drop my drawers right here."

"You do that."

"I will. And why aren't we in the back of your car, driving somewhere official?"

Jeb looks at me. Looks away.

"Uh-huh. You don't know what to do with three kids and a momma who didn't have nothing to do with nothing."

Jeb ignores.

"So let me ask you this. I had you tied good. You got arms like a weeping willow. I know you didn't bust that duct tape and power cord."

Jeb clenches his teeth. Stares to my eyes. I get the red. He could look past me to see Ruth if he wanted, but he doesn't, and the deception isn't what he's saying or doing but what he isn't.

"Uh-huh. I hear you."

"You need to sit on the sofa," Jeb says.

"I need to spray paint a toilet brown, is what I need to do. Then I'm yours. Whatever."

"Sit on the sofa. When Frank gets back you can use the bathroom."

"I'm about to bust open right now. Was in a hurry to get back to the house is why you was able to catch me so easy."

"We wait on Frank."

Noise in the hallway upstairs. "You understand my diet's mostly liquid and what comes out is too?"

Jeb looks at Ruth. Thinks on her. And sure as I knew it, figures she's safe. He gestures. "Upstairs."

I climb the stairs as Mae arrives at the top with Joseph in her arms. Bree and Morgan trail behind in long t-shirt nightgowns, wide eyed and spooked. We cross on the stairs like a prisoner swap.

At the stairwell top Jeb says, "Frank, stay with Baer while he relieves his bowels. Don't let him out of your sight."

"Hey little princess," I touch Morgan's tiny shoulder. "Don't you worry on nothin'. Uncle Baer's here." I reach to Bree next. "You go downstairs and mind your mother. These men is good men, here to help us through some trouble is all. You be good, right?"

Bree nods slow.

"I be back down there with you in a hurry."

I turn back up the stairs and down the hall. At the bathroom door: "It's small in here. You mind a touch a privacy?"

I let out a fart I been saving five minutes, not knowing its precise intentions. "Oh lordy. Oh lordy, cutting things close."

Frank waves the gun. I step inside and ease the door partway around behind me. The window's open a crack. Fixed it last summer. Top half likes to slip downward. I stuck a dowel next to the track—only dowel I had was three quarters of an inch. It didn't fit inside the track, so I rested it next. It keeps the top window from sliding down when you undo the latch to lift the bottom. Window's unique: bottom half go up and top half come down. And a fighting tool's stowed inside.

I drop my drawers and none too soon. While I file a grievance in the toilet, I twist around and work the window to get the dowel out. Finish both at the same time. Rest the dowel on the floor while I stand and spin the toilet paper.

"What's the noise?" Frank pushes open the door. A gust from the window delivers some air to him. His face wrinkles like he's breathing death.

"Just a minute, Frank. I got a loose boot."

I bend, turn my naked hairy split to Frank and grab the dowel. In one doublehanded swing I bring it to his head and he stands dumb and numb while I give him another.

Frank's the one always ready to shoot, always ready to lie and deceive. No way such a man's got the moral above me. I give him one more thwack, square atop his head for good measure. Then pin him to the wall and let him down slow so he don't make a tumult. Wipe good, lift and fix my drawers, fetch the cuff keys from his pocket and learn quick how to use them.

I leave his plastic gun and scoot to the window. Use the dowel that made such a handy head club to prop the top window back open so I can get out the bottom. As I wriggle and kick and get one leg out, Frank rouses and blinks away the blood. Crawls after me. He pulls his pistol and I'm a confessed fool for leaving it with him. I got one foot on the roof and the other kicking off the toilet. I get clear and step to the side as he brings the gun to bear.

Frank shoves his pistol hand out the window and I give it a kick, but he holds the gun and follows with his head outside. I reach and pull out the dowel. The window drops a couple inches.

I grab the top and slam it home like a flat headed guillotine on Frank's noggin. One'll do but Frank brings out my generous nature, and the dowel already proved he's thick skulled. I give him three. He's dead or close. He drops his gun. It slides on shingles and stops next to the gutter. I don't want to go after it.

A burst of cold wind gives me a shove and I wobble a couple steps. Got a front coming in from the east. Rain, from the smell.

I cross to the side of the roof with the tree adjacent. Hard to see in the dark, but I been up and down it enough to guess. I reach to the limb that overhangs the roof. See red and blues coming from Gleason. Lights flashing between houses and trees, wouldn't be visible from the ground. I jump to the limb, swing up my legs. Once I got the grip, work to the tree, then crotch to crotch until I reach the ground. Don't want to leave Mae and the girls or the truck of gold, but those police cars will be here inside two minutes.

The back way to the Ingles' parking lot crosses the road. If I go now, I'll arrive when the police do. Since they're likely looking for an old guy with long hair and rough clothes, I take cover in a copse. Hunker low and wait.

In no time, three police cars come roaring in. Lights swirling and flashing, make a blind man dizzy. They get out their cars unconcerned and wander about. One looks at my truck and moseys to the side. Jeb doesn't yet know Frank's head is busted open, else these boys'd be in a hurry. Copper looks at the bed, shines his light inside and stops a minute, and shines it away, and my heart about sinks.

He doesn't say anything to the others, and now I have a goal: get back with a couple guns before these lawmen split my gold.

Chapter 17

Ernest Swain confessed to Josiah that he'd lost the five hundred-thousand-dollar life insurance death benefit.

Shortly afterward, Josiah Swain became aware of a voice. It explained, *IT WILL RAIN DEATH ON HIM.*

It?

It, who?

The disembodied voice proposed no course of action. It didn't demand anything of Josiah. He wasn't required to sneak into Ernest's bedroom, cock the firearm sitting on the night stand, and fire at him.

That was a relief. Josiah had seen Ernest wearing the pistol on his hip, even around the house. Far from feeling protected, Josiah had felt fear at being so close to an unstable man with a gun.

IT WILL RAIN DEATH ON HIM.

What, Josiah thought. *The gun?*

He could imagine Ernest having a mishap and shooting himself in the foot. Ernest's short temper and quick frustration also made it easy for Josiah to imagine Ernest carrying the gun into the woods and never coming back.

Days passed. Nothing happened.

Ernest didn't commit suicide. In fact, Josiah found him on the hammock with a Sony cassette player on his belly, his face twisted in the happiest smile Josiah had ever seen. It was enough to make Josiah doubt the voice.

He'd probably heard a snippet on the television—a soldier explaining how a bomb would kill someone—and the words came back from memory. Or maybe he'd had a dream. Who knew where words came from, before you think them?

For the next two days, Josiah kept track of Ernest. He rose early. Ate breakfast and took a green spiral notebook to the patio. He sat on a lounge chair with his legs stretched, and listened to cassette tape, after tape, after tape.

At the window of the second story home office, Josiah cracked the window open. He watched Ernest through binoculars as he began his meditations.

Ernest started with Aaron Copeland. He let the cassette play for three minutes and twenty-six seconds. Then he rewound the tape and let it play for three minutes and twenty-six seconds, six times. Josiah saw tears on Ernest's cheeks on the first playing. During the second, Ernest grimaced and shook, and wiped his eyes several times. By the sixth playing, he sang *BAH BAH BAH!!!!* full voice.

Ernest sat up in his lawn lounge, swung his arms back and forth. He threw a few shadow box punches, a couple head fakes.

He nodded, over and over, like he was super sure about something. Then Ernest played a cassette from a set by a guy named Dyer.

The last time Josiah heard the voice and felt the compulsion, it only took two days for his parents to die. This go around, his premonition seemed less efficient. Maybe he needed to find a way to help things along...

The floor rumbled. The window rattled.

Earthquake!

He couldn't ask for a bigger sign than that!

Josiah leaped down the steps two at a time. The audible shock wave hit when he was halfway down. Josiah jumped, released an uncontrolled shout and missed his next step. He tumbled. The wall flew at him. Josiah banged his skull and shoulder and rolled onto the floor. The blast echoed in his brain and his ears rang.

Josiah waited a moment to emerge from the daze. He stepped outside as Ernest drove away in the red Volvo. Josiah saw inside the car. Ernest leaned to the right and looked out the passenger side window, as if searching for the source of the sound.

Josiah looked to the woods as well, and set off with long, powerful bounds. He ran by instinct, sure he had to be within a half mile of whatever had produced the sound.

After a minute of racing top speed, giant raindrops pattered through the leaves. They fell with force. Josiah stopped. Looked up. The sound had been like a bomb. But could it have been a thunder and lightning blast?

There hadn't been any clouds in the sky.

The rain never picked up momentum, just the sporadic crash of a few fat drops smashing through the leaves. But one came from above him, and when it hit, bounced five feet away.

Josiah stepped to a red cardboard tube with a pristine fuse sticking out the side. It looked like a piece of dynamite.

As he picked it up, other leaves crackled, every few seconds. The patter accelerated, and within twenty seconds was over.

IT WILL RAIN DEATH ON HIM.

Emma Swain was getting groceries with her daughter, Mary.

Ernest Swain slept on his hammock.

Josiah was ready.

For the last year, Josiah sometimes got out of bed at night to creep around the house. One time he stepped on a slipper left in the living room. He'd rolled his ankle, hit a wooden rocking chair, and slammed it into the wall. No one roused. Ernest continued to snore. Josiah learned from that.

It was critical to Josiah's plan that Ernest be deep asleep. Standing next to him, he saw one of the small wheels of the Sony Walkman turning. He heard the droning voice of the man on the cassette tape through the tinny speakers at Ernest's head.

Josiah pulled an M100 from his pocket and straightened the fuse. He dug from his other pocket a butane lighter he'd found on the side of the road.

With his thumb on the lighter, Josiah thought about what would happen if his plan didn't work.

What if Ernest woke up?

What if the firecracker was a dud?

All he'd be able to do was pretend it was a joke. He didn't know it was serious. Would anyone believe him? He'd feel comfortable telling it that way, regardless.

The bottom line was that he had to trust. The compulsion had told him his parents would die. Then the compulsion gave him the means to destroy his parents' killer. The fact that the compulsion seemed to be playing both sides was not a reason to doubt it.

Josiah simply *knew* how things would turn out. He would light the M100. Rest it on Ernest Swain's chest, and the blast would shatter his ribs, stop his heart and lungs, and kill him. And it would all be right and good, because Ernest Swain had hired a man to kill Josiah's parents. Ernest Swain had stolen all the money Josiah's father had left for him.

Still, it was a big deal.

Every time he did something wrong, Emma—he'd never call her Mom—threatened they'd have him put in the reform school. Saint Clayton's, over at Chattanooga, where the big kids would beat him up. They wouldn't let him watch television or read his books or do anything. All his time would go toward practicing marching and doing math homework. Josiah knew Emma wasn't happy about taking in her nephew when her brother- and sister-in-law died. Early on, he'd overheard her say to Ernest, "He's family, just not *family*."

Josiah kept his mouth closed and observed. But he always knew he was apart from the others. Not that he didn't have a real family. He was apart in how his mind worked, how he understood things. In a way, he was outside the normal rules of right and wrong. Not that he wouldn't have hardship—he didn't even think in those terms. He was aligned with his existence. As long as he heeded the compulsion, he would walk between the raindrops that afflicted others.

Josiah flicked the lighter, held the flame to the firecracker. Waiting until the fuse burned half its length, he looked from the sparking fuse to Ernest's eyes, then back. Satisfied, Josiah placed the M100 on Ernest's chest.

Josiah trotted backward. He tripped and fell to the ground on his tailbone.

The firecracker exploded.

Parts of shirt and skin and blood flew past him, over him. Ernest bounced in the hammock, his arms popping up in the air. His legs shook. His voice cried an anguished, grating moan that faded as his chest cavity filled with blood.

Josiah regained his feet and ran back to Ernest. He heard a car door slam behind him. Emma was home.

Ernest's eyes were open.

"You killed my mother and father," he said.

Ernest blinked. His eyes dulled. Josiah saw life leave him.

Inside Josiah felt as if he had completed a masterpiece. He had found something essential and perfect about himself, and how to express it. He knew why he existed; what fulfilled him, what sounds were music.

Behind him, Emma shrieked.

Josiah noticed a spiral notebook by Ernest's side. Tucked low, protected from the firecracker.

He should have destroyed the notebook.

Emma arrived. *Oh My God No Oh My God No Oh My God No!*

Chapter 18

Back at the Suburban I swing into the seat and close the door. Put my head back and close my eyes.

Didn't expect you back so quick. Was I right about the gold?

"Maybe."

Well?

"Let me think."

I see in my mind's eye the jugs of liquor I took from the fight circle. I bet a snurkle of that would be a toothsome delight. I reach back and grab a jug, take a long pull and let the numb spread across my tongue and throat and do its calming work.

Put the keys in and give them a half turn.

3:13 in the AM.

Take the keys out.

Didn't want to kill Frank, but he insisted. And it's like them dogs. He wasn't fit. I lived my whole life wincing every time a liar got near me on account of the pain from the juice. I know the depth of these men' souls. Each ready to trick and deceive to have his way. Some petty advantage, most time, but other times it's for stealing. Flat out put you in a hard place so his is easier. That's all mankind, and all woman, too. Selfish and blind. Whole cesspool. No wonder God made the flood, you think on it. Miracle he hasn't done it again. And these boys think they got the authority on me? Take control of me, put me in a cement room with bars and brown paint? March me all solemn in front of a judge who glows red and sparks his own damn self?

Then judge me?

Bull. There's not a man on the planet has the right. All they can do is gang up and use force. That's all the lot of man is good for anyway. And if I let them it's my own damn fault.

Time to ditch Gleason for good. I got a life waiting out west. Some cabin in the mountain wood. I'll head to town and buy some seeds and blankets and edge tools. 'Side that, nothing. Maybe a radio and some salt and pepper, and cheddar cheese.

I grab another pull from the jug. Tired. Chevrolet makes a fine seat. Can almost feel tight backbones uncouple and settle in.

Maybe I'll sleep here and come morning, find a ball cap for disguise and catch 40 West, no one the wiser ....

But that won't work and I know it. Best get out of town now. I twist the key. Headlamps cut out into trees along the road and in some fella's house.

Didn't you say they had Mae in cuffs?

I look at Stinky Joe, lit by the dashboard. "Why, no I didn't."

But they did. And didn't you say Mae helped you get loose, with the lie about the toilet?

"What did I tell you about conscience?"

Stinky Joe looks at me like he expected more.

I wait. Think. "And she held a gun on them while I was gone. So they think she's part of the whole deal. All those boys dead in the wood. And Frank with his head busted. All that's on Mae. My girl Mae."

And if Mae goes to jail, wouldn't Ruth have to take care of Morgan, Bree, and Joseph?

"And one more thing. That's my gold. Worked my whole life for that metal. And if I don't spend it, I want Mae or the kids to buy some stuff with it."

Stinky Joe grins. He looks at me steady and I look back, and we're in it together.

I pop the latch on the back and in the cubby between the last seat and the lift door, drop my Smith & Wesson holster. Check two revolvers and belts. One a .357 with a long barrel and the other a Taurus Judge.

Well, fucky fucky ain't I lucky?

I bust open the Judge and the cylinder goes every other, a .45 hollow point then a .410 shotgun shell. The belt's got twenty more.

I crisscross belts and strap them on so the .357 gets my left hand and the Judge my right.

Another gun looks interesting. I pull it from a butt holster—a pouch that slips above the ass crack—and it's a Smith & Wesson 9mm. Start to jam it down my pants but the gun belts are tight and hell, do I need this much firepower? There's Jeb and three deputies from Gleason—not exactly Wyatt Earp and three Doc Holidays. I leave the Smith automatic.

One more pull from the jug.

"You hang in there, Joe."

Glad I could help.

Walking, I noodle it best I can. The whole plan was to leave Frank and Jeb tied, and them not knowing the Suburban, they wouldn't know how to follow. There'd be no advantage in them dead. Only liability.

But now I got the same liability. The FBI isn't going to come at me with less gumption because I only killed the one.

Walk like I'm supposed to be on the backstreets looking like a one-man O.K. Corral. Each time headlights flash I cut through another lawn. Get turned around, so I have to spin a slow circle and look for all the swirling red and blues to know which way to go.

Closer. I come back on the house like I left. Slow this time, mindful these boys by now found Frank. Put me down, if they can.

I come in along the trees on the upper side, then down the left instead of the right.

They have Mae in the back of a police car with one standing guard with a flashlight, and the kids must be inside. Another flashlight comes up around the other side of the house, slow and careful. Other two must be inside.

Far off, a siren. Ambulance? Do the other two tend Frank?

Alive?

I try and get my brain around how this whole affair's liable to go down. I go in there and my mind isn't made up about killing or not killing, I'll fumble and fart and get my dumb ass in jail. Or shot.

Need to know my mind.

Druther not kill another man. On balance, I don't care for it. But I've already been through the logic: I got to rescue Mae or she spends her life in jail for what I did. Only thing to decide is how far I'll go, so I get there first.

Is Mae's freedom worth all these lawman's lives?

Well, she didn't have nothing to do with nothing. They got her waiting in the back of their car, separated from her kids. On account two FBI boys don't have the sense to see that killing twenty men who like to fight dogs isn't a crime to start with. And everything else escalated out of that.

They left me no choice.

Chapter 19

Sheriff Horace Wycliff Leathers, age 42, of Polk County jurisdiction, stood six foot nineteen and looked to weigh a buck ten. Townsfolk said he hunted geese by slapping them out of the sky. If bad weather was coming, folks would ask him what it looked like the next county over. Horace had a sense of humor about most things, robbery, rape, even the rare homicide. He said having a sense of humor was the only way to reconcile the common man's evil and the beautiful innocence of God's created world. If you didn't have the capacity to laugh at the absurdity of it, even just a little bit, secret, inside... you were likely plain-ass evil too, and part of the problem. And he'd laugh. "You probably don't even wash your elbows."

When he walked fast, he covered six feet in a single stride. His deputy Marcy Keating trailed him like a dog with short legs, taking three steps for each of his. Marcy was an avowed out of the closet lesbian. She liked to say, "Not every man you see on the street is the problem." Leathers heard the sentence almost daily for his first week as sheriff and one day said, "What do you mean by that? Not every man is the problem?"

"Some rape boys."

Leathers didn't know what to say to that. At one time, maybe she said it like a punch line. Now?

By the end of the day he decided to give her the leeway she needed. Let her find her way through the world with whatever peace she could. Through years of service they developed a kinship and enjoyed working together. Over time, she stopped saying it.

Leathers and Marcy entered Swain's back yard with a crisp cadence, though it was late morning. Humid air stuck to the skin. The forest around the back yard buzzed with insect life. And Leathers smelled something.

When he saw Ernest Swain's chest, he recognized the odor.

The pungency of death contained more than the scent of blood. More than any bowel or bladder seepage. Within a half hour of a gruesome death, the smell became darker, somehow. Blood of a dead man smelled worse than that of a living man.

Sheriff Leathers and Deputy Marcy met Emma, Josiah, and Mary Swain on the back patio. Leathers looked over the floor tiles, lawn chairs and charcoal grill. Mary, the daughter, sat off by herself with her arms wrapped around her chest and her knees pulled high. Emma Swain walked back and forth, staring into the distance, not seeming to see anything at all. Her face was pink and her eyes bloodshot. Leathers assumed she'd already passed through a moment of hysteria, and proceeded to shock.

"Did your daughter see anything? Was she a witness?" Marcy said to Emma.

Emma spoke as if each word wafted to her through a fog. "No. We came home right when it happened. We were in the driveway and heard the bomb."

"Okay," Marcy said. "What's her name?"

"Mary."

"Let's get Mary inside the house. Is there a place where she can sit and still see you through the glass door? She doesn't need to hear our discussion."

Sheriff Horace Wycliff Leathers said, "Son, what's your name?"

"Josiah."

"You were here when it happened?"

Josiah nodded.

"Let's go over here." Leathers extended his arm, and Josiah walked along in front of it. Leathers heard Marcy move the Swain daughter indoors. He knew she would next question Emma Swain.

"What did you see, Josiah? That's a great name, by the way. Your parents chose a good one."

"Uh, thanks."

"Your parents passed away a few years ago?"

"Uh-huh."

"Emma and Ernest were your aunt and uncle?"

"Uh-huh."

"You been okay living here? They treat you all right?"

"They're good."

"Okay. That's got to be tough on a young man. Lose his parents, then be the first to find a sight like that." Leathers nodded toward the hammock.

"Yeah."

"Well, I understand, that's all. Sometimes a man's got to look at all the ugliness and heartache in the world and kind of go along with it. Don't fight it until you know what you're fighting. Then give it all kinds of hell. So while you're young like you are, don't let it cut you too deep. Just get through the day. You know what I'm saying? You've got plenty of time later on to make the world a better place."

"Uh, okay."

"So were you outside when it happened?"

Josiah hesitated. "Well."

"It's okay. Tell me what you saw."

"I didn't see nothing, really."

"Where were you standing?"

Josiah pointed.

"You were there? That close?" Leathers looked the boy up and down. "Seems like you'd get debris on you from the blast, that close."

"I fell. Right there."

Leathers strode across the lawn. "Show me."

"I was backing up and stumbled. First I was coming toward him then I saw the firecracker on his chest and thought I was going to be too late then I backed up."

Josiah looked at Ernest's body and stopped talking.

"So you backed up."

"Yeah. I slipped right then. Here's where I kicked to get away after the explosion."

Josiah pointed to a heel mark in the grass, deep enough to cut into the moist earth.

"So if I'm understanding," Leathers said, "you were here, on your back, when the thing went off?"

"That's right."

"Why were you running toward him?"

"Because I saw the firecracker was lit."

"Did you see him light it?"

"No."

"Where were you when you saw it?"

Josiah turned around. Pointed back toward the patio.

"Were you in a lawn chair?"

"No. I came outside. I was standing. I looked and saw the smoke. And I heard it."

"Okay. So you come running up. Did Ernest say anything?"

"No. Well. He held up his hand, like to say stop. But he didn't say it. I think he would have. His mouth was open. He didn't see me until I was here because he had his earphones on."

"So he was listening to the cassette player and didn't see you?"

"He mostly just lays out here with his eyes closed. He listens all the time."

Leathers nodded. "And when you come upon him, the firecracker was already there? And lit? Did you get a good look at it?"

"It was red. Like a roll of quarters, but not so long."

"Let me check if I'm hearing you right. It was an M100 firecracker."

"That's right."

Leathers studied Josiah.

"It might have been. Either the hundred or the eighty."

"Which was it?"

A shrug.

"You collected them in the woods, like every other boy around here."

Josiah nodded. "Am I in trouble?"

"It was an M100. You lit it, placed it on Ernest's chest, and he couldn't hear it. Then you backed away and fell. Then it went off. Were you trying to kill him, or give him a scare?"

Josiah's mouth fell open. He saw himself in handcuffs, headed for reform school. The air went out of him and his thoughts vanished. His mind floated. He heard a roar come up behind him. Blood rushed in his ears. Consciousness slipped over his brain and out the back.

Josiah collapsed.

He roused with a dizzy feeling like when he had the flu and gravity seemed distorted. Like his mind hurtled through an elliptical orbit. He felt himself licking his dry lips and then he heard Emma Swain say, What happened, what did you say to him? Are you even allowed to talk to a child without a parent there?

I asked him if he put the firecracker on Ernest.

You asked him WHAT?

"No," Josiah said, with very little air behind his voice. He flopped his leg. "No." He opened his eyes.

"Keep laying down a minute, until you get your strength back. You blacked out," Emma said. "You have a summer flu."

Josiah looked around the faces above him. It was hard to guess what anyone was thinking. From his perspective on the ground they all looked angry.

But he did notice the spiral edge of a notebook tucked into Emma Swain's purse.

"How dare you!" Emma pushed Sheriff Horace Wycliff Leathers. She was short and he was tall. He bent at the waist and her arms were not long enough to move him. "Ernest was depressed. He sat out here every day listening to stupid tapes for depressed people. He lost the Polk Benton. He put all our money into it, then lost that too. We don't even own this house. He went to bed early and slept in late. He cried watching Little House on the Prairie! And you accuse a thirteen-year-old boy of killing him?"

Leathers backed three steps and Deputy Marcy filled the gap between them. "I'm sorry, Mrs. Swain. We have to ask all the questions. We can't jump to conclusions. We have to ask difficult questions."

"This is outrageous. This is... I don't know. This is terrible. Your behavior is atrocious."

Josiah lifted himself by his elbows. The dizziness didn't return. He rolled to his side and climbed to his feet.

"You know what?" Emma said. "I don't want him on our property. Just because you're sheriff doesn't mean you're allowed on my property."

Marcy shook her head. "I'm sorry, Mrs. Swain. This is such a tragedy. Let's go sit on the patio and you can tell me more about Mister Swain's state of mind in the last few weeks."

Josiah looked at Leathers. Leathers looked back at him, then to Emma Swain.

"I didn't do what you said," Josiah said.

"Okay, son. I didn't think you did."

Chapter 20

The car slowed and cut left. It bounced, as if navigating a rough driveway. Flat on the seat, on her back, Sophia watched through the side windows.

She had a plan.

The driveway smoothed and the car slowed. The engine sound increased and dark fell over the car. Shadows replaced the trees and sky, then resolved into the weathered boards of an old barn.

"We have arrived at the photo shoot," the man said. "Hope you're feeling sexy."

"I'm feeling nauseous. I'm having my period."

He turned in his seat and looked down on her with a slight smile. "Sit tight."

The man exited the car. She watched for him to appear in the window so she could position herself to attack. Instead, she heard a sound like metal rollers. He entered the car and drove forward. The light coming through the back window dimmed, then disappeared.

They were inside a garage. Being in an enclosed space meant it would be more difficult to break free. If she fought at the door, she'd have to push him back and get over him. Or close the door and get around the car before he got up... Sophia's heart raced. She couldn't plan it without knowing her environment. She'd have to think quickly.

It was better to be in a garage than wherever he was going to take her next. Each step would reduce her freedom and make it easier for him to control her fate.

This was still the moment to fight.

The car door beside her head clicked. She sat up, adjusted to the center of the seat, folded her legs to her chest and swung them around. As the man opened the door, the dome light came on. He stepped backward as she kicked with both legs. She hit the car door but missed her kidnapper.

She fell partly out of the car and wrenched her left shoulder trying to stop her fall.

The man frowned. He reached down and held a rag to her face. She smelled chemicals.

Chapter 21

The one with the flashlight moseys to my truck and shines the light inside. He has Mae in the back of his car. Kinda moseys around like a ten-year-old boy kicking rocks.

He looks up sudden, cants his head. Satisfied, he keeps ambling.

Meanwhile the red and blues revolve and make a man wish for less moonshine, or more, one.

I muse on how the whole thing'll play out, but get stumped after I walk up and shoot this copper. Then what? They got the kids in the house. I can't shoot there. So the bad guys stay put, until a couple come out the back, like to sneak up on me?

Okay. Go with that.

I get the Judge in hand and switch from left to right, until the heft feels natural.

Okay Baer. This whole thing goes down inside three minutes, or you spend the rest of your days in jail. Waiting on a Republican governor to enforce the death penalty.

Breathe deep. Stand straight. Been long enough in the dark the copper's eyes have adjusted to the flashlight and the red and blues. I walk bold along the wood and at the closest line to the vehicles cut toward. I'm at the truck grill by the time he hears something. I got the drop.

Step to the side and raise the Judge. I want to squeeze but he stands there. Doesn't swing the flashlight to my eyes. Doesn't say nothing. Stands like some dumb kid.

Can't do it.

"Keep your voice low. You got handcuffs?"

"Y-yes."

"I want you to think on something. You're here because I murdered twenty men who stole my dog. I killed an FBI man. You think I won't kill you?"

"Frank's not dead. You busted his skull but he's not dead. You hear the ambulance?"

There's a trace of red in his eyes but no juice. I press the trigger and realize it's the revolving red and blues that makes his eyes confess to lying. It's the red and blues.

"Well, I damn sure tried to kill him and that's all that ought to matter to you. Point being, you move or call out, I shoot. And so you know, this ain't a pistol. It's a hand-held shotgun. One of those Taurus guns."

"Those are real nice."

"I took it from one of the boys I poisoned."

"Baer, you want me to handcuff myself? Would that be helpful?"

"Yup."

"Okay. So the cuffs are in a leather case on my hip. You want me to get them now?"

"Get them now."

He lifts his left hand, undoes the snap. Metal tinkles. Ratchet sounds.

"Can you do it behind your back?"

"No. Only up front."

"Then do one wrist and I'll do the other."

"Okay. My right is done."

"Turn around, and mind this gun pointed at your head."

"I'm minding it, Baer. I won't forget it."

He turns slow, bends partly forward. Got both his hands at his back. I step closer. Concentrate for the feel of electric but this copper is straight up turning hisself in. I holster the Judge and close the cuffs.

"What's your name?"

"Josiah."

"Well, Josiah, I was ready to shoot you, and I will, soon as I want."

The ambulance gets loud. Blue lights flash down the road and they home in on the red and blues flashing here.

"They're going to bring Frank out as soon as the ambulance arrives."

"Hm. Where you keep the key to them cuffs?"

"Front right pocket. The long tool on my key chain."

"Keep your pecker away from my hand." I reach in his pocket and pull the ring. "This your car with Mae in it?"

"That's right."

Pull him by his elbow. Open the back door. "Get in."

"Baer?" Mae says. "That you?"

Copper Josiah stands beside the door. "I never did this before, with cuffs." He looks back, then forward.

I grab his head and guide him. "Mae, it's me. You keep this copper company a minute. I'll be back for—"

"They have the kids! Baer they have the kids inside—"

Close the door.

Ambulance bounces in the drive and I duck. It swings a U-turn and backs almost to the porch steps. Medic jump out while it's still in reverse.

House door opens and the FBI boy Jeb and a copper fireman-carry Frank across the porch and down the steps. They don't wait on the gurney.

On all fours I shift around the truck bed. Side of the house where I was five minutes ago, a copper searches with a flashlight. What? He looking bent grass? I see Butch and Sundance when they were on the mountain and the Indian below tracks them across bare rock. Make a man feel he better handle the situation now, or it'll never go away. More time they have, the bigger their advantage.

Got that copper Josiah in the car and it's nice he's alive. But if he was dead I wouldn't worry on him getting loose and causing trouble. So how's it going to work with this fella searching the woods? Can't sneak up on him with all the flashing lights. Can't leave him.

While he has his back at me, I scoot to the treeline and pick my way through the wood. Ambulance engine covers the sound and the lights let me not crack my skull on a tree. Twenty-yards-deep I start up the hill parallel to the lawn and find cover behind a giant beech. Kick leaves. Snap twigs.

Flashlight beam cuts past and zeroes in on where I stood ten seconds ago; some leaves are tore up. Light scans ahead to the distance then back and forth looking the lay. Finally back to where I was.

Light beam makes the same path, over an over, out far, in close, side to side.

A twig cracks ten feet off. He's been coming in the whole time. Like a gray squirrel I shift slow and keep the trunk between us. Can't make a sound or the jig's up. One step. Aright. One more. Done.

Peep at the copper.

Got the Judge on him. Kinda itch to see what a .410 shotgun shell in a pistol will do in the dark.

"Don't move. I got the Judge on you. And I can see your elbow there. You move for the gun, I take off your head, right?"

"That you, Baer?"

"That's right."

"This whole thing stinks, Baer."

No red. No juice. Don't know what to make of it.

"What?"

"This whole town's crooked. Stipe and Smiley. Not one of us wanted to take the call, but you busted that FBI fella's head good. Please don't kill me, Baer."

"Well…"

"You could take me hostage or something. Knock me out and take my gun? Something like that?"

"Boy, you know I killed twenty men back there? Stipe's boys—"

"The Good Book says, 'Judge not, or you'll be judged your own self.' I imagine you got some business to work out with the Almighty. But the Gleason police wouldn't be troubled at all if you was to make your getaway—"

"East."

"East. That's right. Getaway east."

I get the juice. Just a tickle.

"You jerkin' me?"

"Nossir. We been watching Stipe and couldn't do nothing because Chief Smiley was in his pocket. Every time we pull one of Stipe's boys in for anything at all, Chief lets him off. Can't even give those pricks a parking ticket, this town."

"I know you told me a lie."

"Well, truth told, deputy Randy James has a hardon for you. Wants to bring you in. He's been angling to get in with Chief Smiley and someday take his place. Kinda like the heir apparent, you know. He wants your ass. But me and Josiah, we'd rather this whole thing went away."

"So you know Stipe and Smiley was corrupt. Why didn't you call the State boys?"

"Got the kids at home. Old lady with child. I can't lose my job now. Or my life."

"Well—"

"What's wrong, Baer?"

"Wasn't counting on you being derelict. Got myself talked in to shooting you, is all, and it'll take a minute to talk myself out."

"All the time you need, Baer."

"Got the handcuffs on your left hip?"

"No, my right. I keep the left for my gun. I'm a lefty."

That works on my noodle a second.

"Okay. Fetch out the cuffs and put one on. Then put your hands in your back. And you so much as twitch, I test a .410 shell on your head."

"Yessir, Baer. My name's Leroy, by the way. Leroy Dupont. Pleasure's all mine."

The ambulance door slams and the driver jumps in. The vehicle drives off leaving the FBI man Jeb and copper Randy with the hardon for me on the porch steps, talking over their next move. If one gets a mind to check on Mae, things'll get dicey quick.

Cuffed, I turn him. "Leroy, I want you to sit behind this beech tree. I need to handle some business with them two."

"I'll just stand here until you come back for me."

"Should I knock you out or something?"

"No need. You got the drop on me. Fair and square."

"You take good care, Leroy."

Leroy and Josiah got me rethinking the whole strategy. I get these last two in cuffs, I can leave them tied up, bust out of town and never look back. Had myself set on capital self defense, but less blood'll do.

Now if I can get these other boys to give themselves up...

"Leroy. Changed my mind. C'mere. We're gonna go in there and make them surrender."

"I don't think—"

"Good." I take his elbow in my left hand and get the Judge in the right. "Easy. Watch your step."

Guide Leroy through the trees. It's easier headed toward the light.

"Now you make sure and speak up when I tell you."

We're at the edge of the lawn and if they was looking they'd see.

"Hey Jeb! Randy. This is Baer Creighton. I brought my bullets, and I got your boy here, too. Got Leroy, and I'm gonna empty this gun in his head 'less y'all put your guns on the ground and comply with my escape."

They stop talking and their eyes get jumpy. Juice on my arms, not like the dogs, but strong. Their minds turn right away to deceit and trickery. Honest man'd fess up. You got me. Mercy. But these two lawmen want to conceive the treachery that'll put them back in control.

"Tell them I got you handcuffed and have a gun to your head."

"Randy! Jeb! This is Leroy. He got me like he says. Got a gun on my head."

"Handcuffs."

"And I'm in my own damn handcuffs!"

"You don't want to die."

"Lord, I don't want to die!"

Jeb nods at Randy. They ease apart. One heads for the cars below and the other inches backward, like to find cover behind the rotted porch.

"Stop! I'll blow this boy's head off!"

"There's no way we can allow you to leave here, Baer," says Jeb. "Whether you want to play it straight or not. Frank and I witnessed you kill twenty men. You need to trust the system. Trust the law. It's on your side. It's there for all of us. Turn yourself in so this doesn't have to get any uglier than it already is."

"Trust the law? Right. I'll get a fair shake from the liars and cheats. Pure thuggery. Now put your guns on the ground."

I push Leroy forward and we walk easy. Both Jeb and Randy glow red. Fifteen feet off, I stop Leroy. Don't like standing behind him like a coward, but truth is, Gleason pays him for his bravery.

"Fellas, I'm running out of time. Here's what I propose. You drop your guns. Then put on your cuffs. I'll leave you in the living room, on the sofa—"

Jeb shakes his head.

"—once I get an hour out, I'll call the State Police in Asheville and they'll come for you. Then you can chase me all you want. That way nobody gets shot right now. Sound good?"

Jeb holds both his hands up, empty. Puts them down at his sides. "Baer, we can't allow you to run. If that means we have to use force, we will. There's three of us and only one of you."

"There's two of you. Got Josiah down there in the car with Mae. He's handcuffed too."

"Mickey's here," says Leroy.

"Where the hell's he?"

"Here."

Behind me. I twist away from Mickey and keep Leroy facing Jeb and Randy. Too many coppers. Mind travels a lot of territory fast. Though it would tickle me greatly if they all cuffed themselves, math works the problem different.

"Mickey, you put your gun on the ground."

"Can't do that, Baer."

"What, you going to shoot your own man?"

He glows red. "If I got to."

Randy shifts toward the cars again.

I'm tired. Damn near dawn and I been putting up with law enforcement monkeyshines all night. I'm through.

I point the Judge at Jeb and shoot.

Chapter 22

Lemuel Carter Sr. delivered the rural mail route that included Welcome Valley Road for twenty-nine years and forty-two days. He delivered mail to the Miller Cousins on Saturday, April 12, 1986.

The Miller Cousins enjoyed small-town fame. Earline, Clystine, and Bambi Miller were sisters. None had ever married. They lived together with fourteen children between them. Twelve men had sired them. In addition, each of the three sister-mothers had different fathers. Only the three sisters knew which child belonged to which mother. With such diversity of genetic material, there was no rhyme or reason to hair color, eye color, facial or body features.

They were a ragtag clan: dirty, poorly dressed, undisciplined. As they aged, they realized the world truly was against them. The three mothers encouraged the children to call each other brothers and sisters. *We all depend on each other, and that's how we'll make it, by God.*

Inside the family, they were brothers and sisters, but townsfolk called them the Miller Cousins. Even called the mothers cousins, though they were half-sisters.

They were the ratty family. The inbred. (A true insult, as the sisters were promiscuous, but damnwell not inbred.)

Several of the brother cousins had learned how to capture rattlesnakes. One had found a cane at a nursing home dumpster. He made another tool by running a rope with a loop at one end through a section of copper pipe. He used the cane to guide the snake's head through the noose. By pulling the rope, he could lift the snake and never be near its venomous teeth.

Catching snakes was great fun, but doing so created the problem of disposing them. It wouldn't do to kick over a bucket and run. There had to be something more entertaining than that.

The Miller house sat in the woods on the outside of a downhill curve in the road. Their mailbox was on the inside. One day years before, Lemuel Carter Sr. had parked his vehicle next to the mailbox while he stuffed it with flyers and other junk. He'd heard a horrific screeching and wailing. He looked back. A gravel truck bounced on its brakes. Lemuel's truck was in its path. The dump truck shuddered to within inches of Lemuel's bumper. He got out and the other driver got out. Each shaking with nerves, they argued about the stupidity of Lemuel parking on the inside of a blind turn. Then the dump truck driver realized he too had parked on the inside of a blind turn. He left.

Ever since, Lemuel swung into Miller's driveway and parked parallel to the road. He trusted his flashing yellow light to slow traffic, so he didn't get hit crossing the road to the mailbox.

On Saturday April 12, 1986, Lemuel Carter Sr. was in a good mood. It was the end of the week. He looked forward to church on Sunday. He took his ninety-year-old mother. They always enjoyed lunch together afterwards. He sometimes thought he'd stop attending service after his mother died. He was thinking about that when he parked at the Miller driveway and walked with letters for the mailbox.

As he approached the black metal mailbox, Lemuel heard a sound like running water, and paused. He looked about the ground for the distinctive colorings of a coiled rattlesnake. He saw nothing.

From behind a tree close to where he'd parked, he heard a child whisper.

Lemuel said, "C'mon on out from behint the tree, there, son. C'mon. I ain't got all day." He grinned, and offered, "I'll beat your ragged ass."

The boys giggled and ran off when Lemuel stomped into the woods after them. Lemuel shook his head at their cleverness. It had been years since someone had surprised him with a rattlesnake in a mailbox. The last time, the kids had hidden the reptile hours before Lemuel arrived in the late afternoon. It didn't give him a fright so much as a sense of pity. The summer heat had baked it.

But the Miller Cousins must have placed their snake moments before Lemuel arrived. It was still ornery, rattling loud and steady. Lemuel heard the warning long before reaching for the handle. It was all in good fun.

Redneck white boys will be redneck white boys.

Lemuel opened the mailbox, stepped away, and walked to the house to knock on the door. When the oldest Miller sister—Bambi—answered, he placed the bills in her hand. "You might stay away from the mailbox a while. By the sound, a rattlesnake climbed up in there."

The following Monday, the Miller Cousins talked about the exploit in school. Their failure gathered renown. It confirmed an already-popular saying, "Dumb as a Miller Cousin."

Josiah, now aged sixteen, heard about the snake incident. That night he suffered a compulsion. It came without antidote. The thought throbbed like a grid of neurons. Each point of light was a truth. They folded together and pointed to a single future. The web created prescience. Aware, Josiah only had to fulfill his part.

The first point: One of Josiah Swain's teachers said he was a spatial thinker. He was good at solving problems that required him to imagine shapes and relationships between objects. Motion, location, patterns. He built mind maps to understand reality. He grasped mechanical relationships by reasoning out causes and effects.

The second point: Fate had already decided Lemuel Carter Sr. would die at work. Fate had used the Miller Cousins, but they executed their duty like a game, and failed. No one can thwart Fate. When something is in the cards, Fate is like floodwaters, probing, moving forward, around, through or over all impediments. One way or another, Lemuel Carter Sr. was doomed.

The third: Josiah was part of the solution. Fate was drafting him to do its work—and creating the opportunity for him to do it with impunity.

Fourth: The Miller Cousins' fame for stupidity and rabblerousing was universal.

Fifth: The Miller Cousins had rigged their own mailbox. They'd established a precedent. People would blame them for future mailbox-related hijinks.

Sixth: Josiah lived a half mile from the Miller Cousins. He still had dozens of M100 and M80 firecrackers that he'd gathered after the fireworks disaster. He'd disassembled an M100 to learn how it worked and knew he could build one with ten times the powder, if he wanted.

Seventh: The Miller Cousins also had access to the M100s that had rained on the countryside after the explosion.

The points swirled and flashed in his mind, assembling into a truth, a reality. He saw the explosion in his mind's eye.

Josiah saw Lemuel Carter Sr. dead in the dirt.

Chapter 23

Orange blast shoots two feet out the tube. Turns out the first shot was a slug, not a bunch of pellets.

Jeb goes down and I swing my gun arm left and squeeze another. The Judge sprays Randy in lead from the .410 shotgun shell. Mickey charges. I spin.

Time I get the gun around, Mickey launches into Leroy and me. Mickey fires and I don't know where the bullet goes. Don't feel nothing. Mickey drives us back toward the house and I see Jeb is on his knees, bent over but getting his bearing.

Maybe had the vest on.

I shove the Judge in Mickey's guts and pull the trigger. It barks and Mickey says, "Uh," and quits just like that.

I push off Leroy, and next shot ought to be the shotgun again. I point quick at Jeb's head and pull.

Jeb goes down.

I check each man quick. Mickey's got no pulse. Bullet must have tore up his heart. Jeb's head is a mess of tangled hair and blood. Randy's alive, but gurgling through a bunch of holes in his neck.

I did it. I'm alive but want to gag at the cosmic size of my evil. I look at bloody men and wonder how… Yet there's no other way it could've gone. They'd have killed me or taken the rest of my life from me either way. So it was theirs instead of mine. But I'm pissed they made me choose.

I run to the police car on Mae's side. Open the door. "You coming or staying?"

"I'm with you."

"Turn your back to me."

I lean in and unfix her handcuffs.

"Josiah, stay put."

I turn back to the house and stop. Ruth and the babies. What'd Ruth have to do with this?

Mae climbs out the car. Rubs her wrists. Jumps up and down, tiny bounces on her toes like a boxer.

"Mae, how'd the FBI boys get loose? I had them taped tight."

"Mom. I was upstairs. Joseph has a sore throat."

Ruth let them loose. And my gold missing from the truck. "Josiah, why was you shining light in the bed of my truck? When you first got here?"

"There's a gold piece back there."

"Still there?"

"I told Randy. If it's not in the truck it's in his pocket."

I stomp to Randy and pat his pockets. Fetch it out. Kneel. "You're a thief, Randy. Go ahead and die."

I come back to the squad car. Lean into the open door. Josiah's scrunched against the far door, got his hands behind him in the gap between seat and door.

"Josiah, this is your lucky day. You keep honest and you'll live through this with a bonus." I close the door. "Mae, when they put you in the car, did they uncuff Ruth?"

"Uh-huh. They had her watch the kids so they could tend Frank and look for you."

"We need her car keys. We need the kids. And we need to leave in less'n five minutes."

Mae runs for the house.

In the commotion Leroy lost his bearings. I trot the woodline where he's wandered. "You making a break for it?"

"Nah, Baer. I didn't want to get shot. Didn't know you'd use me for a shield."

"What you think hostages are for? C'mon. I'm putting you in the car. Same deal as I give Josiah. You treat me right through this, you get your reward at the end."

"Some that gold?"

"That's right." I slam the door and leave them.

Inside the house Ruth greets me at the door with a hug. Her eyes glow and the static electric tingles all up and down me on account the proximity. I push her off. "Gimme your keys."

"What for?"

Don't know if I should answer with words or knuckles.

"Here." She pulls them from her pocket.

I spot my leather holster for Smith and grab it. Go back outside and Ruth follows on the porch and down the steps.

More cops are coming. Feel it in my bones.

"I was trying to make a life for us together," Ruth says. "An honest life. The world's so vile, and I'm wretched for being a part of it. But we never know any different…"

Ruth strides past me and cuts in my path. "I wanted to preserve something of all this hard work of yours. I wanted to keep it for you. Tell me you understand."

I grab her shoulders. Shove her like they need her next week. She skids sideways on the dirt, part on her knees, but in the same move is back on her feet.

"Baer, you owe me this! You owe me understanding!"

I push her key in her trunk. Pop it open. Two buckets rest sideways on about four inches of gold coins spread across the bottom.

"Baer! You love me! I love you! We still have the rest of our lives to work things out and get back to where we were! I hurt you years ago but that doesn't have to be now. We can move forward as a team. I want to be your partner. I always wanted that but I didn't know how to do it. I didn't know how to get past all the problems and the lies. Because I know you see them all."

I take the buckets out. Grab the back of Ruth's neck and drag her to the trunk. Push her in, and she's like a cat over water, got to keep pushing arms and legs back in.

I pull the Judge. Press it to her temple.

She folds her arms and legs. I slam the trunk lid.

Chapter 24

Josiah learned to light a match by pressing the head to the abrasive, then folding over the matchbook cover. Dragging the match between insulated his finger from the flame.

He built a mechanical version using two small paper clips, a rubber band from the broccoli in the refrigerator, and string. He glued the mechanism to a small piece of plywood from the garage. Last, he modified a M100 by gluing wood screws radially to the red cardboard. He affixed the firecracker where the flaring match would light the fuse.

Deployed inside a mailbox, he would use the length of the match as the height on the mailbox door to crazy-glue the other end of the string. Opening the door would pull the match and leave the flaring head under the M100 fuse.

Josiah chose the night of Wednesday April 16, 1986. His plan called for placing the device during the middle of the night. But excitement got the better of him and he slipped out shortly after Emma's bedroom light went dark at ten. Wearing a ski mask and gloves, he eased over the sill of his first-floor bedroom window and dangled until his feet found the ground. He carried the explosive in a brown paper lunch sack.

On the road he hid behind trees or boulders whenever headlights appeared.

Arriving at the mailbox, Josiah placed a small flashlight inside. He stood with his body blocking the light from the Miller house.

In thirty seconds, he crazy-glued the fragmentation device in place. He connected the string in another minute.

Josiah looked around. There was nothing to do now except wait. All night, all morning, and half the next afternoon.

What was he supposed to do in the meantime?

The flashlight off, Josiah sat at the mailbox post with his knees to his chin and stared at the Miller house.

After a moment, he smiled. Nodded his head as an idea took form.

He ran.

Josiah climbed into his bedroom and removed a poster of an insolent Jim Morrison from his wall. Three years earlier, he'd cut out a six-inch circle of plaster. By pushing down the insulation with a rolled newspaper, he'd created a floor. Then he stashed dozens of M100 and M80 firecrackers that he scrounged after the fireworks disaster.

Josiah removed the six-inch plaster circle. He jammed three M80's into his jeans pockets and replaced the cover and poster. Careful in case his aunt was awake and milling around, he tiptoed down the hallway. The deadbolt clicked loud when he unlocked it. He paused. Heard nothing.

Josiah left with the front door closed but unlocked.

He saw all the elements of his plan in his mind at a single moment, like a brush stroke envisioned as a perfect painting.

Where should he stage the firecrackers?

He'd place a couple where the boys would easily find them. That way, he didn't have to plant the M80s inside the house. The Cousins would carry them inside on their own. And he'd leave one someplace the police would be likely to find, but not the boys.

At the Miller house, he crept to the living room window. Hoping no one was sleeping on the couch, he pitched a bright red M80 to the roof. The thud sounded loud, but it was night. Anything would sound loud. Because the fuse stuck out the side of the red cylinder, not the top, like a stick of dynamite, the M80 barely rolled. An investigator looking from the mailbox to the house would see it, but anyone leaving the house would not.

Josiah placed another M80 at the edge of the driveway. The cousins would discover it while waiting for the school bus. The last he dropped at a tire swing where forest met yard.

The next morning Josiah ate a bowl of cereal. He loaded a small backpack with an egg salad sandwich and a plastic one-liter Coca Cola bottle he'd refilled with water. Instead of waiting for the bus he turned up the road, walked a dozen yards, and ducked into the woods.

Within a half mile he arrived at a cave haunted by bats and bones. Josiah sat with his back to the cave's damp wall.

The day was overcast and cool. Last night, after slipping back inside the house at two in the morning, he'd struggled to sleep. He finally drifted off, only to awaken sometime around four in the morning to the flash and clap of a lightning storm. The rain smashed against the roof like fat chunks of hail, and Josiah wondered if the M80 he'd left on the Miller Cousin's roof would be swept off.

Sitting in the cave, Josiah leaned against the rounded wall. His head found a smooth divot. He closed his eyes and slept.

When he roused, his Timex showed he still had hours to wait. He imagined seeing the blast. The flash and smoke. He imagined hearing Lemuel shriek like a little girl, if he said anything at all.

Adrenaline jazzed through Josiah. He stood and dusted off his pants. They were damp. He thought of the match, and how soggy air makes a match head wet, and refuse to light.

But his teacher had said Josiah was a spatial thinker. He understood mechanical things. Spaces. Interactions. Step by step, proof by proof, angle by angle. He'd seen wheels spinning within wheels and had accounted for the whole process in a singular comprehension.

Building his contraption days before, he'd checked the weather, and dipped the matchhead in paraffin.

Townsfolk referred to the youngest Miller sister, Clystine, as the pretty one because she still had all her teeth.

Although known to fraternize with almost any man, her heart belonged to a skinny car thief named Ike. She pined for him because, until late 1986, Ike would remain housed at the Polk county jail. The year before, they'd been wild lovers for two weeks. Ike's incarceration occurred before Clystine's ovulation cycle. This prevented him from becoming the thirteenth Miller daddy.

Because police arrested him while their relationship was ascendant, Clystine's love for Ike endured longer than for any other man she'd been with. Neither Clystine nor Ike remained faithful to the other while Ike was in jail, but they longed for each other's flesh and wrote torrid letters describing the carnality they would enjoy on the day of their mutual release.

Winding down his last letter, Ike wrote he could see them together in their own house, somewhere with a fresh start. A big yard, refrigerator on the porch, and maybe a few junkers of their own in the back yard, for parts.

To Clystine, that sounded an awful lot like marriage. In his next letter, Ike would surely propose.

She'd spent the afternoon downstairs doing laundry. Every time they ran the machine the drain clogged. The iron pipe was barnacled, corroded, plugged with bacon and hamburger grease from the upstairs sink. It wouldn't permit the washing machine's gray water to pass. It flooded every time.

The sisters had a pact. Anyone using the washing machine had to stay with it. When it backed up, the user had to squeegee the overflow to the center drain. The older daughter-cousins slept in the basement on mattresses resting on the cold cement. Whoever did laundry had to ensure their mattresses didn't get soaked.

On the afternoon of Wednesday April 16, 1986, Clystine sat in the basement on a lawn chair. The washing machine thumped toward the end of its last spin cycle. Clystine read a romance novel named *To Cage a Whirlwind*, by her favorite author, Jane Donnelly. She read the sex scene that took place in the unused wing of the house, then read it again. Closed her eyes and pictured her and Ike in the scene. His rough hands grabbing her. His thrusting hips matching the lopsided banging of the washing machine in spin cycle.

Clystine ached.

She looked at her watch. If the mailman was early…

The spin cycle ended.

She climbed the steps. Stopped at the top, and when her lightheadedness passed, yelled, "Turn that television off! Get out the house!"

Clystine tromped outside. She walked to the road, stopped to let a car pass. It was early, but being Saturday, maybe Lemuel had already been by…

Clystine crossed the road and flung open the mailbox. She heard a hiss, bent forward, and peered inside.

Josiah checked his Timex. Soon he would walk to the forest edge and emerge next to the field opposite the Miller house.

He heard a BOOM.

Was Lemuel early?

Josiah ran.

He bounded over leaves and logs. Leaped streams and rocks. Wove between tree trunks. At the section of briars, he folded his arms like to charge through them, then stopped. He could go around and wind up closer to his planned observation post. He cut to the right and in moments stood at the edge of the embankment where woods met road.

Josiah looked downhill. Where before had been a mailbox, now was a post. Beside it, on the ground, a writhing pulsing mass of children hovered over a heavyset body.

That wasn't Lemuel Carter Sr.

From the size, it had to be one of the sisters.

Josiah stood. He looked up the road. Back down hill to the chaos. He stepped backward, then stopped again. Turned.

Having arrived after the blast, his carefully constructed plans were obsolete. If a passing driver saw him, anyone in his right mind would wonder why he was pacing instead of running to help.

Should he approach the Miller Cousins? He was friends with none of them. Any time Josiah saw the cousin brothers in a group, he avoided them out of fear of getting beaten up.

But this was different. This was an emergency. And that body down there was his handiwork. Josiah remembered the thrill of seeing Ernest Swain's chest blown inward, the whole cavity opened, exposing a pit of quivering meat.

Josiah trembled at the thought of seeing what an M100 could do to a woman's face.

But how would he explain that he was nearby?

Behind him, a car approached. Without turning to see it, he knew he had to run toward the others. He'd been seen. He had to behave as if he was as surprised as anyone else.

Josiah ran toward the Miller kids and realized they were the youngest, those not old enough to be in school.

The vehicle pulled beside him.

"Hey boy, what's going on down there?"

It was the postman. *The man who should have been dead.*

"I heard an explosion," Josiah said, running. "I was in the woods."

The postal vehicle surged ahead, swerved into the Miller driveway.

Josiah and Lemuel Carter Sr. reached the mailbox at the same time. Seven Miller Cousins knelt beside the body of a flaxen-haired woman with no face. One of the boys perched above her with his hands centered on her front, doing CPR. Josiah saw he was way too low, pushing on the woman's stomach. Each time he pressed, blood oozed out of a fissure in her neck.

The top of her shirt had burned off. Blood, as if blown from a straw, streaked her white skin.

"CLYSTINE!" One of the mother-sisters screamed from the concrete front door step. The screen door thwacked. The woman charged toward them.

"Son, let me in," said Lemuel. "Let me see what's going on with her heart."

Lemuel pushed aside one of the younger boys. He looked at Clystine's exploded neck, and instead grabbed her wrist. He pressed his index finger to the vein. Shifted up a little. Shifted back.

The other mother-sister arrived. "OH MY GOD WAT HAPPENED CLYSTINE!"

Lemuel held his open hand toward her, then placed Clystine's hand on the ground. He looked up. Shook his head.

"Already crossed," Lemuel said. "Already with the Lawd."

Josiah stepped back, then around Lemuel so he could get a better sight of Clystine's head. "We better call somebody," Josiah said. "Who do we call? The fire people?"

He looked at the length of her. From Clystine's shape and the color of some of her hair that wasn't matted in blood, he thought he knew which sister she was. The pretty one.

"She peed," one of the girls said.

Lemuel braced his hands on his knees. Pushed himself to his feet. "Bambi, we need to get on the phone."

"I'm Earline," the other sister said.

"Pardon, Earline. But we got to get the po-lice out here."

Earline nodded. She smiled taut like a brain-shot pig and passed out backward onto a couple of cousins still beside Clystine. They crumpled under her and shouted until they wriggled free.

"Damn," Lemuel said. "Royal damn. You—" he pointed— "Lift her head. Go on, lift her head. That's her sister's blood she in."

Chapter 25

Sophia awoke sensing not much time had passed. Her heels kept hitting something and she felt constricted around her chest. It was hard to breathe. She opened her eyes and saw a blurry vertical rectangle of light. Each time her heels dropped the rectangle receded.

She remembered being in the police car.

She remembered the chemical rag over her face.

The man was taking her downstairs.

Terror washed through her. The farther away from the light he took her, the more certain her fate. She heard her father say *Fight.*

She sensed opportunity.

The man struggled with her weight. He was medium sized, and almost wrestling her with each step. He lurched, pulled until her feet dropped, lurched the other way. His arms compressed her chest.

Sophia drove her feet into the wooden stairs. She bucked against him. Pushed backward with all her might. They were in the air, untethered, and she discovered her feet were bound together. She couldn't separate them. The man released his arms around her chest and she saw his hand flail before disappearing behind her.

"Bitch!"

They landed. Her back compressed his ribs and wind blasted from his lungs. She drove her head backward, connecting with the man's chin. Jarred, she was still alert. She drove her elbows into his ribs.

Above, old joists crossed a ceiling that seemed more cobwebs than wood. Light came from a pair of bulbs in white fixtures on the ancient looking timbers. She saw white electric lines. She felt him move beneath her. Felt dirt under her hands.

She threw open her legs at the knees hoping he'd used duct tape on her, but the sharp pinch suggested a zip tie. She wouldn't be able to break it. She'd need to knock out her kidnapper to have time to pick the tie's plastic latch.

Sophia raised her head and again slammed it against the man beneath her. Her skull glanced off the side of his, and her head fell backward, extending her neck. Pain shot through her. The man shifted beneath her, shoved her with his arm. Using her elbows, she hit left then right, thrashing. His arms came above her shoulders and pinned hers down. He was so much stronger; she couldn't move. He lifted one hand and drove it hard into her belly. Sophia gasped. Her stomach was a knot. He hit her again, and she had no control at all. She couldn't breathe. Her body shook.

The man pushed her off and rolled. While Sophia struggled to fill her lungs, he rose to his feet, grabbed her hair and dragged her across the dirt. He released her.

She curled like a baby. Gasped. The tightness in her knotted stomach barely eased.

He grabbed her feet and spun her. Held her head in his hands and twisted until she stared into a pit that looked like a grave.

He put his mouth next to her ear. His voice was gritty, as if he spoke through clenched teeth.

"The pit? Or would you enjoy taking some photos?"

Sophia whimpered.

The man stood. He pushed her with his foot then walked toward the stairway. She looked at the hole and the pile of dirt beside it. A shovel and a sheet of plywood leaned against the stone foundation wall. She saw an upside down five-gallon plastic bucket with a roll of duct tape on it. And farther away, in a shadowy corner, an orange extension cord and a metal frame. She couldn't tell what it was.

Then she stared at another device.

She recognized it from a history textbook. It belonged to the colonial period. A pillory? It secured criminals for display, with their hands and head stuck through holes in a board.

She understood why her captor might secure her bent over, with arms and head locked forward.

His footsteps approached. She looked at him. He wore a black police uniform. A short sleeve shirt with yellow rank stripes. A shoulder patch. A badge on his belt. As he strode toward her, she saw his gun.

"I want to take the photos. I want to take the photos." She raised her arms over her head and shrank from him. The man handcuffed her. She brought her arms down in front of her.

He removed a knife from his pocket and opened it, revealing a tiny triangular razor blade. He moved behind her. Pulled her shirt backward and sliced it from her neck down her back. Sophia trembled, expecting the blade to slice her skin, but it never did.

He pulled her blouse forward and let it hang on her arms. A thought raced through her—if she could get behind him and throw her hands over his head, she might choke him—

The man released her bra and pulled it forward too.

She hunched forward, mostly covered by the tangle of clothes. He stepped to her, grabbed her hair and wrenched back. She felt a sharp pain in her neck and wondered what injury she'd caused by driving her head into his. But she heard her father urge her to survive another minute, so she could choose her moment.

Sophia let her arms fall. He could see what he wanted.

"Don't move. Not an inch."

He stepped away. She heard a switch and white light blinded her. The metal structure she'd seen earlier held lamps. The brightness was unbearable. She closed her eyes and waited, expecting to hear the click of a camera shutter.

Instead she heard a zipper.

Chapter 26

Mae's bent over, ass hanging out her car's rear seat. "Mae? What the hell? We gotto go!"

"Not without the safety seat for Joseph."

"We'll buy another tomorrow, somewhere the police aren't about to show."

"Sure, if you can guarantee we won't get in an accident between here and there. You driving half drunk and on no sleep."

I open the other side door and unbuckle the seat. The latch on top. "You got your side done?"

"It's too tight."

"Unbelievable." Cross around the vehicle. "Step aside."

She backs out.

"Go fetch the kids. We're out of time."

I unloose the seatbelt buckle holding the safety seat. Stow it in the back of the squad car. I turn on the engine and wait. Think of the bodies there for the kids to see. Jeb on the porch steps upside down and bleeding like a deer hung by the ankle slits. And Randy, headshot with a half dozen #4 pellets, beside the squad car.

I get out and drag Randy a few feet around the right rear corner, so he's hid from the lights.

Shadows move inside the house. They'll be out in a second and right on top of Jeb. I catch Mae at the door.

"One minute, Mae."

"You was the one in a hurry."

"Shush."

Step back and drag Jeb along to the end of the steps and over the side, then get his feet out of the way. There's a couple gallons of blood puddled down the steps and pooling out to the middle. No way to miss it. I can smell it, but in the dark it looks like motor oil.

Mae's at the window. I wave her forward. She backs out the door with Joseph asleep in her arms. Morgan and Bree walk in short steps, sleepy but ready to rouse into full panic. I pick up Morgan and nuzzle her with some stubble and grab Bree, too.

"We're going on a vacation, girls. Going someplace real nice. Got to get a early start. We got so long to drive. But it's going to be sunshine and warm all the time. And we get ice cream for supper every day."

I put them one by one in the back of Ruth's car. "That's right girls. Settle in there. Easy does it."

"Where's the seat?" Mae says.

"In the police car."

"I need it here."

"We don't have time. We're only going a half mile to the Ingles parkin' lot. Let's go!"

Mae gawks.

"You want, I'll take Joseph with me."

Her nose flickers a snarl, but she minds her mouth. "Go. I'll follow you." She hands Joseph to Morgan. "Keep him on your lap."

At the squad car I stop, circle back to dead Randy and fetch the handcuffs off his belt. Stick them in my back pocket.

Mae comes back from the car door she was about to get in.

"Baer, you have to take their cell phones. The cops. And Ruth."

"Good thinkin'."

Open the squad car. "Where you boys keep your phones?"

Leroy's eyes glow. Then stop. "Front pocket. My pants here, on the left."

"How about you?"

"Same, but on my right."

I open each door and fish in their drawers.

"You'd be best leaving the phones here, Baer," Josiah says. "Gleason police can't do it, but the FBI can track those."

I wedge each phone under the front of a rear tire. Get in the car. "This is posi-traction, right?"

"You don't have to—"

Stomp the gas and spit cell phone parts. And some rocks. We pull out and not a block removed I spot red and blues in the treetops a quarter mile off, over the knoll. Can't see the headlights yet, but I cut the wheel on the first right and Mae swerves after me probably cussing a storm. In the rearview, three patrol cars speed toward Mae's house.

"Where was they coming from? Who was they?"

Leroy says, "Asheville."

"That or state troopers," Josiah says. "Don't know. FBI would have called the state police, seeing how our chief was under investigation. That's my bet."

"So they was actually on him?"

"That's right."

I wonder on that. Woulda thought the whole cesspool was happy with the corruption.

I make a turn this way and another that. Pull into the parking lot on the back side with all the potholes, and come in along the Suburban.

"You wait here. I appreciate you boys being level headed. Lotta folks'd lose their cool."

"No problem, Baer. There's no need for things to get out of hand. We want what you want."

They look at each other and smile. Josiah keeps an otherworldly face. Like his body's in the back seat but his soul is on a cool mountain chewing teaberry leaves.

I step out and Mae pulls in beside me.

I make the whirly signal. "Nah, back it up. Need you—"

She stops. I cross to her open window. "Need to back up so the trunk is next to the Suburban. Back into the space."

Mae grinds the clutch, stalls, starts the car. She backs in. "Keep the kids in the car a minute. I got to get the gold out the back. And put up your window so the kids don't catch cold. We'll be a minute or five. Kill the engine."

I half hope Ruth suffocated or died of gold poisoning but she lets out a kick when I open the trunk.

"Asshole. What's wrong with you?"

"Mind your mouth. Kids in the car."

I reach for her leg to steady her but she kicks me away. Drags herself over the rubber seal and on her feet. Twists her neck like to stretch a pulled muscle.

"Getting old, girl." I slip behind and drop a handcuff on her right wrist then pull the other next to it.

"What? You prick. What the hell? You can't do this."

"I know it's a royal stretch—but try and be a lady."

I unlock the Suburban. Feel along Ruth's forever pert derriere and somehow she managed to fill her back pockets with gold coin. I take out six from each. Then feel along her frontside for a cell phone.

No phone, but her rack's in the same sprightly form I left it thirty years ago.

Deposit Ruth in the very back seat.

At the trunk of her car, I pull out the buckets and drop in coins. Scoop a handful, then another, and my hipbone says, there's two young bucks with strong backs in the car...

I open the squad car door. "Listen. You boys don't know it, but I got about four million dollars gold in the trunk of this junker over here. We need a clean getaway and it'll take me half to dawn to pick them coins myself. Can I trust you to do it for me?"

"Sure, Baer."

"I'll have to uncuff you. Can I trust you? You won't run or provoke nothing?"

"Heck no," Leroy says.

"You?"

"No, I'm with you, Baer."

No red. No juice.

"Four million in gold? How the hell did you get that?" Leroy says.

"Aw shucks. You need to understand fractional reserve banking and the fiat currency is all. I'll explain all it later."

I fetch the handcuff keys, and Josiah rolls part away so I can free him. I give him the key and pull the Judge, then realize the Judge needs a reload so I pull the .357 too. And that gives me the idea they ought to name the .357 the Bailiff.

I put the Bailiff on the roof of Ruth's car and bust open the Judge to refill the cylinder. I alternate the shells, .45 and .410 shotgun, like my predecessor.

"Aright, Josiah. Leroy. See these buckets? Fill them with all the coin in the back."

They stare at the specie. At each other. Then at me, and finally back to the gold.

"Once the trunk is empty, don't use the wire handle to lift the buckets. Each one'll weigh at least a hundred fifty pounds."

"Where'd you get all this?"

"Still shine, avoid paper money, pay no taxes. Now get to work. We got to bust out of here 'fore every state trooper in fifty miles is looking for us."

I open the Suburban back gate. "When you're done, put them buckets in the back."

They bend and coins start rattling. Pretty sound if I wasn't mired in murder and looking at getting caught.

I need a pull off the jug.

Holster the Bailiff and keep the Judge in hand. Step to the Suburban while the boys fill the buckets with scoops of coin. Working like field labor.

"I got the gun on you two."

"We're with you Baer. All the way. No worries."

"Still, I'll shoot you when I want. Is all."

I open the back door. Grab the jug I worked on an hour ago. Gulp a couple mouthfuls and the refreshment hits quick. Don't understand men that can go a day without so much as a thimble of shine. But they're out there, doing harm every day.

"You're going to kill us all," Ruth says from the back. "I always knew you were barking mad."

I sit on the second seat with the door open and my legs out and watch the boys work. I got the power of the juice and seeing red eyes, but knowing deceit doesn't mean you know truth. Not unless you identify all the deceit and nothing but the truth is left.

So far, I know where everybody stands in this escape equation. All but one.

Mae.

"And I guess I always knew what you was too, Ruth. I want to know one thing. Tell me how exactly them FBI boys got loose."

Ruth glows red, and that doesn't mean what she says is useless. It's just one more explanation that isn't true.

"The FBI man couldn't breathe from his bloody nose. He was gagging and turning blue. Rubbing his face on the carpet to try to peel the tape so he could breathe. You wasn't here. If I didn't save him, it's the same as if I killed him. I pulled off his tape, and then—"

"And when did you and Mae go out to the vehicle and move all the gold?"

"I did it all myself."

Ruth glows even redder and I want to throw up my heart.

Chapter 27

Sheriff Horace Wycliff Leathers arrived at the Miller house a half hour after Lemuel. He pulled beside the postal truck. Walked to the youngest Miller girls, who were holding Clystine's dead hands and praying for her soul.

Leathers shook his head.

Lemuel Carter stood beside him. "She was gone when I got here. The kids was already out the house. And Josiah Swain was runnin' down the road."

"Swain?"

"Said he heard it go off. Was up in the wood."

"School day, right?"

"I wondered that, too."

Horace Wycliff Leathers nodded. He turned a full circle, took in the sweep. Then looked back toward the house.

"I saw that right off, too," Lemuel said. "Looks like one of them firecrackers from the Bait Farm. 'Cept it wouldn't a stayed three year on the roof."

Leathers stooped to one of the children. Looked both ways across the road. "Run inside the house and get me a broom, 'kay, Darlin'?"

The child jumped up and ran.

"All right, I need you all to step back away. Everyone. Let's go. Get back across the road. It's not safe on the curve here." To Lemuel he said, "Which sister is this?"

"That's Clystine."

"All right. Y'all need to step away from Clystine. We got law enforcement work to do. If there's a clue to who did this, I don't want y'all to stomp on the evidence. So go on back to the house. Swain, you stick around a minute."

Earline had recovered from her fainting spell. She stood next to Sheriff Leathers like a softball next to a bat. She said, "You got to find the son of a bitch—!"

"Miss. Put your hand down. What's your name?"

"I'm Earline P-for-Proud Miller. That's my sister and you better—"

"Miss Earline, you'll have time to wag your finger later. Right now I need you to go inside and get a bed sheet you won't mind losing. I don't want traffic to see your sister like that, and you got all these kids to think of. And the rest'll be along on the school bus in no time. So put your hand down and work with the team here."

A sheriff's deputy arrived in a Ford Bronco. Leathers waved him to park on the inside of the curve, up the hill from the mailbox.

"Miss Earline, please. Let's go."

Leathers called to the newly arrived deputy. "I want photos of the scene, and do a sweep. Body parts or mailbox parts."

Leathers felt a tug on his drawers. It was the little girl with a broom. He knelt to her and said, "Thank you, Darlin'."

While he squatted, he noticed a red object partly under a dried oak leaf in the dirt under the tire swing. He gestured toward the house. "Darlin', why don't you go inside? We've got work to do and I don't want you to get hurt because one of the big people steps on you." He smiled big and wrinkled his nose. Her eyes got wider than before and she ran back inside the house.

Leathers walked to the red spot, stooped, and called, "Sam? Come over here real quick with the camera."

In a moment the deputy arrived and Leathers said, "First, take a bunch of pictures of the body. Every angle. Do it first so we can get… Clystemine?"

"Clystine. Like Clydesdale and Holstein, mixed together."

"So we can get Clystine off the road. Then I want a couple photos of that firecracker in the mud. Then—turn around, here— you see there's another on the roof? I want a couple of that, too."

Leathers turned away. Turned back. "That horse and cow thing was funny, but I don't think the kids would get it. Savvy?"

"Yes, Sherriff."

Leathers looked across the road. "Josiah Swain. Here, son."

The school bus rolled in, coming uphill, and stopped with the door emptying kids out on the house-side of the road. From inside the bus arose a cacophony, audible through the open windows, as the kids still on the bus discovered Clystine without her face.

"Nuts!" Leathers strode to the bus, walked out in front and around. Earline followed with a bed sheet. She whipped it open and the two of them covered Clystine's body. "We'll hold it down with a couple rocks, time being. Won't be long. We'll move her from here as soon as we can."

Leathers crossed in front of the school bus.

The driver poked his head out the side window. "Sheriff, you need any help? What's going on?"

"Get these kids out of here, Charlie."

Behind Sheriff Leathers, the older Miller kids gathered on the driveway. The bus ground gears and drove away.

One of the boys said, "What's going on, Sherriff?"

"Inside the house. Everybody inside the house."

"Who is that?"

"I'm afraid there's been a tragedy. Now, everyone inside, and Earline here's going to talk with you. Earline, take them inside."

She looked at him with a red face and wet eyes. Nodded once. Opened her mouth and the words faltered, but she coughed once and spoke full voice.

"All right. You heard the sheriff. Everyone inside the house. This's a crime scene and we got to let the man work. Inside. Bucky dammit now!"

A couple of the older boys peeled off and stood by the tire swing, heads low and shoulders round. Leathers watched them a moment, then walked to his Bronco.

He leaned through the open window, thumbed the radio, "Kate, we got a homicide up here at the Miller's. Need you to send the coroner up. And take Marcy off that project at the courthouse. I want her up here, too."

Leathers extracted his upper body from the open driver side window. Turned and saw Josiah Swain.

"You said you wanted to talk to me?"

"Yeah, son. Walk with me this way." Leathers opened his arm as if to corral Josiah, but without touching him. They walked toward the shade on the house-side of the road.

"That was a real tragedy with your father. You been holdin' up?"

"Uncle."

"That's right. Helluva tragedy. But Lord knows he wasn't the first banker to seek an end to his torment."

"I'm all right."

"I hope so. You know, a lotta people try to shame a man that'd do that to himself, but I never saw it that way. You think real hard about taking your own life, and think about what it'd take to do it—I don't know what it is—that isn't a coward. It's sad as hell, and maybe mentally sick and all. But coward means something else entirely."

"Yeah. I'm all right."

"Good. Glad to hear it. I wanted to check because seeing another person blown apart by an M100... That's got to be tough."

"Yeah."

"Most people don't ever see it in their entire lives. And now you and me seen it twice in three years."

They stood at the side of the road in the shade, twenty feet across from the body, with their backs to the Miller house.

"I need you to help me understand what you saw. Somebody out there did this rotten thing, and I won't catch him without your help. Is that all right? Will you help me?"

"Yeah."

"So tell me what you saw."

"I was in the woods up the hill at the cave and—"

"Today's a school day, right?"

"Uh-huh."

Leathers winked. "Hookey, huh?"

Josiah nodded. Smiled.

"Go on."

"Well, I heard the explosion and—"

"Hold on. Just thinking, here. Why'd you skip school today? Any reason?"

Josiah stared. Mouth open. "Uh. Not especially. I didn't have any tests or quizzes and nothing much was going on."

"You like to be alone sometimes."

"Yeah."

"You go up to that cave much?"

"Weekends."

"Okay. So you heard the blast ...."

Josiah looked to the dead body. Then to the sky.

"I heard the blast, and it didn't sound like a gun. I thought maybe one of the Miller boys skipped today, too, and set off a firecracker. They do it pretty often. I guess everyone around here had a couple fall on them after the disaster. So I uh, I thought I'd kind of see what they were up to."

"And?"

"Well, I come out on the road and saw Clystine there."

"And."

"I started running. And Lemuel drove up at the same time."

"Would you say it was an M100?"

"What?"

"A second ago you said you heard a firecracker. You know the difference between ordinary firecrackers and an M100?"

"Yeah."

"And you believe it was an M80 or M100? Is that fair? From the sound?"

"I guess because it was so loud, even in the cave."

"I see. That's helpful, son. Did any of the Miller Cousin-brothers skip school today?"

"I don't know. I didn't see any until they got off the bus."

"Any of them missing? Not on the bus?"

"Uh. No."

"I sure appreciate your help on this, Josiah. Let me ask you to speculate on this. To test your skills as a future deputy—how's that?"

"Uh."

"So what do you think happened here?"

"Someone put a firecracker in the mailbox."

"Who? Why?"

"I think it's one of the Cousins. Last week they put a rattlesnake in there for Lemuel to find."

"They what?"

"That's what everyone at school said."

"That's interesting. I'm going to let you know what I'm thinking here. Just to see if it meshes with what you know about your neighbors. And this goes no further. You hear? I can't tell you this and have you tell anyone else."

"I get it."

"Okay. I get here and one of the first things I see is an M80 or 100 up on the roof. And a few minutes later, I see one on the ground, over by that tire swing." Leathers twisted and pointed. "Seems like everyone in a mile radius of the Fireworks Disaster three years ago has a personal stash of M-series firecrackers."

"Uh-huh."

"You think those boys went out and gathered up a bunch of them?"

Josiah nodded.

"You ever hear them setting them off?"

"Yeah. Fourth of July and all. And sometimes without a holiday."

"I thought as much." He grinned big. "You got a stash of those fireworks?"

"Nah."

"I don't give a hoot in Hades if you do. You seen what damage they do. I know you'd be responsible."

"They fell all over the place. Seemed a shame to not pick them up."

"Accourse—Absolut—" Leathers faced a commotion by the tire swing.

Lemuel Carter had one of the Cousin brothers pressed against a tree by his throat.

Leathers listened.

"You gunnin' for me? You put the snake in there and then rigged a bomb? Kilt your own damn mother!"

The boy hung by his neck, feet lifted from the ground. Old Lemuel Carter Sr. still had it. The boy's mouth was open and he gagged.

"Carter!" Sheriff Leathers said. "Let the boy down. Go on."

Carter glanced at Leathers. Nodded like he didn't know what came over him. Tossed the boy aside.

"He had one of them M80s in his pocket, playing with it. Just like that. His dead mother right there. Aunt. Whatever she was to 'm. He playing with it."

Sheriff Leathers walked toward Lemuel, leaving Josiah. "Lemuel, you still got a good part of your mail route to complete, don't you?"

"I do, sheriff, but this is what's on my mind."

Leathers held his hand up to Swain, now ten feet off. "Wait a second, son. What's on your mind, Lemuel?"

"Wasn't but last Saturday I come here to deliver, and I stopped 'cause I heard a snake. The boys put a rattlesnake in in the mailbox, a feisty one. They was in the woods there and I give em a chase but they got off. Now they put a bomb in the box. These boys tryin' to kill me. That's what's on my mind."

Sheriff Leathers stared at the salt-treated post that held the mailbox. The sheet covering Clystine pulled his eyes. His ears rang like he'd been to the range.

The new information about the snake, confirmed by Lemuel, hinted at a new explanation of the facts. He'd suspected Josiah Swain had killed his uncle—not really suspected it, but considered it—three years ago. And Josiah being so quick on the scene today, it'd be hard not to cast a suspicious eye his direction. He'd already admitted he had a stash of M-series firecrackers. He intimated he knew it was an M-100, not an 80, that exploded the mailbox. Leathers didn't even know that, yet.

Until Lemuel interrupted his questioning, he'd had Josiah on a roll. Leathers had thought he'd pull a confession out of Josiah right there on the road.

But those firecrackers all over the premises, and the one in the boy's hand, and the snake....

Normally you'd think of a snake as a prank. The odds of getting bit aren't one hundred percent, and the odds of dying aren't one hundred either, even if you do get bit. So placing a rattler in a mailbox is idiotic, but not quite attempted murder.

But follow it up with a bomb that removes the better part of a woman's face—that's grounds to reconsider. Maybe the snake was an attempt at murder. The bomb was a follow-up attempt, foiled by Clystine's bad luck, checking the mail before the postman delivered it.

The scenario matched the displayed intelligence of the Miller Cousins brothers.

Leathers nodded. "Lemuel, I'm going to need you to come by the station to make a statement after you finish your route."

Chapter 28

Whole world's evil and corrupt. Nobody untouched. Selfish. Deceitful. Every man, woman, child's a god-cussed snake ready to bite the hand that feeds it. I declare rightful autonomy.

No man. No woman.

Nobody got a right over me. None. If I'm the only honest man in all North Carolina, no one has the authority on me. All they got is corrupt power seized by corrupt means. I feel like God ten minutes before the flood. The whole thing's broke.

Mae? You kill my heart.

"Baer? Looks like we're done."

Leroy has a tire iron in hand. I parse his face. "You fittin' to club me with that?"

"Ah, heck." He tosses it to the trunk. "I used it to fetch a coin from way in back under the rug."

I step. Look. "You get down in around the tire?"

"We lifted it, see?"

Leroy shifts the tire.

"Good. Put the buckets in the back here, and we'll be off."

"We was wondering... What you got in store for us?"

"If I don't shoot you? Maybe cut you loose somewhere in Tennessee, each with enough gold to start something new."

Leroy smiles half-wit. "I was hoping you'd say something like that."

"It'd be better to leave us here with it. Save us carrying it back," Josiah says.

"Better for you. But you're in my employ. So you know what that means. Put the buckets in the back."

They each lift one by the lip. Amazing what a plastic bucket'll hold without the bottom falling out.

They get the gold in place and I see all the guns I left partly under the back seat. I look at the boys. They had no time to make a grab for them. And neither one has given me so much as a spark anyhow.

"Hey, put these cuffs on for now. Then you're in the back seat with Ruth. And if she gives you any lip, run an elbow through her guts."

I keep an eye on the hostages while I move to Mae's window, make the twirly-finger. "Let's go."

Josiah cuffs Leroy behind the back then gets one hand cuffed and the other hangs free. He comes like a dutiful son, and I feel part bad.

"Know what? Here, put your hands up front. No need to have them at your back."

"That's considerate, Baer. It works on the wrists when you have to sit on your hands very long."

I nod. Common courtesy, is all.

I unlock Leroy and cuff him in front, too.

"What about me?" Ruth says. "My hands are numb."

"When they rot off you can have the nubs up front."

The hostages climb in the back seat with her, one on each side. I grab the guns in the back of the Suburban and set them in Ruth's trunk. Won't be needing any more'n I got. But I still like the feel of that Smith compact nine, and accourse, got to keep my old Smith & Wesson. I stow both under the Suburban driver seat and promise the self I'll remember each time I get out.

"The safety seat," Mae says.

I grab it from the patrol car. Shove it in the footwell where the kids feet ain't. "We'll install it on the road. Get in the seat. You're shotgun, Mae."

She glowers and I glower back.

"Where'd the damn dog go?"

"That dog is Joe, and he's already spoken for you once. Show a little loyalty."

I grab Joe and put him in the second seat with the kids. Joe doesn't like it but he has fur and a sloppy wet tongue so the kids don't mind.

Joe looks at me and we connect a minute, and I hear a voice that may be his, may be mine.

Why keep any of them?

Chapter 29

Leathers and his deputies searched a radius of three hundred feet around the blast site. They never found Clystine Miller's face. Deputy Sam did find a folded piece of mailbox. It contained a partly-melted piece of blue rubber band, such as might hold three stalks of broccoli. It was balled around two paper clips. Puzzled, Leathers showed it to a 'Nam buddy who had served in Special Forces.

"That's the easiest detonator in the world," said Hayduke. "You hold a match like this. Cover it with the abrasives on both sides. Then the paper clips. Wrap them in rubber bands. Drag the match through. Veee-Ola."

Leathers wondered: Which of the Miller Cousins brothers could have built it?

ATF sent a man from Chattanooga. He wrote some notes, returned to Chattanooga, and was fired for something he did three weeks before in a honky-tonk. ATF sent no one else.

The FBI, who shared enforcement responsibilities under 18 USC 841-848, didn't show.

The US Postal Inspection Service sent a woman from Charlotte, North Carolina, named Elizabeth Page.

By the time she arrived, Sheriff Leathers had sorted it all out.

Still, Postal Inspector Page needed to interview the boys. Leathers drove her and listened from the car. She sat them on the porch and asked questions. He grinned when she returned to the car after a bare two minutes.

"No way," she said to Leathers. "Mmm-mmm. I ever have a baby that dumb I'll hit its head with a hammer and raise a pig on the milk."

But Sheriff Horace Wycliff Leathers believed evil kept on trying until it achieved its goals. The boys had already confessed to the so-called prank of attempted murder by rattlesnake. Leathers believed their rottenness would inevitably manifest in other violence. Louder and bloodier. If he was wrong to suspect them, the process would find his error. He wasn't judge and jury—didn't pretend to be.

The three oldest Miller Cousin boys, Bucky, Clyde, and Lester never confessed. As part of their plea-bargain, the judge sent them to Saint Clayton's Academy, a military reform school an hour west of Nashville. The school was famous for several alumni having reached the rank of general in the US Army. Three others were state senators.

After the boys were gone, Benton, Tennessee settled down.

Until Lemuel Carter Sr. died by M100 a couple months later.

The death occurred Saturday evening, June 21, near as the coroner could guess. The body was well decomposed, and the temperature of the closed house was in the upper nineties.

Lemuel Carter Sr. lived alone. His wife had recently left him. He failed to show for work for two consecutive days, Monday and Tuesday. His supervisor Frederick Walker had to cover his route. When Lemuel failed to show on Wednesday the 25th, Frederick divided the route into four. He added the segments to other carriers' routes. Frederick then drove out to Lemuel's house.

He smelled death before reaching the porch. Saw flies crawling over the inside of what appeared to be a bedroom window. Standing at the glass, he cupped his hands around his eyes and pressed closer. Inside, he saw feet on a bed. Looking higher, a hole in the wall and blood spatter.

Frederick Walker's breath clouded the glass. He stepped back and wondered how Lemuel had killed himself, leaving his feet on the bed and a hole in the wall.

Frederick walked to the neighbor's house. It was a small box, last painted white in the sixties, with a refrigerator on the porch and a three-bladed push mower rusting under a sugar maple. He knocked. Spoke to Hermetta Washington. Used her phone to call Sheriff Horace Wycliff Leathers.

Hermetta Washington listened to the call and when it ended said, "Mmph. Lawd, I knew it was somethin'."

"What do you mean?"

"I went by Sunday with cornbread like always and Lemuel wunt there. No man pass up on my corn bread. No man. Lawd."

Sheriff Leathers arrived at the Lemuel Carter Sr. house twenty-five minutes later. Detective Marcy rode in the passenger seat.

Frederick Walker and Hermetta Washington stood on the porch, apart.

"I have the key, but we ain't gone in," she said.

"Why do you have a key, Hermetta?" Leathers said.

"Me and Lemuel live side by side thirty year. His wife run off and my man die and I been bringing Lemuel cornbread ever since."

"When'd his wife run off?"

She wrinkled her upper lip. Tried not to smile. "Three, four week ago."

"I understand. Have you used the key recently?"

"Nawh. I only use the key if he tell me to."

"I appreciate that. I do. And just one more thing. You seen anything unusual lately? People around here you don't recognize? Anything get your suspicion up a little?"

"Nawh. I don't come up here 'less Lemuel invite me. Mercy. And I keep my nose in my own business so I don't see no go'ins on outside my own go'ins on."

"I understand," Leathers said. "Miss Hermetta, would you mind unlocking the door so Deputy Marcy and I can investigate?"

She nodded. Twisted sideways like to pass through an ordinary door and cut a path between sheriff and deputy. She unlocked Lemuel Carter's house.

"Oh Lawd, I can smell 'im. Oh my Lawd, that bad."

Hermetta backed away, stumbled on a loose porch board that had bowed upward at the end, and caught herself on a post.

"Thank you, Hermetta," Leathers said. He nodded at Marcy. At the open door he said, "Frederick, I'm going to have to ask you to stay outside."

Frederick nodded.

The smell was a couple shades past the worst Leathers had ever experienced. That included his memory of a town of Vietnamese who'd been helping his platoon. The Viet Cong found out and burned the town to the ground, leaving bodies charred under the ashes. Others hacked and shot to death in the open areas. Lemuel Carter Sr. was worse than two dozen three-day-old jungle corpses.

Leathers gulped air, stepped inside and turned on the lights. Nothing appeared amiss in the living room, save a hole blasted through the wall from the other side. Plaster debris was on the floor, the top of the coffee table, everywhere.

Opening the door roused the flies. Big, black, heavy ones.

"What did that?" Marcy said, nodding at the hole.

"Wild-assed guess? How about an M-series firecracker?"

Leathers placed his palm on the butt of his holstered pistol. Stepped forward, looking at a bad angle through the open bedroom door. He scanned the floor, door jamb, and eased through. On the bed lay a headless black man on a blood-soaked bedcover.

Marcy enter the room behind Leathers.

"Awww."

She turned back around.

Leathers considered. The body was interesting, but the rest of the room held the key to solving the mystery.

The door was open. Why blast a hole through a wall? Did a punch do the damage? A kick? Or someone's head? That wouldn't blast a perfect circle through two sheets of drywall.

That hole came from an explosion.

Blood splatter centered on the damage, evenly filling a circle with a seven-foot radius. Heavy spatter, consisting of brain matter, skull, and hair, accented several areas within the main circle. At the bottom of the wall lay clumps of Lemuel's head—if the victim proved to be Lemuel.

In the corner where floor met wall, Leathers saw something that resembled a nose. Or it could have been an ear.

Leathers turned a circle. He'd noticed blood everywhere, on all four walls, when first entering. But now he wondered at the significance of it. Blood misted three walls, but the one with the damage had the heaviest spatter.

He stood over the body, looking down. The blast had removed head, neck, and upper right shoulder. On the left, the shoulder seemed mostly intact. The bed to the right of where the head would have been sustained heavy damage. Mattress blasted to bent wires; cloth soaked in blood.

The bed abutted the wall with no headboard. An area the size of a quarter was shot through. Leathers leaned and put his finger in the hole. It lined up with the level of the mattress.

He imagined if he dug into the wall he'd find an endcap plug from an M-series firecracker.

He'd seen what an M100 could do to a man's chest. He'd seen what it could do to a mailbox and a woman's face. But this damage seemed beyond the capacity of an M100.

"Look here," Marcy said.

Leathers turned, unaware she'd re-entered the room. "What you got?"

"A suicide note?"

"Naaahh."

Marcy stood next to a dresser that sat long and low against the wall, with three sets of three drawers. On the top was a digital alarm clock, a lamp, and a stack of folded underwear Lemuel had apparently forgotten to put away.

Marcy nodded at a piece of paper next to the underwear.

"No way in hell," Leathers said.

Although open, the paper retained folds and rested uneven. Leathers stooped. He shifted to get out of the light. "You see that?"

"What?"

"Horsefeathers, is what. Blood, under the suicide note."

Another thing wasn't right. How did a piece of paper remain sitting on a dresser while a blast four feet away blew a man's head off? And knocked a two-foot hole through a wall? Looking again at the underwear on the dresser top, Leathers noticed the stack had toppled over. And yet the paper suicide note withstood the blast.

That dog didn't hunt.

"Maybe it was over closer to the bed before the bomb. Then drifted over on top of blood."

He looked at her.

She shook her head.

"I bet when we search the house, we don't find the notebook that paper came out of." Leathers lifted his hands and framed the bed. "Okay, so we have a firecracker—or some other device. How does an explosion on the right side of Lemuel's head have the force to cut through the wall on the other side, eight feet away?"

"I don't know," Marcy said. "You don't think his head went through the wall? Like a projectile?"

They both looked at the hole.

Leathers shook his head, furrowed his brow. He stepped to the doorway and into the living room. "There's no head in here."

"It wouldn't disintegrate, would it? After coming through the wall? That doesn't make sense."

"No, and there's no blood on this side. Only dust and plaster."

They were still, each taking in the room.

"Another thing," Leathers said. "Look around his hands. You see a match book? A cigarette lighter?"

"No."

Leathers looked over the floor. Nothing but blood. "I say B-S on the suicide note. Wait." He saw a glint under the bed and knew what it was. He squatted and nodded toward it. "That's a .22 casing."

"So ...." Marcy said.

"So."

"What are you going to call it?"

Leathers said nothing. He stepped out of the room, walking slowly, head moving left to right. He moved into the kitchen and saw red M100 firecracker tubes on the cutting board on the counter.

"Marcy. Check this out." He stood beside the counter. Counted eight tubes. "I want prints off these."

"Right."

Leathers nodded to the fireworks mess. "What's missing?" he said.

Marcy was still. "Tubes. Packing. Fuses. There's no explosives."

"If I'm to believe the setup here, Lemuel took some time off after the fireworks disaster, went foraging in the woods for firecrackers, and saved up eight. Nine, counting the one that took off his head. And then he drilled into the ends of eight of them. He removed all the clay, and took the explosives out of eight and packed them into a single tube. He used the fuse and charge of the ninth to make a bomb powerful enough to take off his head. Then he went into the bedroom, shot himself with a gun that disappeared after he fired it, then lit a fuse with a match that doesn't exist, and blew off his head. Then he got up and put the suicide note on top of the blood."

"Yeah," Marcy said. "I don't see Lemuel doing that." She paused. "So what are you going to call it?"

Chapter 30

Sophia sat with her head tilted at the ceiling for what felt like a long time. No man had ever seen her, like this.

She sensed the weight of his gaze on her skin, first her bare neck, then lower. She felt musty air, cold on her flesh. She breathed in the dampness. She was in an abandoned house, somewhere in the mountains near Sylva or Cherokee. She hadn't seen much from the back seat of the police car. But she'd seen the faded white paint and shattered window of an upstairs room. She filled in the rest with her imagination. The house was like so many others, once you got out of the civilized part of North Carolina. As if Asheville was an outpost and going an hour west, to Sylva, put you with a different kind of people. Different ideas on wealth, work, and everything.

Sophia remembered a Family Vacation Saturday, as her father called them. He'd driven her and her mother to Sylva to see where the train wreck was filmed for the movie *The Fugitive*, in 1993. Years after the movie, the mangled train cars were still there, sitting off to the side of the tracks. She remembered one that almost seemed to be resting on air. It crossed a gulley. Weeds hid whatever supported it. The town of Sylva was like that in her memory. A sad town that seemed to know it was a way station too far. They'd made a good effort but the hills were taking it back.

Damp stone walls. Dirt basement. Upstairs there was likely crown molding and wood floors. Walls with peeling paper. Water stains everywhere.

Ghosts.

After having her stomach beaten, she ached from holding the pose her captor demanded. She rotated her shoulders. Felt the weight of her chest shift.

"Do that again."

She heard him making intimate sounds that suggested vulnerability. Behind the blinding light she heard rapid motion, his breathing. He was masturbating. Sophia tried to think of her bare skin as part of the environment. Like a hammer on the floor or a knife hidden in a drawer, her environment held resources she could exploit.

The sight of her nakedness was a weapon.

She wished she'd been more of a flirt so she would have a better idea of how to wrap a man's lust around his neck and choke him with it.

After another moment the sounds stopped. Without thinking she said, "Next time you should share the experience."

She heard her voice as she spoke the words. They didn't come out as silky as she wanted. She sounded like she smoked cigarettes for a living and someone punched her in the throat. The man didn't respond and Sophia wondered what harm she'd done. Finally, he came out from behind the bright lights.

"In time." His cheeks were flushed. He moved behind her and pulled her bra and shirt back up her arms, leaving them open in the back like a hospital gown. Then he crossed the basement and from the darkness behind the light brought a ladder. He lowered it into the pit. She saw a lump at his groin and wondered how long after a man finished he should still be ready.

"Look down there." He pulled a flashlight from his belt, turned it on and pointed the beam downward. The pit was several feet deep, enough for her to stand if she stooped at the waist. A blanket covered the bottom.

"That's a floor. It's wood. Over there is a hole. That's your bathroom." He shifted the light. "Blankets. Bottled water. I'll bring food tomorrow."

The man pulled his firearm, and Sophia recognized the squareness of a Glock. He pointed it at her head. "I like you. We have a real thing. You seem genuine. It's very important that I keep liking you. Understand?"

"I understand."

"You pull a stunt like that on the stairs, and I'll bury you here and burn the house on top of you. Am I clear?"

Sophia nodded.

"Don't move." He shifted in front of her and untied her tennis shoes. Tossed them aside. Then he released her belt buckle, then slid the belt from her pants. He pitched it beside her shoes. Next he withdrew the razor knife from his pocket. He pulled her shirt forward again, then cut off her bra shoulder straps. Cast it aside. "All right. Any more metal anywhere?"

She shook her head.

"Get in the hole."

Sophia inhaled as if it might be her last breath. Released the air. She crawled to the edge of the pit with the ladder and dangled her body over the edge. It was difficult to move with feet bound and hands cuffed. She found the rung. Grasped the top.

"Stop."

She froze. He came toward her and studied her hair. Ran his fingers through it. He extracted a bobby pin and ran his fingers through again. He found another. He allowed his hand to rest on her head and, as if emboldened, lowered it to her cheek. She leaned into it, hoping the human connection would work on his mind the way her father said it couldn't. Anything she could do to reduce that stress and connect with him would help her long game.

Because that's what it would be. She had to keep her mind right for a month, or longer, if need be.

"How far am I from the bottom?"

"Hop down. You'll be fine."

She looked at him again. This time his eyes were kind. The emptiness was gone, replaced by something warm and human. He was like a boy.

Sophia hopped.

She landed on the plywood floor.

"There are plenty of blankets and water. You like McDonalds?"

"I'll be grateful for anything."

"Good girl. Kneel down."

She did.

He pulled away the ladder and stepped away. She heard noise. He returned with a full sheet of plywood. He stood it on its edge along the length of the pit, then standing at the end, said, "I'll see you tomorrow. And in case you get any ideas, I'm going to cover this in cement blocks. The windows are too small for you to fit through. I'll chain and padlock the basement door, when I go. And explosives are set through the house. Some in the floorboards. Some in the walls. Triggered by motion or weight. So if you try to escape, you'll die. Period. Better to build a relationship, and we'll keep it going that way. Someday, if I can trust you, you won't be in the hole."

"Thank you," Sophia said. She nodded at him, and again saw through his eyes to the blackness beyond. She realized her shirt had fallen forward again, exposing her. She moved her arms but couldn't adjust her top back over her shoulders.

"Let me help with that," he said.

The plywood roof came down, and the man's pantleg lifted, revealing a holster with another gun.

Except for a circle the size of a quarter, all the light disappeared. She heard the thumps as he placed cement blocks on the plywood. So many she worried whether it was strong enough to hold them. She counted thirty, all over the plywood surface, but concentrated on the edges.

When her eyes adjusted to the darkness, she found a plastic bottle of water and drank.

Sophia sat on the blankets and wept.

Chapter 31

Drive Interstate 40 headed west like I wanted, ten hours ago. Before I had the fool idea to give gold to my deceitful daughter. I wanted freedom and now I'm slave to hostages and liars and thieves.

And why can't I pull over and shoot them? Leave them along the road? People'd say *I* was wrong.

Or leave them at a Hardees?

Why not?

Can't get my brain wrapped around Mae. Her whole life, all I did was love on her. Fix her roof. Feed her kids.

Unmitigated gall.

"Morgan, hand me that jug."

"No, Morgan," says Mae. "Don't."

"You tread a thin line."

"You aren't driving drunk with my babies in the car."

"I'm more dangerous sober."

We pass a Hardees sign.

I need sleep worse every second, but that won't happen for at least a hundred miles. I got a plan for that. There's a truck stop past Asheville, and I have a list of supplies in my head.

Sky in the rearview turns gray. Clock reads 4:39. This is the time you can think you're alert and thirty seconds later wake up dead. But I need distance.

Ten minutes down the road, snores come from the back of the Suburban, from the copper hostages. Soon the whole vehicle snores, leaving me and my anger keeping the wheel attuned to the road.

Pass Asheville and truckers are firing their engines and joining the onramps. Business dudes in suits chugging silver coffee mugs. In a hurry to get their slave on.

Another Asheville exit and onramp. Another. Finally the sun breaks full into my side and rearview and slices through the fuzzy in my brain. Ahead, on the right, I see the TA sign and switch the turn signal. Right on Wiggins and left into the lot.

It's like I woke them. Headlights on. Men walking butt-low and fast. Trucks side by side; gas pumps have vehicles waiting. I pull to the side, out of the bustle.

"Mae, you got money?"

"You don't have any money?"

"I got a ten spot in my billfold. The four mil is illiquid."

She lifts her purse from her feet. "I have a debit card."

"You don't want to do that," Leroy says, half a yawn in his throat. "First thing they'll do is look for us to use our credit cards."

"They can see that?"

"They'd know before you finish pumping gas."

"So with the time it'd take to get here, you're saying I could get away with it?"

"No."

"I'm fooling. Something in the morning sunshine make a fella giddy."

"I have a twenty," Josiah says.

"Preciate it, but I'll need a touch more. I got an idea. Go back to sleep."

I pull the latch and open the door. "Mae, outside."

Mae joins me outside the vehicle, up by the engine.

"I have to trust you on this, Mae. You got to keep these people in line. You know I can see deceit, and this truck's chock full. But I have to go inside and make a trade."

"Trade what?"

I lift the butt holster and slip out the compact Smith 9.

"Ohh. That's pretty."

"I'm going to sell it, one of these truckers."

Mae's eyes turn to the entrance. "Let me do it. You're on the radio by now. And we need to cut off your hair, give you a tight shave and a ballcap or something. Buy you a suit so you don't look like a—what they'll be looking for."

"That's good thinking. But I don't have a shave kit."

"Another thing," Mae says. "We need to trade some of those coins for cash, right away. Today. Otherwise all we have is guns and gas stations, and that—I won't put up with that. Not with the kids."

"You got some good ideas."

I look at the sun breaking through the trees. A state trooper steps out of a patrol car parked next to the TA building. Mae must have seen him before she volunteered. He does a three sixty, situational awareness and all, and goes in for his morning donut.

"Mae, here's the thing. You been fighting me all morning, and now you want me to give you a gun and send you in with the state trooper. Can I trust you?"

Mae breathes out and slumps a little. Tilts her head a mite. Shakes it sideways and her nose gets wide. "I left my whole life," she says, and her voice is a cigarette grumble though she don't smoke. "I carried my kids past dead bodies for you."

"Turn around."

She does.

I lift her sweatshirt top and push the holster down her back into her butt. "Jostle it around a little to get it snug. The pressure from your bottom's enough to hold it in place."

"Is it loaded?"

"Accourse. But it has a safety switch. So unless you got a spare hand in your ass likes to pick things, you're fine."

"What's it worth?"

"Maybe four, five hundred, new and legit. But we'd be lucky to get fifty or a hundred. We only take cash. And I want a jug of coffee."

Mae walks to the travel center and I keep an eye on her while I open the door and let Stinky Joe out to handle his business. It's cramped in the vehicle, and if I dropped off Ruth or one of the coppers there'd be room for the dog. And less people to lie to me. But these coppers have been helpful and Ruth'd spill her soul even without the aid of all her spite and treachery. Then I'd need a new vehicle, direction. This ain't... No.

Behind the glass Mae passes the state trooper without so much as a sideways look. My heart settles a little.

"Joe, c'mere!"

He carries a sammich wrapper in his teeth.

I have to turn gold into food and water. Coffee. Men can use leaves, but toilet paper for the ladies. Sleep supplies. Blankets. I got a whole clan to look after.

Hardees looking better. Or the woods.

I let Stinky Joe in the vehicle.

"I need to use the restroom, Baer," says Leroy. "It's morning and I got a pretty regular bowel."

"You're going to save it until we get to the wood. No civilized services for y'all."

"But Baer, we've been helpful as we can be."

"And long as I got the guns you'll continue."

I climb inside. Hit the door latch that locks them all. Twist back and give my grandson Joseph a howdy shake on the knee. His face puckers red and a sound like to peel paint comes out his mouth. I look to Morgan and she takes Joseph on her lap and corrects me with a look.

Got that safety seat on the floor.

I recall my old camp with the tarp stretched ground to tree. Sleeping bag and crate with old Fred, the fire circle where we had conversation. Somewhere out west I'll have it again.

I get out the vehicle and come around the other side. Grab the safety seat. "Bree, I need you in the front seat a minute. Can you climb up there?"

She wriggles and cavorts. Three seconds later she somersaults into the front passenger seat. Ta dah.

I strap the safety seat next to Morgan. She watches and I see she isn't studying me but what's behind. I turn.

"Good morning."

It's the trooper.

"Noticed the gun belts. Wanted to say hello."

Out the corner my eye, Leroy elbows Josiah awake. They're in uniform but so long as the trooper doesn't peek in the vehicle, they're out of his line of sight.

"Howdy, officer."

I cinch the seat tight. "Climb in back, Bree."

Close the door. Let the tinted windows do their work.

"Yeah, officer. This one's a Judge, is the name of it. You ever see one of these?"

I pull it by two fingers. "Let me bust this open."

With the cylinder hanging I dump the shells. "You got the forty-five and the .410. About as pretty a situation as you can see."

"Mind if I get the feel of it?"

"Nah." I hand it to him.

"Where you headed?"

"West. Got the grandkids and the daughter for the day. Thought we'd visit kin in Cataloochee. Their grandmum's sick and don't have many days left. But the Good Lord's been waiting on her and soon enough she'll be with'm."

"I'm sorry to hear that."

Mae comes out the travel center. Stops by the window and stands looking.

"I appreciate that." I wave to Mae. "Here's my girl right here."

Mae walks with bags in hand, coffee in the other.

Trooper hands me my Judge, and I got a handful of shells in the other.

"Be careful with that. Have a good day with your family."

He leaves as Mae arrives. "Thought you couldn't lie."

I open the front passenger door for her and scoot to the driver's.

"Yeah. Since last night, it comes more and more easy. You get much money?"

She puts the bags of goodies on the floor and pulls a wad of cash out her pocket.

"Should be about a hundred and twenty left."

"Huh?"

"I got one-fifty. See that spikey-haired red over there with the pitchfork tattoo on her neck? She digs the Second Amendment."

Chapter 32

Sheriff Horace Wycliff Leathers had reasons to feel shaky in his post. He faced a fall election challenge from a Benton businessman and outsider named Stanley Ulrich. He was the CEO of the Benton Furniture Factory & Outlet, and deacon of the Benton Baptist Church. He'd staked ground as the law and order candidate with business savvy and high integrity. The press ate it up.

Law enforcement credentials? He had that too. Served fifteen years as an officer in the Military Police.

Leathers had the advantage of incumbency, familiarity, and name recognition. But the challenger was a millionaire. He had millionaire friends and newspaper friends. His background checked off every block.

The prick was good-looking too. Like Charlton Heston as Moses, before he came down from the mountain with white hair.

But Ulrich was no Moses. He played dirty. Leathers suspected Ulrich had bought a series of newspaper hit pieces. They began in spring, and questioned Leathers' use of resources for personal benefit. The articles started before Ulrich declared his candidacy for the fall election—perfectly in keeping with his apparent shrewdness.

Then another hit piece got his blood boiling, for its simple vileness and corruption.

A photograph accompanied the article. The photo showed Sheriff Leathers with a beer in his hand. His arm draped over the shoulder of a gorgeous, well-endowed woman in a tank top. Leaning toward the camera. The woman was not his wife.

The photographer snapped the image with Leathers transitioning from smiling to speaking. He looked like a pervert.

The writer questioned Leathers' commitment to "family values." The piece avoided mention of the woman, and thus didn't allege an illicit romance. The photo said everything.

The article's author and the newspaper that printed it didn't care that the photo came from a family reunion. The woman was his sister, whom he hadn't seen in five years.

After that came a flow of negative articles about his office and leadership. Next came op-eds and letters to the editor that used the same template. They began with begrudging accolades for Leathers' service to Polk County, followed by a presentation of a problem that wasn't real. What about big-city crime creeping into Benton? What about all the drug traffickers passing through on Interstate 75, on their routes from Chattanooga to Knoxville? They sometimes detoured to Benton….

Each missive closed on a question designed to make Leathers appear flat footed.

What is Sheriff Leathers doing about it?

After a couple months, Leathers became curious who his competitor for office would be. Regardless of who wrote the news, the one who benefitted was the one who made it happen.

Also fearing a challenge in the fall, Benton mayor Charlie Burnett began holding town hall meetings. He walked Mainstreet in the evenings chatting people up. He held a press conference and demanded Benton police enforce a zero-tolerance policy. Despite the newspaper's histrionics, the town in 1986 had no problem with drug abuse, bar fights, or even regular small-town criminality. So Burnett campaigned against speeding limit offenders, jaywalkers, and noise ordinance violators.

Mayor Burnett had pressed Leathers to close the Miller Cousins mailbox bombing as rapidly as possible. It was obvious the Miller boys did it. Leathers reminded the mayor that while he offered respect, the mayor wasn't his boss, and His Honor needed to back the hell off.

In Leathers' estimate, Mayor Burnett was a small time political whore. He'd want Leathers to solve Lemuel Carter's murder in a day. Given the scant probability of that, he would push for Carter's death to be written up as a tragic suicide.

"Yeah," Marcy said. "I don't see Lemuel doing that. What are you going to call it?"

"I'm not *calling it* anything. This is the third death in three years caused by an M-series firecracker from the disaster. Today's victim—Lemuel—was connected to the second victim."

"Right. He was the first on the scene."

"Nope. He was second on the scene. And that's not the connection I meant."

"What?"

Leathers held her look. "He was the target. Remember the Miller Cousins tried snakes first. That was the main evidence that put them in Saint Clayton's Academy."

"He was the target of a firecracker bomb, and now he's dead of a firecracker bomb."

"That's not the only connection. Lemuel wasn't the first on the scene. He was the second. The first was Josiah Swain—the adopted son of the first victim to die by firecracker. Ernest Swain."

"Sounds like we need to see if Josiah has an alibi. If you're going to call it homicide."

Leathers shook his head. "I'm going to get Sam in here to help you. Then I'm going to catch up with Josiah Swain."

Chapter 33

We park at an open lot beside the Hardees at Monterey, Tennessee. Saw the sign from the highway and grabbed the turn. The lot is flat and open, suitable for a gas station.

The drive-through line reaches the road and the parking area's full. Every town has one high class eatery that pulls them in.

Stinky Joe stretches in the dust next to the vehicle. Eyes closed under October sun. He's worked harder than he's accustomed. He snoozes in the dirt, paws flipping like he trudges along the dream, not yet found the scent he seeks.

The hour is nine. The sun bold. Delirious with fatigue and buoyed by the fact I'm alive despite my stupidity, I've agreed to change my appearance. I have to trade gold for fiat currency. Got to sleep. I close my eyes while Mae snips at the tangle in back. Don't ken her process, cuts here and there.

In a minute Mae's got me short cropped. My whole mop's on the dirt. I come to the sideview mirror and it doesn't look bad for scissor work, though a little closer the skull than I'd cut myself.

Turn my head and get closer to the mirror. Good crop growing in my ears and nose. Other than that she's snipped it all less than an inch long.

I look back at my reflection. If there was a little Nazi sign on my forehead people'd mistake me for Charlie Manson.

"Mae, you got to cut the beard close enough I can get it off too. Can't leave me looking like some serial killer."

She smirks.

"I'm a mass killer. Technically."

Her smirk doesn't improve, and I don't feel any lighter for joking of it. She works the scissors and in no time I feel metal against my skin.

I check in the mirror and next time I'm near a basin and soap I'll have a smooth shave. Be interested to see what's down there.

"That'll do until we can get you some different clothes. Maybe see a barber."

Now that I look civilized I may as well smell my clothes and pits.

Rank.

"Aright. We need enough food for everyone until supper."

We load up and Ruth says, "I can't feel my hands."

"Good."

"Mister Baer," Josiah says, "If we don't fix her circulation problem, you'll have a bigger headache than you can imagine. Besides, you got Leroy and me back here. She won't be no trouble."

I pass the keys to Morgan and she passes them to Josiah. They shift and wriggle. Ruth twists sideways and Josiah works the key to her hands.

"Cuff her up front and pass them back."

"I'm hungry," Bree says.

"Me, too," says Morgan. "When will we get there?"

Mae closes her door. I drive to the Hardees drive-through window and order two of everything plus a gallon of coffee. Cash.

A man gets out of an F-150 built back when they ran on coal and steam. He walks in front of the Suburban to the Hardees door. Gadsden flag on the truck window.

"Hey fella. Hey there."

He looks.

I cut the wheel so's to miss him and pull forward. "You know where a sovereign citizen can trade gold for fiat paper 'round here?"

"Why you want to do that?"

"Got a couple maple leafs at the moment, and the gas stations all want paper."

He looks back to his truck and then rolls his eyeballs part into his skull. When they float level says, "Only place round here, you got to go all the way to Cookeville."

"All the way?"

"Shit sakes." He steps sideways. "No way around it."

"How far?"

"Least twenty minute."

I whistle. "That far? What's the place?"

"It's called the Quick Cash. It's a pawn shop."

"They do gold?"

"Sure."

"How I get there?"

"Take the highway west. You get off the next exit. That'll be twenty-four. You go right there, not left. You go right and keep going until you're in town and watch for the Dairy Queen on your left. Well, right there you turn right. Go a couple hundred yards."

"Who do I ask for?"

"I dunno."

"Preciate you."

He waves.

I sip coffee and it's so hot I gag. "Go ahead and pass the food back."

Josiah says, "You a sovereign citizen, Baer?"

"No. But he was."

I wait on traffic and given opportunity, cut left and jam the gas to beat a Cadillac. Right onto the onramp. Mae keeps her gaze on the road like a good copilot. Got the kids in the back and everybody restless. Stinky Joe wants a burger. I keep drinking coffee but even with the sunlight and caffeine it's a losing battle. I'm ready for a good zonk.

"BAER!"

Mae lurches for the steering wheel and I grab it hard. Jerk it steady.

"What—?"

"You fell asleep. PULL OVER."

"I'm awake."

"You're going to kill us."

"Maybe. But not in the Suburban."

"You need sleep."

"How am I going to sleep when I can't trust a one of you to not cause trouble?"

"You're paranoid," Mae says. "What's got into you?"

Josiah says, "Baer, you could find a dirt road. Pull over. Climb up on the roof and lock us in with the key fob. The alarm would sound if we unlocked the door from inside. So you can grab a nap on the roof. Twenty minutes is all you need."

"That true? It'll set an alarm?"

"It's made that way to prevent theft when someone breaks a window and unlocks the car door without using the key fob."

"Beats dying in a car accident," Mae says.

We come upon a dirt road and I take it. In a mile, it's nothing but wood on the right and pasture on the left. I pull over and park. "You people eat your food. And if the alarm doesn't work I'll feel you open the door."

Electric current on my arm, not a lot. I look them over and no one's eyes are red. Just the juice. Could be anyone. And could be any untruth.

I climb the grill and over the hood. Lock the vehicle with the keys and lay across the roof, skull on warm metal. First time my head's been close to bare in forty some years. Don't feel right. Not natural, man to have short hair.

Got the Judge in my right hand and the Bailiff in my left.

Sun is bright and cuts between leaves and dances on my eyelids. Little breeze here and there. Vehicle shifts as the folk inside settle for a snooze of their own. I drank enough coffee, now that I want to sleep I can't.

Highway lines zip through my mind. When they fade I see Randy's face tore up from a .410 shell, and that black pool of blood below Jeb's head. He sits up and says, "Ain't you going to hang me in the trees?" And Randy rolls sideways and belly laughs. He points. "That's a good one. Ole Baer isn't the one that put them in the trees."

Back of my head aches now and I feel the click of the car door latch through my head. The alarm squawks. I jump. Sit up straight with two pistols ready to fight. But the alarm cuts the brain like a butcher's cleaver and I drop the Judge to fetch the fob out my pocket. Press buttons until the horn stops blasting.

The back window pops up.

"Baer! It's been an hour," Mae says. She's opened her door. "We need a bathroom break. And we're choking to death in here."

I look at the fob. One of the buttons shows a lift gate. I look at the back of the suburban.

"Ahhh."

"BAER!"

I shake the sleep loose my head and swing my legs around.

Dismount the Suburban roof. Sun's moved across the sky. I'm groggy like a flu hit me, but it's the sleep not letting go. Knees buckle as I slide off the hood to the ground, and I'm on my back looking up dizzy at Mae. She steps away and the door slams and she's back. "Are you okay? I closed the door so no one can see. You're safe, okay? What happened?"

"Maybe the blood pressure."

"Stay flat for a couple seconds, until you get your bearings."

"Close the back window."

Heart steadies out in my chest, and I dwell on all the trouble I'm in. All the men back at the fight pit. Two FBI boys dead and a copper too. The wild-ass crazy of the last twenty-four hours, all because I couldn't let a bad man get away with being bad. Now I'm the fool stuck out across the line.

I have to solve the problem. Got to get loose of these people. I scratch my head. Pebbles stick in the skin. I miss my hair. Collar on my neck is chafey. I get up on my elbows. The Suburban door opens. I get on all fours and, with the blood pressure recovered, on my feet. Morgan jumps out, then Bree. Joseph wails. Stinky Joe hops down. Josiah pushes the seat forward and climbs down, then Ruth and Leroy.

"Don't stand next to the road with those handcuffs on."

"You all right Baer? Saw you take a tumble."

"Nah. Had to pass out a minute. You know."

They circle me and it feels wrong. Like a big family.

"Step down in the woods and do your business. Stay away from the girls. And if you run off so be it. I'll drive away."

"No, Baer," Leroy says. "We're with you. One hundred percent."

"Fine. You go off that way and the girls go right. Mae—take them. And if Ruth runs, holler. I'm still of a mind to shoot her."

Stinky Joe sniffs about and comes up with his tail working sideways. I squat. Good to bend the knees deep. Hug him tight and scruff his face with mine. Scratch hard about his ears and neck. Got his tongue out lolling and lapping and now my face is clean and sticky. A dog's tongue slap'll cure all.

"Joe, you keep an eye on these lyin pricks, aright?"

Leave a gun with me ....

Stinky Joe grins.

"How did Mae turn on me, Joe? How did she try and rob me blind after all I done?"

I rough up his back and Joe sigh-growls like he's warm next to the fire. "You're a good puppydog."

I stand. Get the lay. Brain's coming back strong. Clarity in my eye. One day soon, I'll be West. I'll be rid of these liars and alone like I set off last night.

"All right. Shake it off. Back in the vehicle. I got a plan, and you'll know it once you're in the truck."

The girls come back first, but I keep them out until Ruth arrives limping.

"You're an asshole, Baer."

She walks like one leg is short.

"Twist an ankle out there?"

"Why don't you let us go? What can we do to you out here?"

"Inside."

"No!"

"Kids, inside. Morgan, Bree—up inside the vehicle."

They climb in and I close the door. Lead Ruth by her neck to the back of the Suburban and spin her. Get close. "You want to die?"

She studies me hard. Shakes her head flat-ways.

"Get in the truck."

"I better get inside first," Leroy says. "So she can sit in the middle."

"Get in."

Leroy pulls himself through the opening.

Ruth looks past me—her and Josiah hold a long stare. She moves her head to my ear. "It isn't what it seems, Baer."

Ruth steps inside and I steady her with a hand on the hip. Josiah files in next. Mae jumps shotgun and last Stinky Joe doesn't want left behind. All inside, I join them. Drink coffee. Wriggle into the seat.

"Here's the way I see it. I need cash. We go to the pawn shop up the road, like the old feller said. Once I have the cash, we find a place to hole up a day or two. I got to change my looks and clothes. Y'all need a bath. We need food and sleep. Once we're set, I cut y'all loose. Josiah, Leroy, you been good to me and I appreciate it. Once we get situated a bit, we'll go out a couple mile and I'll give you a mess of gold and leave you to your own. Sound good?"

"We appreciate that, Baer," Leroy says.

Josiah nods. "You been good to us, too."

We're all good people, shucks.

Put the vehicle in drive and head toward the pawn shop.

"Maybe the radio has something," Mae says. "News."

She pushes the knob.

Chapter 34

Lemuel Carter Sr. had survived the snake in the mailbox, and the bomb in the mailbox.

Yet he had to die.

Josiah knew he'd failed from the moment he saw Clystine Miller sprawled on her back by the mailbox. Josiah had felt a sense of doom talking to Sheriff Leathers. He'd been all good-buddy while interrogating Josiah, but Josiah knew he was under suspicion. The questions about skipping school, and especially getting him to admit he'd collected a few of the M-series firecrackers... Josiah had thought it would look even worse if he didn't admit to gathering some. He'd expected Leathers to whip out his handcuffs and drop him to the ground with a knee to his back. But it never happened.

The evidence he planted did its job.

He'd made the scene lie. Not the firecrackers Josiah placed on the property, but the history between Lemuel and the Miller Cousins. Part of staging a crime scene was what you brought to it. Another was recognizing a pregnant situation that, with a little nudge, could tell a new story. In one light, the rattlesnake in the mailbox was a stupid prank. But illuminated by a bomb blast and firecrackers around the scene, the snake in the mailbox was a failed murder attempt.

Get law enforcement looking one direction, it'll be hard for them to look another. And in the future, if you don't make the boneheaded error of being at the crime scene, you won't be an automatic suspect. They'll look where you make them look.

Good lessons, when Fate tasks you with killing the mailman.

It was May and school had let out. Josiah's days were free. His aunt, Emma, had taken two jobs, one as a waitress, and the other at a furniture store in Benton. She was gone most of the time. When she wasn't at work, she curled up on the couch. She'd read her Bible, then sleep with a finger inserted to keep a page.

Josiah looked up Lemuel Carter Sr. in the phone book and found he lived on the outskirts of Benton. Close enough to town to have a house number on a named street, instead of a Rural Route number. Josiah needed to learn everything about Lemuel. Somewhere, his background held a situation that could look like something else.

Josiah wanted to sneak into Lemuel's house while he was delivering mail all day. The last thing he wanted was for Lemuel to come home with Josiah snooping in his house. But he couldn't risk a neighbor seeing him come or go, and that meant it couldn't be in the daylight. Even weeks before the murder, his presence there would announce, *Look at me. I make a good suspect.*

Josiah didn't want his name to enter the mind of Sheriff Leathers. He needed something to put him in the area for another reason. Something to make him anonymous.

Josiah knew he had the perfect solution the moment he thought of it. What do all adults want to see in kids? Religion and work ethic. Well, religion could screw itself. He'd seen all the good it did Emma. But work ethic... There had to be something he could do in town that would justify him being near Carter's place. Maybe a burger joint or something would hire a teen.

Emma had stopped getting the newspaper after Ernest died.

Josiah wondered. The neighbor two houses down on the right side of the road, Noah Campbell, had a newspaper mailbox.

Everyone knew the Campbells were the richest folks in Benton. Noah did something in construction. They didn't have kids.

Josiah rode his ten-speed past Campbell's newspaper box and saw it was empty.

Mrs. Campbell pulled weeds in the garden, part stooped and part squatting. On impulse Josiah swerved onto the gravel driveway.

Josiah had a lump of trepidation in his throat. But he thought his strategy would work. Adults seemed to admire industry in young people.

"Well hello, Josiah. How are you today?" Mrs. Campbell stood erect, then leaned backward, stretching.

"I'm looking for a job. I was wondering if you still have yesterday's newspaper. We don't get it anymore."

"Oh, why certainly. Of course."

It was that easy. In minutes he had the paper. Mrs. Campbell pointed out a couple classifieds she considered telling her nephew about. She smiled at Josiah with sadness in her eyes. She knew his real parents had died in a car accident when he was ten, and his uncle committed suicide three years later. Josiah recognized it as a look that said, "I pity you so much, I'll believe whatever you tell me."

"Thank you," Josiah said. "Can I keep this?"

"Of course!"

He stuffed it under his arm for the quick ride back to the house. There, he opened the classified section on the kitchen table. Like he'd seen Emma do three years before, he circled any ad he thought might be in the right area. The problem was, he didn't know exactly where Lemuel lived. He knew the address, but he couldn't place it in the greater context of Benton, Tennessee.

He'd need to scout it out.

He ate a PB&J, filled his water bottle and set out on his ten-speed. Two or three miles would take ten to fifteen minutes, depending on how fast he rode. Josiah pedaled hard, adrenalized by the mission. He had a specific place within fate. He'd aligned his work with his destiny. He needn't worry about anything.

He didn't know if a map of Benton existed anywhere, and didn't want to ask anyone for directions.

Benton was not a large town. Josiah got lucky. Approaching town on Welcome Valley Road, he discovered a turn he'd never seen before, Pankey Lane.

That was where Lemuel Carter Sr. lived.

Josiah rode the rest of the way into town, another mile to the dead center.

He stopped at the Main Street hardware. Brick. Big windows. *Help Wanted.*

"You Ernest's boy?" The old man said. He wore coveralls with a t-shirt. Had yellow teeth and a box of Marlboros on the counter by the register.

Josiah nodded.

"Damn shame. No offense. What that man did. You got transportation? I can't hire help 'less I know he'll be on time. Can't miss work for nothin'. I don't care if the Messiah shows up on your lawn with a nekkid angel lady plays a harp—you got to come to work on time."

Josiah nodded.

"And you don't got no back problems neither? Last boy couldn't lift a soggy sack of pig piss."

"You sell much of that?" Josiah said, and smiled.

The old man smiled back. "Yeah, alright. Take the sign out the window. Might as well start now."

Josiah worked seven hours until the hardware closed. On the way home, he detoured for a quick ride up Pankey Lane. The farther he rode the lesser maintained were the houses. Finally, when he saw Lemuel's place, he wondered if he'd made a mistake. It was small. He made sure to only glance at the house and looked around to make sure no one was outside. He rode another hundred and fifty yards and the road ended. That was a new concept... a road that just stopped. He turned around, and sat with his butt on the seat and one foot on the ground. He drank water from his bottle.

The area seemed to be farmland overrun by houses. A wooded section gave way to an open area with a few homes, then the road ended in another wooded area. Lemuel's place was in the first.

Josiah rode home. Told Emma about his new job. She looked at him with tired eyes and her mouth parted by an unspoken question. She closed her mouth, question unasked.

"I need to be there first thing tomorrow," he said. "I'll be leaving at eight."

"Do you want me to drive you?"

"It's no trouble. I like the ride. Plus our schedules don't match."

"Be safe."

He smiled.

Chapter 35

Sophia Ellen Whitcombe lay on a thick blanket atop plywood. Another blanket draped over her bare back. Her eyes had adjusted to the light. She'd fallen asleep with a sense of hopelessness and woke with no sense of elapsed time. She shivered. She'd used a stack of blankets as a pillow. She grabbed one. It was hard to move at all, with her hands and feet bound together. She shook the blanket open and covered herself.

Then she had to use the bathroom. She moved to the other end of her grave-sized pit, unbuttoned her jeans and wiggled them down with her underwear, all at once. She leaned and squatted, pressing her bare back to the dirt wall. She peed. Waited a moment before pulling her pants back up.

When she got them in place she felt cold wetness and smelled pee. She'd peed on her pants.

"YOU ASSHOLE!"

Stooped over, Sophia jumped up and down, pounding her feet to the plywood floor and bouncing her back against the plywood roof. "I'll KILL YOU!"

She screamed until she hiccoughed. Her throat raw, Sophia pulled her pants back down. She'd leave them until they dried.

Her anger gave way to thoughts of vengeance, and then escape. Her revenge would come when her Navy Seal father hunted down this pud-pulling pig. Beat him to death with his bare hands.

Except her father said rescue never happens.

She had to escape. She would survive until she found the opportunity—but she resolved to be clear with herself. She would escape. Rescue was not an option. Neither was death.

Sophia thought through her situation. Her kidnapper had taken her after school at three thirty. It took an hour to get to Sylva. After hiding behind the lights and jerking off, the man probably went home for the night. He couldn't disappear for days at a time in the police car—not if he was a real cop. He was gone for the night.

Then again, he didn't wear a wedding ring. He could come back any time he wanted.

Or maybe the uniform and car were just props... Maybe he lived in this run-down house, and only put on his costume when it was time to grab a girl.

Maybe he had a microphone and camera hidden in the hole with her.

Had there been others before her?

Sophia pressed her bound hands to the dirt wall, as if seeking a connection. But the earth was cold.

She had to escape. Doing so would require long term focus. Sophia committed herself. No more childish outbursts. No more whining. Regardless of whether God watched over her or even knew she existed, someone had buried her in a pit. She could die, or she could live. If she lived, it would be because she kept her wits. She had to believe, so she did.

Time to make progress. She had to be content if it took weeks, or longer. But she had to make progress at every opportunity.

How long had she slept? She had no idea. Her body wasn't super stiff like when she'd slept all night on a tent floor without a mattress. She remembered her father's family weekend outings. He taught her to fish with a trotline, how to eat pine nuts and grubs together, so they weren't as nasty. What she'd give to be there now.

Sophia half-smiled. She'd get through this. She'd eaten a grub.

Sophia found the bobby pin she'd hidden by a belt loop on her pants and pulled it off. With her fingernail she popped off the plastic covering the metal end. Sitting with her knees at her chest, she felt along a zip tie holding her ankles together. He'd used two. She traced the plastic with her fingertips until she found a square section. She inserted the end of the bobby pin and picked at it until it gave a little. She spread her knees to create more pressure. One zip tie gave, the other held. She switched and inserted the pin into the second tie and worked it the same. In minutes of alternating, she'd freed her legs.

Sophia opened her knees and flexed until her lower body started to feel like her own again.

Next, she twisted her wrists and felt for the lock hole on the handcuffs. She pressed the tip of the bobby pin along the metal until it dropped into the hole. Then felt inside for a nub that would catch, that she could then press down to release. She'd seen people do it in the movies and was sure there had to be a way.

Her fingers tired. She dropped the bobby pin. *Damn.* She felt along the blanket under where she thought her hand was when she'd dropped it. Then started making circles, larger each time. Finally, she found it down by her feet.

Sophia tried a different approach with the handcuffs. Her father had said it was scarier because you have to make the cuffs tighter for it to work.

She slid the pin along the top of the teeth that ratcheted the cuffs tighter. When it would go in no farther, she jammed it. The cuff clamped harder on her wrist. As she kept the pressure on she pulled her arm away and the handcuff popped free. She'd jammed the ratchet. Sophia did the same on the second wrist. It was easier, now that she knew what to expect.

Sitting with her shoulders aligned with the length of the pit, she extended her arms. Then swung them in circles, rotating at the shoulder, until her muscles loosened.

When she'd been cursing her captor, screaming and slamming her back into the plywood above her, it hadn't moved at all. But what if she made a focused effort? If her captor had placed most of the blocks on the edges of the plywood, she would only need to lift half of them. Standing at one side, she might be able to topple them over. He hadn't used cement—she'd heard them grate on each other as he stacked them.

Sophia stood hunched over. The plywood met her back halfway up. To make the best use of her leg muscles, she needed to be higher, so the flat of her lower back met the plywood when her thighs were two thirds extended.

She'd need to raise the floor of the pit.

She pulled up her pants. They were damp, but she was on a mission. She folded the blankets and put them on the potty side of the pit. Then standing at that end, she lifted the sheet of plywood that formed the floor. She leaned it against the pit wall. Then she felt along the side to remind her of the pit's contours. She'd need to widen the dimensions to get the dirt to elevate the floor.

She stopped. What would happen when the kidnapper peered into the hole? Would he sense the size was different? Could she risk it?

Sophia sat for a moment. It was crazy to think she could escape. He'd thought of everything. He would notice the pit had changed.

Then Sophia thought of the site of the train wreck from *The Fugitive*, and the train car that seemed to float.

It had support on two ends. The ground under the middle was hollowed out.

She'd do the same thing. She'd acquire the dirt she needed not from the walls, but from the floor. She'd hollow out a section in the middle and heap the dirt at the ends. Unless her captor had perfect depth perception, he'd never see it.

Sophia felt along the dirt floor and built a mental image of the areas she would hollow out.

She froze.

A sound… like feet on an old rickety floor.

He was back!

She scooted to the end of the pit, lowered the plywood. She spread the blankets and searched for the zip ties and handcuffs.

Where were they?

Footsteps, down the stairs. Slow.

Sophia froze.

Could she overpower him if he was expecting her to be bound? Not without tools.

She needed to re-bind herself.

She felt along the blanket. Nothing. But there was a hard shape beneath. She lifted the blanket, and another, and found the hand cuffs. But the zip ties weren't with the cuffs.

She heard a cement block slide above her. How many had she counted? Forty? A couple minutes' worth?

Sophia thought hard. If the ties were on the blankets when she folded them, they might have fallen to the dirt. She might have put the plywood on top of them. Again, she went to the toilet end, lifted the plywood and felt along the dirt.

There!

But it was only one tie.

He'd already moved ten blocks. She was running out of time. The zip tie was black and would be against her blue jeans. He wouldn't notice if there was only one.

She lowered the plywood. Climbed back onto it and flattened the blankets again. She put her legs together and zip tied them. Then she waited until she heard a cement block slide, counted until the next. Fifteen seconds. She counted seven seconds and clasped one cuff. Seven seconds from the next cement block she closed the other.

Sophia wriggled under a blanket as best she could. Then as she waited, thought of one last thing. She removed the bobby pin from her pants and felt along the dirt wall. In the corner above the plywood floor, she pressed it into the dirt.

Sophia pulled back her hands as the plywood ceiling lifted. She shielded her eyes from light that seemed bright as sunshine. It was only the yellow bulbs from the joists.

She blinked until her eyes adjusted. She saw his feet, his calves.

"Guess what, little darling?" he said.

Squinting, she removed her hands from her eyes. She saw the lump in his pants and felt a combination of pity and fear. His constant hardon explained much. The man was always on. It was driving him to evil.

She said, "I guess you're ready for our photo session."

"Yeah. Are you ready to bleed?"

Chapter 36

Mae twists the dial to a talk radio station teaching the horrors of modern liberal corporatism. If it isn't one *ism* it's another. Politics give a man cancer, if he hasn't got it already.

"Turn it off until ten."

Road's gray and the yellow line leads like a rainbow to a different pot of gold.

All my life I mused if I ever had the chance, I'd go west.

Grew up dirt poor but managed to see some of the movies and most of the television shows.

Shane.

Laramie.

Rawhide.

I know the woods by my still and the nearest ten miles. The land has its good and bad. Get accustomed to the bugs; less the bites. I once had to cut out a chunk of leg the size of a silver dollar on account the rot from a brown recluse. Still, I like hemlock and the scent of damp forest dirt. Crick water. Trout fried in cast iron—with cabbage.

But since I was a boy I kept alive the thought of living west. I didn't feed it, not like a pet. Maybe like a nuisance I never killed.

West—they got the big spaces. Climb the mountain trails by Montreat and stand atop the Seven Sisters, there's a lookout that lets you see twenty miles. But they say out west, everywhere you stand the view is ten times that. All the mountains are tall as gods and the canyons deep as oceans. Air clean, and you can walk all month and not cross another man's path. Nor find his beer cans or cigarette butts.

Don't know what I'd do, thirty days without the red or juice.

Behind me the kids bicker and slap. Mae turns around and corrects them. I see Ruth in the rearview, eyes burning love holes in my head. The two coppers on either side of her, Josiah like an old prophet, cool and friendly. Bet he lights candles at church and helps the old ladies to their seats. And Randy—daddy of the year, provides for the babies and reads to them at night. These boys doing life right and trying to make their kids decent people.

And me and all my butchery.

Highway cuts through rock. We hiss along, hardly any noise. Some trees have shed their leaves and the bare limbs bring me low. The dream of going west is coming true. Got a daughter, grandkids, and the woman I pined after for thirty years in the back. In handcuffs no less.

But the bare limbs bring me low.

This isn't the way I dreamed it. And I see now, if I'd have left instead of all that killing... If I could restore those people's lives and disappear to the red rock west, we'd all be happier.

Mae presses the radio back on. A smooth voiced woman enlightens us.

"In breaking news, police are on the lookout for a Gleason, North Carolina man. Law enforcement calls him their only suspect in the murders of twenty plus men, including two FBI officers and one police officer. He is armed and dangerous and may be traveling with multiple hostages. The suspect has long hair, a beard, and is likely traveling with a young woman and three children. If you see this person, do not attempt to apprehend him yourself. Instead, call the Gleason police. In other news, the hunt continues for the missing sixteen—

I hit the knob.

"Wait! I want to hear that." Mae punches the radio back on.

—Whitcombe, gone now for six days. Conflicting tips have police scattered, with the most reliable indicating she was last seen hitchhiking east on Interstate Forty, an hour away, near Hickory. Another tip, discounted by police, has her last seen entering the back of a Gleason police car. The tipster has a history of anti-police activism, but police say they investigate all leads, regardless."

I hit the knob.

"Good thing we cut the hair."

We're at the exit the man with the Gadsden flag told us about. I pull right.

"Watch for the Dairy Queen."

We tool along, and I muse on my passengers. I want rid of them. All. I want the life I had before the evil found me. I want Fred back. Stinky Joe's a smartass pup. He'll grow into a solid dog, but Fred was stoic like no other. Had wisdom. I'll do right by Joe but, by God, I miss Fred.

I want to sleep next to a fire. Wake to the sky above and a sore back below. It's what I know.

"There's the Dairy Queen up there," Mae says.

I wait. Turn right.

Ruth. Just about got my mind made up on her thievery and deceit.

I stop in front of the pawn shop. Realize I have no choice but trust Mae. I either send her in for me, or leave her with the hostages and gold. I don't trust her to not get took trading maple leafs for fiat currency. Pawn shops are generally run by fine people, but they're there to profit. They operate from the belief a person who doesn't know the value of what she owns doesn't deserve to keep it.

On the other hand, just say them coppers in the back decide they want to make a break for it. Take the gold and hostages of their own. Then I'd be out my family, four million, and Stinky Joe.

And they'd be taking my revenge on Ruth.

"Mae, I need you to go in there and trade two coins. They're going to tell you the price of gold is down and come up with all kinda nonsense. But each coin is exactly one ounce of gold, and pure. When they sell that coin to someone else, they'll ask eight ninety. They'll say all manner—"

"Eight ninety?"

"Eight hundred, ninety."

One of the coppers whistles.

Mae says, "Okay, Baer, I got it."

"Well, that isn't all. I need some clothes. Electric shears if they got them."

"Anything else? What about supplies for the trip. Sleeping bags, stuff like that?"

"Nah. This isn't the place. Not yet."

She gets out. Opens the back. Coins tinkle. I check the mirrors, case anyone's around to see her pull gold from a bucket. The street's empty.

She walks inside, and I recall her and the redhead that bought the gun. Mae's got smarts. I shouldn't talk down on her. But I have to hold the plan close, as I don't trust her a lick. Not after what she did with Ruth to rob me blind.

Gaining and losing a daughter in the same day cuts a man raw.

"You know, Baer, about that radio report," Josiah says.

"Yeah?"

"Some friendly wisdom, here. You know Leroy and me are on your side. Gleason police is corrupt and lawless. And those FBI boys back there—they put you in a box and give you no choice. We know that. But nobody outside us here knows that. And there's a code in the law enforcement community."

I listen. He stops like he wants me to talk, but I let him hang in it.

"There's a code, says a man kills a cop, he doesn't make it to jail."

"I wish you'd do it," Ruth says. "Reach up there and choke him. Put me in the trunk. Sit on my hands four hours."

"There you go, Josiah. I'll give you advice, right back. Don't spurn a woman. She'll peel off the lipstick and slip out that bifurcated tongue, and you'll see what she is."

"I'm being straight with you, Baer. You need to have a plan to get out of here, lay low, and never be seen again. The FBI has every tool in the book. They have cameras in the sky. Microphones in the weeds. Kid you not, those boys got this country wired. Only way you're going to make it is live where man don't ever set foot. You need a cave in the Rockies."

I scan the side mirrors again. There's a vacant lot behind us. On a whim I turn the ignition, gas the engine, look both ways. I back out, pull forward, and back into the same slot.

Josiah got me thinking I need to be two steps ahead, the rest of my life. Wonder how an old fart's going to do it.

But I recall my talent for spotting deception and hope it—coupled with solitude—will keep me free. I leave the engine run with the air blowing.

In the left sideview Mae exits the pawn with an armload of clothes and who knows what all. She opens the back gate and stows it. Resumes her post at shotgun.

"How'd you make out?"

She shows me a wad of bills, bigger'n expected.

"Per ounce?"

"Eight hundred, per. That's ninety percent."

She sees my wheels turning.

"I already thought of that. I took ten coins, in case they were square with me on the first."

"I loathe holdin' paper money, on principal. But I like your thinking."

I pull out and drive the quarter mile back to the Dairy Queen, and park with the engine running, windows up.

"Listen, people. This is where you and me untether. I'm going to buy you as much cheeseburger as your guts'll hold. Then I'm going to stow Mae and the kids in town. Then I'm going to drive each of you someplace close to nowhere. Give you sixteen coins, each. That's a pound, if you're not a math whiz. Generous, given the situation. I do it right, you'll have a day's walk to find a telephone, then you can say whatever you want to law enforcement, and I won't hold it against you. That'll make us square."

"That's generous," Josiah says. "Cue the dance girls."

I like Josiah, on account he doesn't give me sparks, but there's something queer about him.

"Mae, will you go up there and get two big burgers and a deck of fries for me, Josiah, Leroy, and Ruth. That's eight burgers, four fries, four drinks, and whatever you want for you and the kids."

Morgan and Bree pick at one another. Need out their seats. And little Joseph sees an opportunity to wail, so he takes it. I'm at the limit of my endurance with noise and commotion. I'd love a walk out and about to clear the head. But I don't want the attention two gun belts would bring, and can't leave them in the Suburban.

Mae returns with big bags and, soon as she's inside, Stinky Joe is rapt. The powerful smell makes baby Joseph curious enough to stop his noise. The whole Suburban community comes to a single mind.

"No food until we get where we're going."

"Baer," Josiah says, "won't it get cold?"

"Accourse."

"I need a bathroom break," Ruth says. "You can't expect us not to have to go to the bathroom. We need toilets. We need to wash our hands."

"No."

Consult the map and see a shortcut to the highway.

No sooner than five miles there's a *Rest Area Ahead* sign.

"I demand we stop at this rest area, Baer. That's a demand. I won't stand for this. You're not even being civil. This is kidnapping. What kind of example are you setting for the children? How are they going to remember you? The man who held a gun on their grandmother and made her crap herself, and sit in it all day, because he's too mean to let her use the bathroom? I said I was sorry to you and this—"

"Stop your jawing. I'll stop."

Ruth stays her mouth.

"Josiah, Leroy, you need the bathroom, you'll have a chance in the wood when I drop you off. No more special favors. I'm sick of it. I'm just plenty sick of it."

"That's all right, Baer."

I exit at the rest area. Don't want to be close to people, and for the first time in six years feel lucky. Not a soul's here. Not even a trucker. I park a little ways from the restroom entrance, and take my time coming around to open the door for Ruth. Get her out. Leave her in cuffs, time being.

Mae opens her door and I give her the .357. "Keep an eye on them, and don't let them jaw too much. You'll be safe in a hotel soon. All this'll be over."

I close Mae's door and follow Ruth to the entrance.

"You have to undo my handcuffs, Baer. I can't use the bathroom like this."

Fetch the key from my pocket and remove her cuffs.

"I got thirty years of spite locked up in the liver. You run off, I'll hunt you down. Try to flag someone down, I'll shoot you. The story of Ruth and Baer is going to end the way I say. Clear?"

She holds my look, eyes steady. I step out of her way and she skitter steps like a woman got to poop.

My heart's about sick of causing hurt, death. Being alive seems to commit a fella to someone else's harm.

The way things are ordered.

I sit on a bench and keep an eye on the Suburban. Can't see through the back window, but the front passenger seat is a clean view. I figure Mae'll be the canary lets me know the coal mine's falling in.

I think the plan through. I'll leave Mae in a town somewhere, then haul Josiah, Leroy, and Ruth to a different location. Give each what he deserves and come back for Mae.

If she's there—

Ruth's at a pay phone. Heart jumps in the throat.

She gets through, it's the end of Baer.

I jump and stretch the legs fast. See a sorry end, bars, shadows, electric chair. She's giving me up this moment, saying location, vehicle. The lungs burn and the heart pounds, but I run like it's death behind me.

Chapter 37

Three weeks after gaining employment at the hardware, everything was in place. Josiah had learned enough of Lemuel Carter's back story to locate vulnerabilities. He would point Sheriff Leathers the exact direction he wanted.

The fated night arrived.

At eight in the evening, Josiah knocked on Lemuel Carter Sr.'s back door. He'd approached by foot, having left his bicycle a quarter mile away across a grassy field. He wore a small backpack and carried his dead uncle Ernest's Junior Colt .22. He heard footsteps and the creaking floor inside the house. The porch light came on.

There would be no accidents tonight. He'd learned from his mistakes. He would prove himself a capable student of his avocation.

The curtain on the door window parted. Lemuel's wrinkled, unamused face studied Josiah.

He hadn't thought of this moment, how he would make Lemuel open the door. But instinct took over. He felt his countenance change of its own accord. He half-frowned. Half pouted. He looked like a kid desperate for help in an unfair world.

Lemuel's expression changed at once. He unlocked the door. Opened it. "Josiah?"

Josiah put his foot forward to block the door. He raised his gun arm. Lemuel pushed against the door and finding it blocked, reared back and slammed it hard. The impact crushed Josiah's foot in his sneaker, but the pain didn't distract. The door bounced open and Lemuel backed away.

"You weren't going to cheat Fate forever," Josiah said. "You escaped something you shouldn't have, twice. Move to the bedroom."

Lemuel winced. He held up his hands and stepped backward, facing Josiah the whole time. They moved through the kitchen and although Josiah wore thin gloves, he touched nothing.

"Why you want to do this, son?" Lemuel said. He passed from the kitchen to the living room. The bedroom door was to his right.

Josiah waved him into the room.

"You don't got to do this, son."

"Which drawer holds your socks?"

"What?"

"Your socks?"

"That one." Lemuel nodded.

"Open it."

Lemuel did.

"Now sit on the bed."

Lemuel remained standing.

Josiah shifted his aim from Lemuel's chest to his head. Lemuel sighed. He sat.

"Toss that pillow to the other side of the bed."

Lemuel did.

"Now lay down flat on your back."

Lemuel again sighed, the universal signal of resignation, of not being able to imagine a way out. Not caring to find one. Lemuel leaned back, swung his legs up. "You going to shoot me in my bed? That it? What I ever do to you? I don't got no money."

"I'm not going to shoot you. This isn't about money. Relax. Okay?"

Lemuel reclined onto his back, but his body was rigid. His arms straight, but taut. Josiah remained alert.

From the open dresser drawer, he pulled a stack of folded underwear. Then a stack of socks. He took a sock in hand and placed his backpack on the floor. From it he removed a rope.

"Ah no! No way. You ain't—"

"SHUT UP!"

Josiah pressed the .22 to Lemuel's forehead. He pushed the barrel downward. Lemuel's eyes expanded into giant white orbs and in a high pitch he said, "No-no, no-no, no-no."

Josiah grabbed Lemuel's left wrist and pulled it toward the bedpost. He got most of the way there before Lemuel pulled back.

"I said no! I won't be handled. You gonna shoot me by God shoot me but I won't be handled!"

Josiah shoved Lemuel's arm.

"Go to hell, white boy. Get it over."

Lemuel began to sit up.

Josiah again pressed the snub .22 to Lemuel's forehead, used his weight to press the man's head back against the bed. Lemuel resisted hard. Tears rimmed in his eyes.

Josiah pulled the trigger.

The .22 bullet penetrated Lemuel's skull and broke into pieces that cut through his brain. The lead crossed his brain in fragments. None had the energy to penetrate the other side. They ricocheted back into the brain, shredding it. Lemuel's eyes narrowed on Josiah. In a second, they were empty.

Lemuel's body spasmed and Josiah stepped backward. Though he'd seen Ernest's death spasm, he'd forgotten it. He pointed the gun at Lemuel again, lest he shake himself upright and attack.

But after a few seconds the quaking ended, and Josiah roused himself to the remainder of his mission.

He hadn't wanted to use the gun. Aside from being unartful, it carried the risk of interfering with Josiah's careful plan. If he used the gun, he'd have to leave it as the suicide weapon, and he didn't want to do that. He had no idea if there was a way to trace the gun back to Ernest, and then to him.

But the situation had demanded he pull the trigger. Lemuel had been gathering his courage. Josiah believed he could have overcome Carter in a physical contest. But the real risk of a fight was that he would leave evidence behind. Or Lemuel could have marked him in a way that connected him to the crime. A black eye might be nothing alone. But what if someone had seen him scouting the house?

Josiah stood still while his racing heart calmed and the ringing in his ears subsided. There had been no muzzle flash. The sound was loud, standing right next to it in a confined room. But Josiah doubted the report traveled very far outside the house. Lemuel's closest neighbor was a hundred yards. They would suspect it was a car backfiring.

He closed his eyes a long moment. Opened them. Jumped into action.

First, Josiah slipped his hand underneath Lemuel's head. The bullet had not exited out the back. Good.

Josiah placed the unused rope back inside the backpack. He extracted two M500 firecrackers. He called them M500s because he'd modified them. Always curious about how things work, he'd drilled into the end of an M100 and had discovered most of it was clay. Only a tiny part was the explosive, held in place by a cardboard tube.

For this job, Josiah had wanted something special. Wearing his aunt's yellow plastic gloves, he removed one end cap from five M100s. Drilled out the clay and dumped the flash powder. On the fifth, he expanded the hole and combined the powder from all five into one tube. Packed it with fresh clay and glued the end cap with Elmer's.

He made two more M500s.

He deposited the cardboard tubes, fuses, clay and endcaps, into a plastic sandwich bag.

Josiah took one of the new improved firecrackers to the cave where he'd spent the day waiting for the mailbox bomb. He also brought a honeydew melon he'd wrapped in duct tape to simulate Lemuel's head. He placed the M500 immediately adjacent, lit the fuse and bolted from the cave. The deafening blast spattered him with cold melon meat.

Now, in Lemuel's bedroom, he placed one M500 by each of Lemuel's ears. He bent over and kissed Lemuel's forehead. Then he took his backpack to the same door Lemuel had opened for him and stationed it there.

Back in the bedroom he pulled out a lighter. About to hold the flame to the first firecracker fuse, he held off. The delay between lighting the first and second fuses could pose a problem.

He stared at Lemuel's head. Thought.

Josiah held both M500s side by side, so the flame would touch both fuses at the same time. When they flared, he placed one on each side of Lemuel's head.

Josiah dashed to the kitchen. He forgot to plug his ears. The blast hit him with a double wave of physical force, two separate explosions a mere split second apart. His eyes felt the concussion. His field of vision distorted as if space became warped. He saw the wall blast into the living room and imagined the wet sound of brain spatter, all at once like a sizzling slap. He coughed. The ring in his ears left him deaf.

Blinking, seeing dust fall from the ceiling, he ran back into Lemuel's room. The body on the bed was headless. Blood spatter covered the wall. And somehow the blast had taken out a section of the living room wall. Josiah stood a moment, looking from the body to the hole; then, he understood. The M500 on the left side of Lemuel's head exploded after the first one. By the time it went off it was next to the wall. The second explosion atomized blood in flight and fired it back the other direction. It misted the ceiling and other walls.

Adrenaline shot through him. He was getting better at his craft. After imprinting the room in his memory, he returned to the kitchen. Grabbed his pack and reached for the door.

The evidence!

Josiah stopped. Bent forward and braced his hands on his knees.

Think.

He went to the living room and nudged aside the curtain at the front window. He looked at the neighbor houses. Headlights came down the road.

Josiah eased the curtain back. Watched headlights through them. The car pulled into Lemuel's driveway.

Josiah felt the .22 in his pocket.

The car was backing up. It turned and headed back out.

He released a long breath. The street was a dead end. It made sense for people to turn around.

Josiah returned to the kitchen and found a wooden cutting board in the sink drying rack. He placed it on the counter top and dumped the two baggies from his backpack. Eight empty M100 tubes, the crumbled clay and dust from the insides of ten M100's, and the fuses that had led to their explosive packs.

Josiah pulled a folded piece of tablet paper from his backpack. He unfolded it and ran back into the bloody bedroom.

In the weeks before this night, Josiah had surveilled Lemuel Carter Sr.'s house. One evening the week before, while Josiah watched with binoculars, he'd seen a woman come to Lemuel's front door. She carried something in her hands, like a food dish wrapped in grocery bag paper. Lemuel let her inside and they sat on the sofa together in front of a window opened a couple inches. Josiah had listened to them.

"Do you think she's coming back?"

"I found her at her sister's place in Seattle. At first her sister said she wasn't there, but I heard her, so she put her on the phone. She ain't coming back. She knows about us."

"She wasn't treating you right. Got no claim on a man good as you."

"She gone for good, Hermetta."

They talked about other things, then one of them started making slurping sounds. Josiah retreated with enough information to form his plan.

Later that week, while Josiah watched after dark from the field, Lemuel wandered over to the woman's house. Josiah approached it from the back under the cover of moonless night. Lemuel and the woman were in the bedroom. He heard banging against the wall.

He backtracked to Lemuel's house and found the back door unlocked. Inside Josiah found a letter addressed to Norma Carter. He also found in the trash a hand-written letter that Lemuel had penned to her but had not mailed.

He took the letter. At home over the following week, Josiah spent hours practicing writing in Lemuel's hand. He wrote multiple drafts of a suicide note, then reviewed them all to find the most effortless script.

In Lemuel's un-mailed letter to his wife, he'd addressed it to Norma, but in begging her to return, he'd called her Tootbaby.

Nice touch.

Now, looking down at Lemuel's headless corpse, his ears ringing full volume, his heart jumping and thrashing inside his chest, Josiah placed the note on the dresser.

I don't deserve to live. No man should cheat on his wife. Norma—Tootbaby—I'm sorry.

—Lemuel

Josiah backtracked. He looked for anything that would signal Lemuel's death was other than a suicide by firecracker.

This was a good job. He'd done well.

He would never again ride his bike down this road, or even look this direction.

Josiah lifted his pack from the kitchen floor and backed outside.

Chapter 38

Shoulder Ruth aside. She's on her ass looking up past legs that kept their curves but got a couple veins. I cover the pay telephone handset's mouthpiece. Listen.

"Mam? Mam? Are you okay?"

I hang up. Grab Ruth by her crown and lift her straight. Then switch to her neck. "What'd you tell her?"

"Nothing. I wasn't able to tell her anything."

I get a shot of electric. Her eyes pulse red with her heartbeat. Scared out her mind.

I squeeze her neck and the red switches from her eyes to face. She gags. I loose her. Bring the Judge to her temple.

"I told her the truth. You've kidnapped us all."

"Location! You tell her where we are?"

She coughs. "Rest area on Forty. Past Cookeville."

Red. Juice. "You tell her what vehicle? You say Suburban?"

"You hit me. I didn't have time."

No red.

I grab her wrist and run. She drags her feet and I stop. "Force me and I'll drop you. C'mon!"

She livens her pace. Mae's got the Suburban door open. "What's going on?"

"Your mother made a phone call."

I shove Ruth in, slam the door while she tries to negotiate Stinky Joe and Josiah. Race to the driver seat, engine roars, put her in drive and haul ass.

"I don't know where the nearest trooper is. We get off the ramp, we're good. They don't know the vehicle."

I sweat. The old heart pounds.

"What were you thinking, Ruth?" Mae says. "We're all in this. All of us."

"Turn on the radio."

Mae does.

"Keep it low until the news."

"They won't broadcast something like this on the news," Josiah says.

I let him think I'm that stupid. Eventually the swarm of cops and FBI boys will realize of all the dead men's vehicles, Burly Worley's black Suburban is missing. Someone links that up with the location of the rest stop, Baer Creighton's situation gets snug.

We make it to the interstate and a semi takes the other lane to let us merge. There's another behind so I floor the pedal and the Suburban surges. Speed limit. Easy does it. Nothing to call attention.

Need to rethink the plan. Everyone out. Now. Everyone but Mae and the kids. This nonsense has come to its justful resting place.

First exit I see, I take. Cut the wheel left. Set the trip meter to zero. Drive like Sunday afternoon, not a care in the world. Out seeing the country. Thinking how it would feel to never see Ruth again. Permanent never, like Ruth Jackson never happened to Baer Creighton.

Ten miles in, the road turns to dirt, and five miles later, ends with a turnaround. A doubletrack of ruts and weeds keeps going. I take it.

Trip meter at sixteen point three miles from the exit, I stop.

"Giver me a bag of sammiches."

Exit. Outside, I open the back door. "Ruth, here's where you and me part forever."

Tears roll on her face. Morgan cries. Now Bree starts. Stinky Joe looks at me like I put his paw in a sausage grinder.

"C'mon, now. Out!"

Stinky Joe jumps out.

Ready to pull the Judge again.

Mae says, "Ma, it's all right."

Ruth looks at her and nods. Some communication went on I didn't see. But screw it, I got a bullet for each somebody who gives me fuss.

Josiah helps Ruth, adjusts his legs out of the way and leans hard. She climbs up past the kids' seat and steps out. I put the bag of burgers in her hand.

Close the door. Draw the Judge. Put my arm on Ruth's shoulder and walk with her, so the handgun's big in her line of sight.

"You know Ruth, I've had the curse my whole life. You lie, I know before you do."

"There's something I have to tell you *right now.*"

"I got questions first. Explain how you and Mae was going to do me."

"Mae? Baer, listen! Josiah's the one—"

I raise the Judge with the hand I got around her back. Tap her skull with metal. "Explain how you and Mae was going to do me for the gold."

"Baer, damn you. That wasn't Mae."

"What?"

"Mae didn't help me. Josiah and Leroy did. Baer, this isn't about Mae or the gold. This is about Josiah—"

"Stop! You answer my questions as I ask them. Stop."

"Baer—I was calling the police about JOSIAH."

Woman make no sense. "How'd you and Mae move the gold? How'd them coppers get free? The whole story."

Ruth glares.

"I went inside Mae's house after you told me to go to hell. Jeb was turning blue from the blood in his nose. I unfixed the tape on his mouth. Jeb told me to undo the tape on Frank's mouth. Frank told me all you'd done. He said my actions made me an accessory, and I'd go to jail like I murdered those men myself. Jeb was gasping and coughing so I unfixed his arms and legs, then Frank's. The kids were crying upstairs so they wanted me to tend them. But they wanted to know where you went. I told them there was no way you'd leave the gold, and they didn't believe there was any gold. So I showed them. We made a deal to move it all to my car. I thought it'd be protected there, locked up, instead of sitting in the open. I didn't know you'd haul us on a road trip. I thought even if you didn't want me, if I had the gold, you'd have to come back. I didn't want your gold. I wanted you."

"So where was Mae for all this?"

"Inside the house."

I'm stumped. Stop walking. Pistol in holster.

No red. No juice. Her voice carries a note I want to believe. After all the killing, I want to forget and do the forgiving that comes with it.

"Now can I talk? Can I say what I need to say for the sake of my daughter and grandchildren?"

"Sure. Accourse."

"Josiah has a gun," Ruth says. "He keeps it on his ankle. You never searched him, and he's had it the whole time. He hasn't used it because he's waiting, but I imagine he's going to figure out what we're talking about. When you go back to the suburban, he'll have Mae at gunpoint, with the kids in between."

She holds me from turning.

"There's one more thing, Baer. You know the kidnapped girl, from the radio? A witness said a Gleason police officer did it."

"I was occupied last week."

"Josiah's the one! That's why I was trying to call the police. The girl's still missing and Josiah's the cop that took her."

"Wait. How you know that?"

"It came on the radio while you were asleep on the roof. During the newsbreak the announcer said as much. They think the kidnapped girl is part of all this. They think she's with us. I looked at Josiah and he didn't even look back. He said, 'Think of these kids, before you open your mouth.' He lifted his pantleg and I saw his gun."

We stop walking. I release Ruth from under my arm and turn.

Through the passenger window, Mae's got her hands up in the air, like someone got a bead on her.

She drops my three fifty-seven to the ground.

Chapter 39

The day after finding Lemuel dead, Sheriff Leathers took stock.

In a perfect world, he would get a search warrant for Emma Swain's house. The warrant would seek a spiral notebook matching the paper of Lemuel Carter's suicide note, a .22 firearm, a quarter inch drill bit with white clay dust on it, the M-series firecrackers Josiah had already admitted to, and any souvenirs Josiah may have taken out of Lemuel Carter's house.

Unfortunately, to invade the privacy of Emma and Josiah Swain, Leathers needed to meet the burden of probable cause. He didn't have the evidence. Nowhere close.

What did he have?

Nothing connected Josiah Swain to the residence of Lemuel Carter Sr.

Marcy and Sam had processed the crime scene. They bagged evidence, dusted the house for fingerprints, and asked for an expedited autopsy. The following day they went door to door the entire length of Pankey Lane. Not one person could recall seeing anything out of the usual in the last few weeks.

Leathers and Marcy visited Frederick Walker, Lemuel's supervisor at the post office.

"Do you know how we can get in touch with Lemuel's son, Junior?"

"No, hell, he's dead. Been dead."

"When did that happen?"

"Years and years ago. Moved to Nashville and Oh-Deed on heroin."

"When did his wife leave him? Did he talk about that?"

"His wife left him?"

"Thank you. You've been very helpful."

They'd lifted dozens of fingerprints but working them was no panacea.

First, they needed to know which prints they had collected came from non-suspects.

They printed Lemuel's hands. Easy. Next, Hermetta Washington had been in Carter's house, but wasn't a suspect. They needed hers.

Hermetta needed convincing. She became less helpful as the day dragged on. By evening she obtained legal counsel from Pastor Jefferson Monroe Washington. He wasn't a lawyer or a pastor, but he'd marched in Selma. He was by chance up from Chattanooga and visited Hermetta's church.

After assuring Hermetta in a typed letter that she wasn't a suspect of any crime, she agreed to put her fingers to the ink.

They then had to pull prints for Lemuel's estranged wife. They looked for items only she would have touched. Shoes she hadn't taken with her to Seattle. A mirror from her side of the bathroom. It wasn't a foolproof method. Until they could get fresh prints from Mrs. Carter, they'd have to use what they had from her unique items as a proxy. It might help them narrow down the remaining prints that might belong to the killer.

Given ten fingers for each person they were aware of with a reason to be in the house, there were thirty possible control prints. After printing Lemuel and Hermetta, they could only be sure of twenty of them. If they pulled more prints from the house, they had no real way of knowing if they belonged to Mrs. Carter, to the killer, or to some other unidentified person who had a justifiable reason for being in the house. They could guess, but that was it.

The prospect of matching a print to some unknown person was almost nonexistent. The FBI had some computerized databases. But if Leathers requested their help, he'd have to wait three to six weeks to get the results.

Technology promised to make it easier to identify bad guys in the future, but it wasn't much help to Leathers today. About the only hope of fingerprints providing solid evidence was if they found a one that matched a suspect they already had in mind.

Next problem: they didn't have Josiah Swain's prints.

The rest of the case against Josiah, as Sheriff Leathers imagined it, was by legal standards thin. No thicker than a hunch.

Yet Leathers *knew*.

He'd closed the first two death-by-firecracker cases. Leathers was on record for both. He'd thought it possible Josiah had rested a lit firecracker on Ernest as a kind of prank. A kid wouldn't know the full damage the blast might cause. At the time, Josiah had no motive.

The other possibility, that Ernest had taken his own life, had a lot of motive. According to Emma Swain, Ernest had lost a half-million dollars. The regulators fired him. He lost seventy years of equity in the Nelson family business. All the family's wealth—that he'd married into—was gone. Many humiliated, emasculated men muse about the other way out. The only peculiarity was that he'd done it with an M100 firecracker. Suicide by M100 was rare enough Leathers couldn't locate any statistics. Dynamite, yes. Firecracker, no. Nevertheless, he'd endorsed the suicide explanation.

The second death—Clystine Miller—was what Leathers had suspected of the first but hadn't proven. Clystine died because a teenage boy or three had no idea the power of a M100 firecracker.

It was a prank gone bad. The Miller Cousin brothers had plea-bargained less than three weeks before. They were already at Saint Clayton's reform school.

In hindsight, Josiah Swain could have placed the firecracker in each instance. He was first on the scene in both deaths. If it wasn't for Ernest's depression and the Miller boys trying to punk Lemuel at the mailbox, Josiah would have come under heavier scrutiny in both cases.

All that was water under the bridge. Unless Leathers found evidence tying Josiah to Carter's death, he had no reason to doubt his earlier findings.

Especially not with an election in a few months.

Last, for the killing of Carter, no one who knew him had motive to murder him. Lemuel Carter Sr. knew thousands of people, but Leathers, the deputies, and Lemuel's neighbors were aware of no one with ill feelings toward the man. He'd attended Clystine Miller's funeral. The boys who had confessed to hiding the rattlesnake for Lemuel didn't fault him for showing his respects.

Least of all did Josiah appear to have a motive against Lemuel. The only thing that tied them together was their presence at the site of Clystine's death.

Leathers had nothing to go on. No way he could argue probable cause to a judge.

In retrospect, Leathers saw behind the scared teenage glint in Josiah's eye. That wasn't fear. That was a canny little snit, getting better at killing people.

No doubt, Josiah Swain was beyond dirty-elbow evil.

Leathers had to start at the beginning: a conversation with Josiah. Get facts on paper. See if he said anything that didn't add up. Based on how Emma Swain went lady-batshit on him three years before, he braced for the conversation.

Leathers had only two ways to play it. He had the right to talk to a minor without a parent present. But if he knew Emma preferred to be there, a shrewd defense attorney could pick him apart for trying to confuse a teenage boy. Also, it might look like he was gunning for Josiah, since this would be the third questioning. The fact that the boy was at each of the crime scenes would go a long way to explain that, but still, judges got funny about kids.

Leathers' father had owned a house and started a family when he was seventeen. Sheriff Leathers had set out as a runaway when he was fifteen. A middle teen boy is at his peak of wiliness and moxie. But more and more people thought of teens as thumb-sucking infants, needing the same legal protections.

Leathers thought people had it backwards. They believed babies were born good and then a sinful world tempted them into corruption. Leathers knew children were born narcissists. Deep inside they would always be selfish. They only had a chance at righteous living if their society demanded it of them. Christian morality provided one set of rules. Various levels of government provided the other, in the form of civil law. Rigorous adherence to both, through strong enforcement, was society's only hope against man's inborn evil.

Leathers drank coffee and rested his head on his hand.

If he went after the boy without his guardian present, that risked the judge throwing out his confession. If probable cause for a search warrant also came out of the interview, they'd pitch it, too. The case would come down to the justifiability of the investigation's starting point. Whether law enforcement violated the boy's rights.

His best shot at getting Josiah to talk would be alone. But if he wanted to be able to use what he said, Leathers needed Emma Swain present.

The day following the discovery of Lemuel Carter's body, Leathers phoned Emma Swain six times. She was always at one job or another. Finally, he reached her at eleven at night.

"I need to ask you to bring Josiah down to the station for some questions."

"What's this about?"

"A homicide investigation. We have reason to believe Josiah has information that will help us solve the death of Lemuel Carter."

"That's horrible. I heard about that today. What could Josiah know about that?"

"That's why we need to talk to him."

"What time is it? Eleven. This all seems very irregular to me."

"I tried calling you several times through the day. I knew you'd want to be present, so I waited. But I need to talk to the boy right away."

"You mean *now?*"

"I do."

"Uh. Should we have a lawyer there?"

"I don't see the need, but you have the right. I want to ask Josiah some background questions."

"Background, at eleven post meridian?"

"Let me get to the point. Bring him in or I'm going to come pick him up."

"Oh. I see."

"Mrs. Swain?"

"Okay. I'll bring him."

"He's good for it," Marcy said. "Emma's just doing what she thinks is right."

Leathers had spent the half hour since the phone call sitting with his feet on his desk and his head bowed, a mug of coffee at hand.

He nodded and spoke as if to himself. "I could buddy up to him. See if he's so stupid or nervous he slips up. Or I could sweat him, cuss him, and tell him he's going to the electric chair unless he comes clean."

"We're not a capital punishment state."

Leathers looked up at her. Blinked. "You think he knows that?"

She tried not to smile. "If he did it, yes. But I still say, shake his cage."

"Yep."

They heard the door open. Leathers dropped his feet and Marcy stepped out front.

"Bring them back here," Leathers said.

Marcy came through the entry first, motioning Josiah forward. Emma followed him with her hands on his shoulders, as if to steer him. Josiah twisted free of her grasp. Leathers noticed. Nodded.

"Thanks for coming in. Marcy, could you grab a Coke for Josiah? Emma, like a Coke?"

"No thank you."

"I don't want one either," Josiah said.

"Give him one anyway," Leathers said. "Might get thirsty."

Behind Emma and Josiah, Detective Marcy Keating pulled a Coke from the 1950's style refrigerator in the lunch room.

"Do you have caffeine free?" Josiah said.

Marcy switched cans. Wiped down the new one and delivered it with her fingers touching only the top rim. Leathers nodded.

"Marcy, you want to press that button?"

She depressed the record and play buttons on a Panasonic cassette player.

"All right. It's Wednesday the twenty-fifth of June. Eleven forty in the post meridian. This is Sheriff Horace Wycliff Leathers. I'm joined by Deputy Marcy Keating, Emma Swain, legal guardian of Josiah Swain, and Josiah Swain. Josiah, where were you on Saturday, June twenty-one?"

"That was last Saturday?"

"Yep."

"I went to work at the hardware. Then I went home."

Leathers looked at Marcy.

"What hardware?"

"On Main Street."

"You work there?"

"The last three weeks."

"What hours?"

"On Saturdays, it's all day. Eight to nine thirty."

"Your mother drive you to work?"

"I ride my bike."

"You ride a bicycle home? At night?"

"I got a generator and a headlight."

"What time did you get home, last Saturday?"

Emma Swain said, "He was home at nine forty."

Leathers shifted in his seat. Took a drink of coffee. "Miss Emma, if you wouldn't mind, please allow Josiah to speak on his own behalf. You can counsel him, but please let him speak for himself. Good?"

She nodded.

"Josiah?"

"I got home at nine forty."

"Any reason you remember the time?"

"I missed most of Mike Hammer, but I saw the last couple sets of commercials."

"Ah. You like the detective stuff?"

"Yep."

Leathers held his stare an extra beat. *Yep.*

"I don't recall, Josiah. How did that episode end?"

"Mike caught the lesbian at the airport."

"Put the handcuffs on her?"

"No, the other guy used one of those plastic things."

"A zip tie?"

"If that's the name."

"I saw that one, too. How long does it usually take you to ride your bike home? Ten minutes?"

"Give or take. Sometimes I get tired, after being at the hardware all day. Sometimes I take it easy."

"I bet. What is that, three miles?"

"Closer to two."

Josiah spoke with a nonchalance that surprised Leathers. He'd expected the stammering kid he'd spoken to by the Miller mailbox. This kid had a toughened edge. He was sparring with Leathers, but making it look like he didn't care.

"So, help me understand something. What's your route into town, on your bike?"

"I take Welcome Valley Road."

"And that goes right past Pankey Lane."

"I've seen it."

"You ever turn up Pankey Lane? Ever ride your bike there?"

"No."

"That's interesting."

Josiah shifted in his seat. He lifted his hands from his lap and, with the right, reached for the caffeine free Coke. He stopped before touching it. Instead, he rested his hands on the table.

"Why is that interesting?"

"I have two witnesses said you were up there after dark, nosing around."

"That's not true."

Emma Swain said, "Who are these witnesses? Nothing but trash lives on that road anyway."

Leathers looked downward. "And Mrs. Swain, you also say Josiah was home at nine forty?"

"Yes."

"And Josiah, you got off work at nine thirty? Not earlier?"

"No, nine thirty. Mr. Gore is a stickler about getting his money's worth."

Leathers took a moment to digest the information. Josiah had told him how the Hammer program ended. That meant he caught the last five minutes. If he usually arrived home at nine forty, that meant there could be as many as fifteen minutes unaccounted for.

Except that both Mrs. Swain and Josiah had said nine forty.

Who watches Mike Hammer after blowing a man's head off with a firecracker?

Was Leathers wrong?

"I demand to know who my son's accusers are," Emma said. "Right now. Who said he was up that street?"

"Josiah, I want you to think real hard on this next question. You get it wrong, it's going to have serious consequences on your life." He looked at Emma. "Serious consequences. The state of Tennessee is not a capital punishment state. But it is a state that tries minors as adults. Especially sixteen-year-olds accused of horrific crimes." Leathers turned back to Josiah. "Tried as adult means sentenced as adult. So the question is this: You ever get friendly with a man, in the backside? Did you like it?"

Emma gasped.

"Your cherry sixteen-year-old ass will be the freshest meat at the state pen in Nashville. You know how horny you get looking at your girly magazines. Those inmates will be that horny looking at you. Who's going to save you when you're sleeping behind bars with them every night for the rest of your life? Let that settle in a minute."

"This is outrageous!" Emma said. "I want a lawyer."

"Josiah, listen to me. There have been three suspicious deaths by M100 firecrackers. You've admitted you collected them. You were first at the scene of the first death. First at the scene of the second death. And now we have two witnesses putting you at the scene of the third. And all you've got to say is some story about watching Mike Hammer. Even let's say you saw the last five minutes of the show. It took you fifteen minutes to ride home from work. That leaves you ten minutes to light a firecracker. Plenty of time."

Emma jumped up. Her chair barked backward. "Josiah don't say a single word! This is a frame up! You want a lawyer. Not a single word."

Leathers continued. "Confess to what you did, and the court may go easy on you. But you fight it, we'll send you away forever. Your choice."

Josiah opened his mouth.

Leathers leaned.

"Lawyer," Josiah said.

"Confession is good for the soul. If you got one," Marcy said.

"Are you going to arrest him?" Emma said.

Leathers looked at Marcy, then Josiah. They held stares. "You're free to go. But don't go too far."

After Emma and Josiah left, Marcy opened and drank from the caffeine free Coke that Josiah hadn't touched.

"Did you see how he placed his hand on the table? Pretty sure we got the whole right hand."

Marcy nodded. "I can see his prints without the dust."

"That's some dirty elbows," Leathers said.

Marcy turned. "You've been saying that for years. What do you mean?"

"People don't wash their elbows. Means they're evil."

Marcy's hand went to her elbow. She wrinkled her brow.

"That's right," Leathers said. "Nobody does."

Marcy held his look. "Yeah. Not every man you see on the street is the problem."

"Let's grab these prints, then go over what we got from the scene. If we get a match, I'll have a warrant by dawn. If not, I don't know what."

"If not," Marcy said, "Lemuel Carter committed suicide and left a note."

Chapter 40

"Bleed?" Sophia looked up at her captor. She'd managed to get the plywood floor down, the blankets spread, her hands cuffed and legs zip-tied together before he lifted the plywood. She still felt a rush of euphoria from having defeated him in this tiny thing. And he'd been ambivalent toward her when he'd left, allowing his hand to linger by her cheek. She'd somehow hoped that would carry through into niceness.

"Blood sacrifice," he said. "That's what happens when girls disobey me."

"I haven't—" she stopped. "I'm sorry. What can I do?" Her throat was scratchy again. She needed to remember to warm up her voice before he arrived next time, so it would be smoother. She sounded pathetic, and no man wanted to keep around a pathetic girl. She needed to drink more water. She needed every resource.

"That's a better attitude. You stink. We need to get you clean for the shoot. Then you can eat. You like cheeseburgers?"

She nodded. "They're good."

Sophia noticed a five-gallon bucket with suds at the top and rolling down the side. Another was beside it, possibly for rinsing water. Maybe that's why he came down the stairs slowly.

"Good. Do as I instruct, you'll be eating cheeseburgers and chicken nuggets. Large fries and ketchup. I spare no expense for my girls. Even got you the honey mustard and barbeque sauces."

"I like them both," she said.

The man stepped away and returned with the ladder. He placed it in the pit, on the bathroom side, but angled to miss the hole. "You're going to have to jump from rung to rung. Then I'll pull you out."

He smiled.

A thought flashed through Sophia's mind. Once she was at the top of the ladder, she could grab him and push him into the pit. Then—

He'd climb out and hit her.

Sophia said, "Okay, I can do it."

Placing her cuffed hands on the highest rung she could reach, she pulled and lifted her legs up a rung. Her shirt gaped at the open back and came forward. It draped her shoulders and inched down her arms as she pushed her body higher. She felt herself wiggle behind it and could tell she was exposed at the side. He didn't seem to look. Sophia wondered what alternate universe she was in. One moment her captor demanded a blood sacrifice. In the next he refused to look at the flesh he'd kidnapped her to possess.

"See. Pretty easy," he said.

She climbed one more rung and was almost out of the hole. She wondered if he would look at her ankles, if he would notice the missing zip tie.

"Where do you want me to go?" she said.

He looked at her. The charming smile was gone; his eyes were vacant. He was calculating, as if he'd collected the sum of her words and deeds and was this moment computing her fate.

She feared the fact that he had allowed her to see his face from the start. It meant he was confident she would never leave this basement. Sophia forced herself past the thought. He would get complacent. She would lull him to it. She had to keep buying time.

He continued to stare at her until she looked away.

"I'm trying to be nice," she said.

"No, I don't think so. I don't think you're of the right frame of mind to do as I ask. I need to teach you a lesson."

She looked downward. Anything she might utter would provide the trigger for his next escalation. If she was silent and still, whatever shyness that kept him behind the lights would reassert.

If God was with her.

"I called the police and gave them a tip," her captor said. "Used a pay phone. I described your clothes, your bookbag. Your hair. They believed me."

"Why—would you do that?"

"So they knew where to look."

"What? Really?"

"Yeah, in Hickory."

Hickory was two hours away, the other side of Asheville. He was playing with her.

He said, "You stink like piss."

She was still.

He grabbed her hair and twisted back her head. "Didn't you learn to use the bathroom growing up?"

"I-I missed the hole. I hit my jeans. I-I'll do better next time."

He turned away. "Disgusting." He extracted the knife with the triangular blade. Grabbed her neck and shoved her to a kneeling position on the dirt floor. Then stretched her sideways, on her back.

He held the blade above her face.

"No," she said, turning sideways. She lifted her hands above her face to block him.

"Conceited little slut, aren't you." He rested the blade at his side, then drove his fist to her stomach, like last time. She couldn't help it. Her knees shot forward, and she rolled to her side, gasping, the pain locking her in a fetal position. He lifted the blade, tugged her pants at the waist, then dragged the blade across the denim. She felt the blade slice her skin as he worked downward over her thighs. She held her breath so she wouldn't cry out.

At the knee he paused.

"You know, right here—" he squeezed above her calf— "if I cut you right here, you'd bleed out in two minutes. And it's easy, too. You ever want to take a leg off in pieces, that's where you do it." He continued to cut away her pantleg. The calf area had enough slack he didn't slice her skin with it. Close to her ankles he stopped, then cut a circle around the leg, then jerked the pantleg free of her. "Of course, a bigger knife works better."

He turned her and did the same with her other leg. Blood seeped from where the blade had cut into her like a stripe along the outside of her thigh. She felt her panties bunched up. Her breath came in short gasps and dizziness encroached. She wasn't getting enough oxygen and her heart was racing.

He studied her ankles.

"Ooohhh. Aren't you the clever one."

He looked over the edge to the pit.

"You got one of them off. Didn't do a lot of good, did it? It's okay. Not your fault. I'm not going to blame you. But when we're done today, you'll think twice before you try to get loose again."

This is how I die.

She wanted to blot out the thought. She wanted to look forward to living. To outsmarting this incarnate evil. But she was bound and couldn't breathe, and she knew he was going to slice her open as soon as he wanted to. He was going to hurt her until he tired of it and then he was going to destroy her.

"See, if I could trust you at all, I'd remove the ties and cuffs and you could bathe like a regular human being. But you're not trustworthy."

He shifted her to her back and cut away her sleeves. He placed the blade upside down next to her skin and dragging it upward with much less chance of cutting her.

She was naked except her panties and a section of jeans over her ankles, beneath the zip tie.

"Did you piss your panties too?"

She shook her head.

"I don't believe you." He placed the blade next to her hip and jerked until the lacy fabric fell away. He moved to her other hip, and she sensed the whole thing about her smell had been a ruse. He'd planned it all along. He followed a path. He had a routine.

So why pretend it was her fault?

He stared at her nakedness, but she didn't feel like it was a tool she could wield to destroy him.

Sophia noticed the ever-present lump in his groin. How had he kept it through the exertion of cutting off her clothes?

He followed her gaze.

"Ah. All this time, I thought you were looking at my crotch. All this time." He reached into his pocket and withdrew a red tube. She couldn't place it. Then he turned it and she saw a wick. It looked like a fire cracker, lit from the side instead of the top. "It's a long story," he said. "But you're right to pay attention."

He smiled again, and his whole face distorted into a monster's.

She told herself to keep her mind strong. Keep the long view.

I don't have a long view if he kills me today!

He reached down to her and placed his hand on her breast.

"God, you stink. Disgusting."

Sophia knew she was out of time.

Chapter 41

Don't know the situation inside the Suburban. Mae's hands are up. But I suspect what Ruth said about Josiah and Randy is true. They want the gold and have been waiting the right opportunity.

If they get off with the Chevy, they'll have hostages. Dead weight, if they plan to run for it. This isn't about Mae's pretty. With four million in gold, they could buy all the single mother-of-three country girls they want. Nah, they're after two things.

Gold and four wheels.

Only way I keep them from taking off and leaving four bodies a mile down the road—

Pull the Judge and point. Run at a dead clip like the kids and Mae's lives depend on me crossing fifty yards in four seconds. Sand grits my joints and there's an ache in the back of my head from the nonstop strain.

I loose the Judge's cylinder on the run and see a forty-five round on top. Close the cylinder, slide to a knee ten yards out. With both hands trying to steady muscles and nerves, I draw a bead on the Suburban. Got to trust the metal to prevent harm inside due to ricochet. I aim at the front of the passenger side tire and pull the trigger.

Tire pops. Mae screams. Babies inside scream. The tire's done hissing, time I roll through. Come up on my feet with the Judge lagging. Point again but got no target.

Crouching in front of the vehicle I point the Judge at the driver side tire and stop. I need the vehicle, too.

They got one gun inside or two?

What'd Mae do with *her* forty-five? The one she had when I met her at the door when this whole nightmare started? Her purse?

I get the key fob out and clasp it in my left hand. Got the Judge in my right. Need to cover distance quick, but tactical.

The Suburban straddles a wash in the middle of the doubletrack. Not deep, but enough to boost the clearance. I low crawl under the Suburban, hope to heaven the commotion doesn't clue them in. Come out under the back and, so far, they haven't opened the doors. Though I hear feet stomping and the Suburban rocks a bit.

Stand behind the Suburban looking in. One on the left— Leroy—is closer. Josiah appears to have moved up a row. I point left and press the fob where the picture indicates the rear window. The latch pops. The glass gate opens and I got the gun on Leroy's head.

But Josiah's out the side door and has a gun on me. Hands still cuffed.

"Where'd you get that piece?"

"Put it down, Baer. It's over. Put the gun down and you, Mae, the kids go free. I'll give you the same deal you offered me and Leroy. A couple cheeseburgers and some coins. Fair?"

Leroy, also in handcuffs, lifts the baby up so if I shoot his head, Joseph gets shot, too. He says, "Don't make me hurt this baby. Don't make that my only choice, Baer."

I lower the gun. Rest it on the Chevy's rear window sill, pointing downward.

"You got me. You know Josiah, there's just one thing?"

"What's that?"

"Looky looky up there. Lady riding shotgun has a forty-five."

Josiah turns his head. Mae's snuck a silver tube out the window.

Stinky Joe growls.

"I guess this is a standoff," Josiah says. "Leroy, choke the baby until Baer and Mae drop their guns."

Leroy twists toward Josiah. If either one gave off any red or juice, I'd wait to see who's playing who.

But neither signals deceit.

I take a last guess at how my pistol hand's aligned through the seat to Leroy's spine, and pull the trigger. Leroy jolts. I pull it again. I don't know if I hit him with pellets or a slug. Joseph screams like to ward off a grizzly. Mae fires and catches Josiah at the shoulder, spinning him. I pull away from the window and line the Judge's front sight on Josiah's head.

His pistol hand is useless. Gun on the ground.

Mae's already grabbing Joseph, checking Bree and Morgan, each so deep in terror they forgot their voices.

Ruth runs toward us from where I left her. "The girl!" she screams. "Where's he keeping the girl?"

I step to Josiah, kick his ribs. "You got a girl somewhere?"

Ruth arrives and falls at Josiah. He spits blood. Ruth lifts his arm, sees the entry wound near his armpit.

Mae might have taken out his heart, lungs, the works. Or maybe not. A rib can change a bullet's trajectory.

Ruth places her hands on Josiah's neck. "His heartbeat is good. Strong. His lungs will likely have problems but we have a little time. Where's the girl?"

"Hospital," Josiah says.

"You keep her in hospital?"

"Take me…"

"Oh man," Leroy says. He moans. "Oh man. I can't move. I'm bleedin' out."

Front tire shot. I'd have to find the jack. Lift the Suburban. Swap tires. Drive a half hour to the highway, find a hospital.

"Ruth, stand back."

I point the Judge at Josiah.

"What are you doing!" Ruth says.

"Back off. We don't have time to get him to a hospital. You want him to talk, I'll make him."

Ruth stretches out part astraddle Josiah, and I can't fathom it. Oughtta shoot them both.

"I'm bleeding out," Leroy says. "I wouldn't have harmed the boy. We was desperate is all. You got to get us to the hospital Baer. We're lawmen for crissakes. *Lawmen.*"

"You got the girl, Josiah?" I say. "You admit that?"

He holds my look. Nods, and no juice.

But he never gave me juice the whole time.

Ruth grabs him by the shirt. Pulls. "What's the girl's name?"

"Sophia. Whitmore."

"And you're the one who took her?"

Another nod.

"What'd you do with her?"

He spits blood. "Buried."

"Where?"

"Hospital."

"You'll tell us exactly where if we take you to the hospital?"

He blinks. Nods.

"You aren't going to get there," I say.

I lift Ruth by the pants and drag her off. Swing the Judge to Josiah's face. Draw it down his body and stop at his foot. Pull the trigger.

Kids in the Suburban scream. It's a .410 shotgun blast, and Josiah's foot is pulp in the dirt. He jerks and inhales hard, raspy. Coughs blood and sound with full venom.

Ruth scrambles away.

"Where's the girl, Josiah?"

I point the Judge at his other foot.

Ruth screams, "STOP!"

She's got the three fifty seven on me—the one Mae dropped out the window when I was talking to Ruth. I holster the Judge. "He won't live long enough to reach a hospital. You want him to talk or not?"

"You can't terrorize people to get what you want."

"Me? ... *Me?*"

"We've got to save the girl," Ruth says. Tears well and fall.

I look to the trees. The sky. Could walk off and never look back.

But there's a girl in a pit.

"Your high minded stupidity is going to kill her. But I'll get the jack and tire tool."

Chapter 42

On the night of Thursday August 7th, 1986, Horace Wycliff Leathers learned the citizens of Polk County had fired him. Leathers telephoned challenger Stanley Ulrich at one in the morning. The phone rang seven times and Leathers was about to hang up when the line clicked.

"Sheriff Ulrich?"

"Uh, not yet. Who's this?"

"Leathers. Congratulations. The numbers are in. I wish you the best."

"I appreciate the call. And I look forward to liaising with your office in the interim period to ensure the citizens of Polk County are best served."

Of course. Yippee whatever. Goodbye.

Leathers was not a man to find solace in alcohol or religion. He trusted the people to make a good choice or to regret it if they were wrong, and either way would be good enough for him.

He went to bed. Woke the next morning at dawn knowing he had three and a half weeks to clear out. Of all the official business still waiting for the sheriff of Polk County, one item rose to the top of Leathers' priorities.

He wanted to know one thing.

Why?

Of course, he'd gone on record that Lemuel Carter Sr.'s death was a homicide. Not being able to bring charges or even admit he had a suspect had left him open to attack.

There was nothing quite like the feeling... He'd worked night and day to bring a killer to justice. The only spare time he had to read was on the toilet. Every day, every crap, a new article about how he led a do-nothing department.

Nothing like it.

After Josiah left his fingerprints on the desktop, Leathers and Marcy compared them to every print taken from the house. They went back twice to search for more.

Nothing matched Josiah.

Estranged Mrs. Carter came home to collect life insurance and settle the estate. She allowed the department to fingerprint her. They compared her marks to those they hadn't yet cleared, and she matched them all. There were no prints left.

The killer left no trace. Except on Lemuel.

Leathers, along with Marcy and Sam, canvassed Pankey Lane and came up empty. After studying a map, they knocked on every door between the Swain house and Main Street Hardware. Several folks had seen a boy on his ten speed. None could identify Josiah with certainty, nor could any say they saw him at a specific time.

Without being able to search the Swain household for evidence, Leathers was out of moves. It rattled him. If a killer didn't confess, wasn't seen by a witness, or didn't leave evidence, there was nothing anyone could do about it.

Murder with impunity was not merely possible. Given a halfways smart killer, it was likely. What spooked Leathers was that Josiah was only sixteen years old. He hadn't even acquired skills, yet.

Then again, no evidence linked Josiah Swain to the murder.

Was Leathers wrong?

Or was the lack of evidence... skills.

Leathers came to an evidentiary dead end. He exhausted all possible avenues to get the probable cause he needed for the search warrant. In the end, Leathers admitted he could be mistaken about Josiah. He went back to square one with the Carter investigation but couldn't identify any other persons of interest.

The newspaper was relentless. Although there had only been a half dozen news stories about the Carter murder, it seemed every couple of days a new piece cast Leathers in a poor light.

One evening he stopped at the grocery store for a few items before heading home. He ran into the newspaper publisher, Les Carry.

There were few customers and only one checkout line open. Leathers stood behind Carry.

"What'd I do to piss in you folks' Wheaties?" Leathers said.

Carry turned half back to him, shrugged.

It wasn't an idle question. Leathers wanted to know. A reporter Leathers had never heard of wrote the first stories. Joseph Miller. The newspaper then published anonymous letters to the editor that shared the same style.

"What's with your guy? Who is he, anyway?"

"Who?"

"Miller."

"He's been here a couple years. Corporate sent him."

"Corporate? I thought it was your paper."

Carry shook his head.

"I'm a minority shareholder. I'm lucky to have a job. When the fifty-one percent owner says his son is coming to cut his teeth on the ground floor, that means you've got a spy. A new boss. You don't control anything. That, Sheriff Leathers, is why you're getting beat up."

Out of a job in a couple weeks, Leathers cleared his schedule for one last investigation. He went home, took off his brown and tan uniform and replaced it with denim and a white cotton shirt.

He massaged one of his wife's black wigs onto his head. Threw on a baseball cap with an adjustable band to accommodate the added girth. Then he sat outside the newspaper until Miller left.

Leathers followed the man to his home. He waited three hours and peed twice into a two-liter Coke bottle. Then Miller emerged dressed to the nines and with a snap to his step. Leathers tailed him through residential streets. As Miller made his final turn, Leathers guessed the house he'd stop at. The whole truth of his election loss was clear.

Stanley Ulrich hadn't played dirty.

Sheriff Horace Wycliff Leathers had crossed the wrong woman: Justine Moon.

Two years earlier, in August, she'd called the Sheriff's office wanting to press charges. An eighty-eight-year-old woman named Dungy had taken her Papillon—a fluffy ten-pound dog with the attitude of a lion—out for a whiz.

Justine Moon was a runner who continued her training schedule deep into her pregnancy. The first trimester had been difficult. Her energy was down. But it returned in the second trimester. Then, seven months pregnant, she watched the Los Angeles Olympics. It was the first in history to include a women's marathon.

Justine found her motivation. She increased her distance despite the human being growing in her womb. That day, she felt pain radiate down her left leg.

She also noticed she was sweating faster, and heavier.

Justine Moon was a stream of consciousness communicator. Leathers had wished she would say why he should arrest eighty-year-old Dungy. Moon got around to it.

Dungy had lost control of her little white demon Papillon. Upon seeing Justine hobbling along, it yipped at her.

"Did the dog bite you?"

"No."

"Then what's the problem?"

"I miscarried. That dog caused my miscarriage."

"Uh."

Leathers declined to arrest Dungy.

Later he'd heard that Justine Moon had followed through with a hundred-thousand-dollar civil suit. The judge threw it out.

Watching Joseph Miller practically dance his way to Justine Moon's doorstep, Leathers understood.

Once more, it all came down to dirty elbows.

Everybody was flat evil—and if he didn't laugh about it, there'd be no way to take it.

Chapter 43

Burly Worley, rest his evil soul, paid extra for the full-size spare tire. We haul ass with Leroy dead and Josiah working on it in the shotgun seat. Ruth sits with Leroy and Stinky Joe, who hasn't said a word since the shootout, in the back seat.

I said we ought to leave Leroy, and Ruth said he has a mother and a wife and children. So he fouls the air in the Suburban, and Ruth rides next to a corpse.

Mae, Morgan, Bree, and baby Joseph are in the second seat.

This time I know I ripped my back muscles to hell. Had to move the gold to lift the platform to lower the spare tire. Then move the gold back. All while Ruth begged Josiah to talk about the girl, where he put her, is she still alive, all that.

Josiah smiled at her.

Discombobulating: Josiah never let off a lick of electric, nor red.

"Can't you drive faster, Baer?" Ruth says.

I push the pedal a touch, so she feels it. But getting pulled over for speeding now would be akin to sewing a pocket in your underwear, for stupid.

I recall a situation where I didn't see the red because I didn't want to see it. Tell yourself you love a woman, you'll see her smile, not the gun she has leveled at your mess.

But Josiah was carrying a pistol the whole time. Every single moment was deception. Not a lick of red. I kept my suspicion up the whole while—but he played me so good I thought he was the moral fella that I wasn't.

And it isn't the curse waning. Not with me about electrocuted when the dogs were ready to rend me at Stipe's fight circle.

There's no account that makes sense. Except the one. Josiah don't perceive good and evil. For him, there's only what he wants and what he doesn't. There's no code higher.

And me? I fret on whether I'm human at all. Especially with all the killing. No better than Josiah: I had a bad impulse and rode it all the way to twenty-some dead. If I ever was a good man, I'm not no more.

Except I don't buy that. If the whole world was mad and I was sane, they'd just flip the words.

And that's precisely what happened. Used to be, a man would call out evil and his neighbor pronounced it right and good. Now his neighbor says, look at you, all high and mighty.

Killing evil men doesn't make me less human. Makes me more. Every damn one of us ought to burn with outrage. Every one of us ought to destroy the evil where it crops up. But they tell us to sit back and let the lawman handle it. Or better yet, tolerate it. Those evil people got feelings. Those evil people didn't have it so easy like you. Evil knows all the excuses. Without we destroy it, we got no virtue. Only misery and death.

"Map says turn up here. We'll catch the highway back to Cookeville. They have a hospital."

"No," Mae says. "I'm through. The kids are through. Leave us in town before you get on the road."

Josiah gurgles a laugh.

"She's right," Ruth says.

I try to piece it together. How we'll work it out and stay a family. I been a daddy all twenty hours, and blew it.

You'd think a woman would understand why a man has to hold the line.

"Sure, Mae. Accourse. I saw a hotel off the exit. A couple. That good?"

"That's good, Baer."

Nothing like the voice of a let-down woman, make a man cringe. But to do other, I'd have to be other, and I ain't.

We arrive at a nothing town with a Motel 6, a pair of stop lights, a BP and a Citgo. Late afternoon. Got my eye peeled for coppers but traffic is nothing. Josiah's front seat is near horizontal, so I pull right up. Open the door and Mae says, "Baer, uh, I'll check in alone, okay?"

I'm covered in dirt and grease from changing the wheel, and blood underneath. But it isn't that. Mae has a cast to her brow. She's shut down the thinking factory.

"Uh. Alrighty. Hold on." I cross to Josiah's side, open the door, the glove box, and pull out the Suburban owner's manual. Remove the paper part from the canvas case. At the liftgate I look around. All clear. Open it, fill the canvas with gold. Bag weighs ten pounds if an ounce.

"Mae, c'mere. Mae, darlin'. I want to be your father and take care of you, but you're a grown woman and don't owe me nothing. Your mother and me delivered you to a bad situation."

"You don't have to—"

"I spent all day believing you betrayed me with the gold. That you and Ruth was in it together."

Her face dances angry.

"But now I know it was Ruth and them coppers. And maybe Ruth wasn't even after the gold. I don't know anymore. It is what it is. Not what it ain't. Or is rarely so. I can't abandon you. Don't want to and couldn't live with myself if I did. But if you want to take off because it's better for you and the kids, here's your chance.

I'll be a couple hour. No, tell you what. You stay all night and I'll check back tomorrow. I'll come back with new wheels and a fresh start west. But if you want to leave, there's more than a hundred thousand dollars of gold in this case. That's a new start for you, where ever you want to go."

Mae's face paints red and her eyes tear. She hasn't slept much either and if there's a God above he'll give her peace and let her brain work to make a good call.

"Take this," Mae says. She pushes a handful of fiat paper in my hand. "That's about half what I got for the coins."

I put the canvas bag of gold in both her hands.

Chapter 44

After killing Lemuel Carter Sr., Josiah improved. His compulsions were rare. He found he could enjoy murder on his own, without them.

Regardless, more deaths by firecracker would push the limits of Polk County's credulity. During the year after Carter's death, Josiah worried someone else would commit murder by firecracker. The new sheriff might reopen investigations into the first three.

No one did, and it confirmed an awareness that dawned within him. Josiah noticed other people seemed to exist at lower thresholds of power. Some were meek as kittens. They padded around and hid when dark clouds thundered. Others were scheming and deceptive, but still weak. They wanted to lurk. Avoid confrontation but manipulate people or situations to get what they wanted. Still others sought confrontation. They enjoyed putting other people in their place. The last category... Josiah only knew two people in the very last domain, those who took life.

Him and Ernest.

He couldn't fathom how weak it must feel to exist on any of the lower levels.

Rummaging through books at a Goodwill store, Josiah found a copy of *Helter Skelter*, by Vincent Bugliosi. The book detailed the work of Charles Manson.

Josiah read it.

Helter Skelter alerted him to an amazing genre of how-to books about mass murder and serial killing. He read them all and soaked in their lessons. He couldn't stop reading, and at night as he drifted to sleep, couldn't resist plotting.

The most profound lesson he learned: police were getting good at connecting dots between murders. Once they had a clear picture of a killer's motive, they could link different homicides. One woman might have died by stabbing. The next, strangulation. The third, drowned in heavy cream. If they each had short red hair and were staged in various poses of sexual humiliation, they likely belonged to the same killer.

Most serial killers had difficulty camouflaging motive. Josiah theorized serials kept killing because they sought the same satisfaction, each time. Take Ted Bundy. Rejected by a pretty rich girl, he spends four years rebuilding himself. He becomes a scholastic and political force that checks off all the right boxes to win her back. He makes a trip to San Francisco, surprises her and she falls back in love with him. He proposes. She accepts.

Then he spurns her. The whole engagement, a ruse. He'd spent years rebuilding himself and his image only to win her love and break her heart, as she had broken his.

Afterward, the killings. The pretty rich girl had been a brunette with long hair parted in the middle. Suddenly college girls all over the area start going missing. Bundy learned to exact the same satisfaction without the four-year period of grooming.

The problem for Bundy: He killed the same victim, over and over. It was easy for authorities to connect the killings, and then, the evidence.

Like the others, Josiah was unaware of exactly why he felt the compulsions he did. He considered himself unique, built for a specific purpose. If he had been built to paint, painting would be fulfilling. For Josiah, taking life felt good.

And reading the books, he realized he was not alone. Others had walked these grounds before him. Josiah would learn from their mistakes.

To master his art and evade capture, Josiah would need to vary his process. He would also have to camouflage something he was only beginning to grasp: the reason he had to kill. It must appear different each time.

Otherwise, tiny mistakes would accumulate. Detectives would add a partial footprint from one killing with a sighting of medium sized male at the next. The next incident would add his skill with a handgun at large distances. Or the color of the car leaving the scene. Each outing would flesh out the definition of the killer, and after enough entries, the description would be full. The picture, clear.

But that would never happen if the killings were never added up.

Josiah needed to keep the victims different in type. The staging of each scene would be random. Or appear random. The method, gun shot, stabbing, strangulation—that had to change each time.

If he controlled the basics, no detective would ever add them up.

Josiah thought about the supposed genius, Ted Bundy. He loved to murder white-skinned college brunettes with long hair parted in the middle. What a dumbass. Throw in a red headed mother of five. A bald black man.

Inspiration sparked within Josiah.

He'd read so many books and studied so many killers, why not do a tribute tour? One victim matching each of the hall of fame killers...

Josiah's return foray occurred in 1989. Florida electrocuted Ted Bundy on January 24, and Josiah felt called. What a perfect time to unleash himself.

He was a freshman at the University of North Carolina at Asheville, studying criminal justice. He'd thought Ted Bundy's plan to become a lawyer was good thinking, and planned to do the same.

He lived in a cement block dormitory. A cube with two desks, chairs, and beds. He had a wall closet. His roommate was a nerd with severe acne, long hair, and halitosis. Josiah tried to avoid being in the room during waking hours.

He'd worked at the Benton Main Street Hardware through his high school career. Before graduating, Josiah bought a car to help him remain employed while attending college. He'd chosen the most nondescript, forgettable vehicle on the lot. A 1984 light blue Ford Tempo. At college he picked up work at an Ace Hardware. Between his twenty hours a week there and his eighteen credit hours of course work, he had little time to spare.

The compulsion, now an avocational calling, held his focus together. The need was getting hard to hold back. He'd mentally replayed his first three murders thousands of times, and they were stale. He needed new material.

Ted Bundy was gone.

Time for a new player to haunt the scene.

But not like Ted Bundy. There would be dozens of copycats in January alone. No, the attraction Josiah felt now was for the Zodiac.

Josiah didn't need to revisit his books to know exactly which Zodiac death scene he wanted to recreate. Of all the serial killers he could mimic, Zodiac offered the most interesting choices. Plus, none of the Zodiac's crimes were too complicated. That made sense because Josiah didn't want to take huge risks while getting back into the game.

While finding kids at Asheville's lovers' lanes was enticing, the murder of cabbie Paul Stine was a better fit. Simple, and the necessary ingredients were at hand.

Josiah rigged a makeshift holster by bending a coat hanger with several zig zags. He wrapped the end that inserted into the gun barrel in duct tape. The holster would conceal the .22 under his pants. The bent hanger came up over his waistline, folded under his belt, then slightly back above the belt. When the .22 was in place, its weight locked the holster so it wouldn't move.

He wore a reversible winter coat, black on one side and forest green on the other. Underneath, a hooded sweatshirt. He placed a hand towel in the cargo pocket of the coat.

He walked along King Street to Merrimon Avenue. After two and a half miles, standing in the middle of Asheville, at nine at night, he waved to a cab that was crawling by.

He jumped in. Looked through the battle-scarred plastic partition. The driver was a woman.

"Where to?"

Josiah hesitated.

A woman?

He'd expected a man. From experience, men were easy to kill. But a woman?

Emma Swain had protected him. She'd taken Ernest's notebook. She'd lied to back up his alibi when Josiah came under suspicion for Lemuel Carter's killing. She'd worked two and three jobs to provide for him. Somehow, Josiah sensed this woman in the driver's seat might be doing the same for a kid of her own.

And women were soft and the one he'd dated off and on in high school had tasted good everywhere he'd tasted her. Women liked to cuddle and say things like, "I feel safe with you." And it sounded good to the ear because some deep biological aspiration responded. He was supposed to protect women. That's what men were supposed to do.

And yet ....

If Josiah only killed men, it would become a signature. It would link his crimes together.

"Where to?"

"Oh, sorry. My coat was making noise. Man, it's cold out. Saint Mary's Episcopal Church."

"Over on Charlotte?"

"That's right."

"Oh. What's going on there tonight?"

"Theater group. You know the show. We did *A Christmas Carol* all through December. We decided to wait until after New Years for the cast party."

"Uh-huh." She put the car in gear. "Yeah. I didn't hear about it."

"We didn't get a good turnout. Mostly people from the church."

They were there in five minutes.

"You sure you got the date right?"

"I dunno. Guess I'm here first. What time is it?"

"Ten after nine."

"Well, if you don't mind, swing around by the entrance. I'll wait at the door a few minutes and if no one shows, I'll walk home."

"You sure? Don't look like anyone's coming."

Josiah looked outside at the church, then through the other windows. No one in the area. No headlights. Nothing.

"It's not until nine thirty. Sorry, thought I said that."

He looked at her brown eyes through the mirror, partly obscured by a roughed-up area of the plastic partition. This was going to be harder than he thought. But the moment passed, and the compulsion steered him.

The woman slid open a window in the partition. He leaned forward as if to fetch his wallet and kept his eyes locked on hers, his smile friendly. He pulled the .22.

"Sorry. Tight jeans."

He pushed the safety off with his thumb before lifting the gun.

The woman's eyes narrowed. She smiled too.

Fake, like his. She reached across the seat, maybe to a purse. Maybe her own gun...

Josiah pushed the .22 through the divider. She screamed. He aligned the barrel with her head. She jerked toward his arm. He squeezed the trigger three times.

The blast wasn't as bad as he expected, confined. The .22 was small and the partition kept most of the sound on the driver's side.

The woman slumped. For the moment there was almost no blood.

Josiah looked around outside the cab. No one was about.

He shoved the pistol under his waist, but the barrel didn't find the duct-taped wire holster. He prodded. Nothing. Stuck it again. He looked around, outside. One more try. Miss.

He stuffed the pistol in his outer coat pocket. He'd put it away later.

Josiah found all three shell casings and put them in his pants pocket.

He dangled his arm through the partition, grabbed the woman's purse, and pulled it through. He removed her wallet, then a small pistol. Josiah held it to the light from the church. A revolver. Good. In the future, he wouldn't have to pick up brass.

Josiah removed the hand towel from his coat pocket and wiped down the purse. He left it in the back seat. Then he cleaned everything he'd touched inside the cab. Last, with the towel between his hands and the handle, he opened the door.

Unlike the Zodiac killer, he did not leave a note.

He walked two miles back to the dorm. Before going inside, he found his Tempo in the parking lot and hid the new gun and the .22 under the seat.

He walked inside to his room and went to bed.

Josiah's next outing was six months later. He'd decided to stay in Asheville year-round and take summer classes, so he could finish in three years.

One Saturday in July, he set out at five in the evening. He drove five and a half hours to Thundering Springs Lake outside of Dublin, Georgia. After consulting a map, he tooled at normal speeds on South Lake Drive. Spotting a turn that approached the water, he took it.

His headlights reflected off the glass of a parked car. Josiah turned around. Another quarter mile down the road, he entered a secluded drive that approached the water. He parked there, with the front of the car ready to exit. He walked with a hand at eye level, aided by moonlight, overland. He found the parked lovers on a narrow blacktop road between trees.

Careful lest his feet betray him, he approached. He heard them inside. The car had a worn-out suspension. He listened a long moment, thinking about a change of plan.

The girl really seemed to be taking a pounding in stride.

No... Stick to the plan.

Josiah shined a flashlight inside through the window. It was down a crack for ventilation. Josiah said, "Roll down the window, son. It's against the law for you to be here."

The window came down the rest of the way and with the .38 he'd taken from the cabbie, Josiah shot the boy and the ... boy.

Nice, Josiah thought. That'll sure look like a different motive.

He drove home and went to bed.

Josiah killed randomly, and each time learned more. From his criminal justice studies, he discovered better ways to disguise his activities. He learned how law enforcement had identified and captured each of his predecessors. And what frustrated investigators about the scenes of the killers they never caught.

But all was not sunshine and roses.

By the time he worked at the Gleason police, he'd grown tired of randomness. Year after year of sudden interactions, pulling out a gun or a knife. A bullet, a few slices and stabs, and then it was over. He couldn't take mementos. He couldn't revisit the scene. His victims all died so fast.

Josiah wanted something more.

He wanted a relationship.

Chapter 45

Waking up, Sophia took a long time to realizing her location. She didn't know until she felt the pinch of the binding at her legs and her hands locked together at the wrists.

Finding it difficult to breathe, she sensed blood clotted her nose. She couldn't tell if her eyes were open, so she blinked. Her left eye remained cemented shut. Her throat was raw, and every time she swallowed it felt like there was a lump in her neck. No light came from the hole. She extended her arms about her head, searching for the wall corners, but there were none.

Had he buried her in a different pit?

She couldn't remember what had happened. Sophia took stock of her body. She lay on a blanket, uncovered, naked but for the denim at her ankles. Bound as before, her feet were higher than her head. In the blackness she wasn't sure what was level, but she felt off-kilter. Sophia moved her legs and a muscle spasmed in her shoulder. She stopped. Her neck rested at an awkward angle.

A shiver started at her center and undulated through her. While she had been in the pit, her starving body had withdrawn blood to the core and reduced functions to conserve energy.

As full awareness came upon her, Sophia remembered her captor had thrown her. She had landed on her head and shoulder. She seemed to have kept the same position until waking. Her neck and shoulder muscles felt torn.

She clamped her teeth and straightened her body. Her feet found the wall and she understood: He'd thrown her in with her head landing on the toilet side of the pit. Sophia sat up. Her brain pulsed white flashes of agony. She'd throw up if anything was in her stomach.

Sophia concentrated on breathing. Being alive, *right now*. When her consciousness felt stable and the pain a little farther away, she reoriented herself in the pit.

She smelled soap on her skin and waves of memories crashed through her. He'd used a large yellow sponge, like to wash a car. He forced her to stand against the stone foundation. He stared at her breast while he scrubbed back and forth. The sponge dried. The rubbing burned. He dipped into soapy water and made her part her legs. He scrubbed the insides of her thighs. Each time he pushed hard into her groin with his thumb, before rubbing down her leg again. He watched her face each time he shoved his thumb inside her. She gave him no reaction. Finally, he stood behind her, raised her arms, and wiped the sponge over her armpits.

He stepped away from her while she still faced the wall, then cold, fresh water splashed over her shoulders, front and back. She shivered. The flow of water stopped, and she heard the clang of an empty bucket. She stood in a muddy puddle. He wrapped her in a towel. It was terrifying and sensual. She couldn't fathom the disparity between his touch and everything else that screamed harbingers of death.

If he had only been nice, she would have been attracted to him. That confused her.

He posed her like before at the edge of the pit, face angled toward the ceiling. He told her to move sideways, back and forth, and disappeared behind the bright lights.

After a few minutes he returned. Sophia anticipated a kindness like the last time, before he returned her to the hole. Instead, holding her cheek in the palm of his hand, he balled his fist and smashed it into her face.

Thinking of it now, Sophia wondered if he'd broken her cheekbone. Her whole face felt swollen and she barely had the power to move her eyelid.

She breathed in.

I'm alive.

She'd found hope believing if she could buy enough time, she would someday lull her captor into complacency. She would locate his mistakes and exploit them when he least expected.

But he had to give her enough moments to make that happen. He'd gotten over his reluctance to touch her. Maybe it hadn't been fear at all. Maybe it was the way he killed girls.

His ritual.

In her heart, Sophia knew she wouldn't get another chance. She had to escape.

She remembered her thought when she climbed out of the pit last time: If she left her feet unbound, he wouldn't notice until she threw him into the pit. She could run for the shovel and hit him with it while he climbed out.

But going that route meant she'd be committed. If she couldn't find the shovel, she'd have to improvise and find something else. Her fate would come down to her cleverness in a single moment of terror. After days and days of malnourishment.

If she failed, he'd know she could get out of her bindings when she wanted. He might kill her on the spot. If not, he'd think of a better way to secure her.

She couldn't risk it. She had to find the option that gave her the best chance of escape on the first try, with the least amount of risk.

Another strategy seemed to have more promise. If she could move the earth below the plywood floor, she could elevate it. Standing with her legs bent and her lower back firm against the ceiling, she was in a power stance. She might have the leg strength to topple the blocks holding the plywood in place above her. Then it would just be a matter of escaping the basement. Her fate wouldn't come down to a single split-second decision.

Sophia felt between dirt wall and blankets at the corner where she'd hidden the bobby pin. She found it and jammed the handcuffs free. She worked bobby pin point into the zip tie ratchet, thankful her captor had not added another. She ground it until the tension loosed, then pulled the tie off her legs. She removed her cutoff pantlegs.

She folded the blankets so they'd take less space and moved them all to the toilet end. She stood the plywood on its side and felt along the dirt floor for the dimensions she'd arrived at last time. Sophia ground her fingers into the packed earth.

It tore like dragging her nails into baked mud. The dirt crumbled a little under her fingernails, but it would take a year to move an inch.

Sophia thought of the water bottles. The water would soften the dried dirt and the plastic screw top would scrape it. She felt along the wall to the water bottles and removed one from the plastic netting. Opened it and drank. The sensation of the cool water running down her throat in the blackness transported her. Her body floated through space and her awareness blossomed. The sensation ended with the sixteen ounces of water.

She opened another and dumped part on the area she intended to remove. Then she used the empty bottle to grind into the wet dirt.

Something resisted the pressure.

Pushing her fingers into the mud, Sophia felt a pliable yet solid object, thin like a string. Lifting it, she felt along its dimensions.

It was a necklace chain with a pendant. Maybe some kind of polished stone.

Cradling it in her hands, Sophia rinsed it with more water. She wondered at the girl who had left it. How long ago?

Where had he moved her, after it was over?

Sophia wished she had something to hide in the pit.

So the next girl wouldn't feel so alone.

You can't think that way.

She rubbed the necklace in one of the blankets and when it was dry, placed it around her neck. Sophia resumed digging and her mind cleared. She stopped.

Water pallets: She'd seen them at Sam's Club. Pallets stacked on pallets. Water was dense and heavy, and at Sam's they stacked pallets four high. The bottles could withstand tons of weight.

Her captor had left her a dozen bottles of water.

Sophia removed each from the plastic web and positioned them along the sides of the pit. They would support the plywood. In the middle she placed the blankets, folded with another row of bottles between. She hoped the blankets would support the bottles while she lifted the plywood in place on top.

She lowered the plywood flat on the bottle tops. Solid. The plywood pressed flush against the back wall of the pit and on each side. If she made sure to press downward, and not to the open side, her new floor would hold.

Sophia crawled on top of the plywood and shifted to the far end, where support was best.

She straightened her legs.

Perfect!

She came to full pressure against the plywood ceiling before straightening her legs.

Bracing her hands to her knees, Sophia pushed with all her might. Vertebrae popped. Her brain throbbed with pressure. The plywood roof shifted, but the weight was too much. She couldn't raise it.

Sophia rested on her knees. She had moved the ceiling. Progress! The euphoria of hope made her strength wax, as if all she needed was some blood circulation.

She held the necklace at her breast. This was it. Everything came down to moving these blocks. Every ounce of her being, of her life… she needed it all in this moment.

Sophia again placed her lower back to the plywood ceiling and straightened her legs. Instead of trying to lift it higher, she adjusted her stance. She shifted the plywood and all the blocks on top an inch to the side.

She stopped for a moment to reorient herself. Was she moving the plywood closer to the foundation wall?

Facing the toilet end, the foundation was on her left. She was moving the roof to the right.

She did it again. Again. Again.

When her strength waned, she rested.

Sophia sensed a different quality to the air. A difference in the ambient sound. Almost like… wind?

Feeling along the plywood's edge, she discovered she'd created a small gap between the pit and the plywood. Through it, she could fit her fingers up to the pad of her hand.

Sophia Ellen Whitcombe growled. Her energy surged and her eyes went wide in the darkness. She drove her back to the plywood and thrust, thrust, thrust, grunting each time. *I Will Not Die Here I Will Not Die Here I Will Not Die Here.*

The edge of the plywood cut into her back. Cool air rushed into the pit. Sophia looked upward and detected a faint difference in the blackness. She reached above and found empty space.

Standing, she placed her hands on the edge of the pit and the plywood and pushed until her legs swung free. She lifted one then the other out of the pit and sat dumbfounded on the side, next to the foundation.

She heard her father.

Every environment has its resources.

She was in a new environment ....

Then she remembered her captor's voice, saying he'd rigged the house with explosives.

He'd said he padlocked and chained the basement door.

She thought of the basement windows. Even if she could get to them, they were too narrow for her to wriggle through.

She placed her hand on the foundation wall. She couldn't move stone.

The joists... she could use the cement blocks and plywood to build a platform, like she'd used the water bottles. On it, she could use the shovel and maybe the metal from the device that held the white lights to batter loose a couple floor boards...

But first, it made sense to try the door. He could have underestimated her and failed to lock it.

Sophia stood, walked short steps to the floodlights. She found a switch. If her captor was near, he might see the basement lights illuminated. She would pray that he wasn't near.

"God?"

Sophia flipped the switch.

She had to close her eyes. The brightness was sickening. She squinted, but she couldn't turn it off because she needed to see if she was walking into traps.

Sophia redirected the powerful lamps toward the stairwell. She picked up one and carried it under the steps to look for hidden wires or explosives. None. Next, she adjusted the light and looked upward at the joists. There was a thin white line she thought was the electric wire for the lights, but nothing else.

She heard a sound like distant thunder. She stopped. Waited. Footsteps above her. A sound like chains.

He was back!

Sophia turned off the light. She ran to where she remembered the shovel. Tripped. Sprawled out and grasped the shovel handle. Hurried back to the stairs. The door opened. Ready to swing with all her might, she held the shovel over her head. Her life came down to this one moment. She would kill her captor and save herself. She saw her father's eyes, gazing with hope.

The man crept down the stairs. Was she too far forward? Would he look back toward her? No matter—he already knew she was free.

He turned on the two basement lights.

Sophia stepped out of the shadows and, as hard as she could, swung the shovel around at her captor's feet. The man snarled and fell onto the steps. She lifted the shovel again and he rolled toward her, fell over the edge of the steps and down upon her. She tried to swing the shovel again, but he was already on top of her. Sophia adjusted her swing midair but smashed the shovel into the steps. Her captor stood and punched her in the face. Her head snapped backward. He punched her again and she fell. He kicked her belly and she lost her breath. He kicked her again. She felt him lift her head, by the hair, and slam her to the floor. It didn't hurt.

It didn't hurt at all.

Sophia felt her mind yielding to darkness. She fought to stay aware, but she heard him behind her head.

She felt his fist connect with her skull, and she saw no more.

Chapter 46

Late afternoon. Eyes burn with tired. Stomach's a fist. Haven't had a drink in—

Mae's not here.

"Ruth, hand me that jug. Ought to be on the left there, all the way."

She lifts it. Frowns. Puts it down.

"Ruth, I been stilling all my life. Drinking half my sustenance every day. I don't get some hooch in my gullet I'm liable to—

"Here." She passes it forward.

"Give me some," Josiah says.

"Go ahead."

Ruth pulls the cork and shifts forward on her knees, tries to get the jug comfortable at Josiah's head. We got his seat laid back so he'll choke to death if he gets a pull.

"You got to lift his head."

"Pull over, Baer," Josiah says. "Help me drink. I'll tell you what—" he winces— "what I know."

Josiah has his eye on death. I grab a handy exit, cut right and stop the vehicle in a gravel lot with no buildings in sight.

Put down the windows and kill the engine. Get out, lift Josiah's seat a bit, check the tourniquet on his leg. He still drips blood but hardly enough to kill him. It's the hole in his armpit and all the damage inside that's done him.

"Take a swig."

I hold the jug at his lips and watch with pride as he gags on the high proof tonic. I pull the jug. He finishes his swallow and says, "More." Grins. Eyes roll.

"No more!" Ruth says. "Where's the girl?

"Sophia." Josiah smiles. Eyes closed. "This one was Sophia."

"Where is she?" Ruth says.

"Give me another drink."

I hold the jug at his lips. He swallows. Liquor spills around his mouth and on his neck. He gulps again. "Let that catch before you take more."

"Where's Sophia?" Ruth says.

"Gone."

The drink fortifies Josiah and he gets dreamy, with a mean force back behind his voice. "I knocked her out and buried her. She's gone by now. They never last a week."

"Animal!" Ruth screams.

I take the jug and step back from the door. Ruth climbs out from the back seat and takes my place in the open doorway. She pelts him with thin fists and he hiccoughs.

I gurgle off the jug like nobody ever say a word again. And when I stop and let the fire permeate the soul, I find I need another pull to make sense of the last. Josiah giggles like a country girl squeezing a dead frog. Ruth sobs and cusses and hits him, but I bet I killed more than him. I drink another gulp and the medicine hits my blood and the blood my brain, and I feel better. Can see the sense of what I did and am about to do.

I have to make him see it. One more pull for me, one for him, and I'll make him understand. Seems like all my troubles through all my life manifest from this one little evil piece of septic squash. If I can make him confess his errors, it'll justify my travails.

With a hand on Ruth's shoulder I ease her back. She falls to crossed legs on the gravel lot and hunches with her face in her hands. Shoulders shaking.

"Here," I say. "This is your last snurkle until we come to consensus, so make it count."

I hold the jug at his mouth and Josiah gulps. Rolls his eyes again and exhales hard.

"You're a killer, Baer. You're one too."

"I know it."

"And if I'm a killer and you're a killer, what's the difference?"

"Virtue."

He laughs like I worked his throat with a wood rasp. "You kill because you want. Like me. You got it in your bones."

Josiah spits blood with enough force to hit the windshield. Man with that vitality could make the ride to the hospital.

But we aren't going.

"I kill because I want. Because I can. And you kill for your dog. Just another way of saying you wanted to do it. Virtue has nothing to do with any of it."

His left hand moves and I pay attention. He roots in his pocket and takes out a red firecracker. Sits it on his lap and pulls a Bic lighter from the same pocket.

"I always wanted to know," Josiah says. "I took my first three with firecrackers. Kept this for last."

He flips the Bic and gets a flame. I grab his hand. Pull the lighter and burn my thumb.

"My uncle had my parents killed when I was ten. I got him with an M100 like this one. And after that I got a hog by her mailbox. Then the mailman. The power in one of these would surprise you."

"Sick," Ruth says. She lurches to her feet and elbows close to Josiah. She spits in his face. Punches him with the side of her fist.

Josiah coughs.

"You. Me," I say. "We're supposed to wreak havoc. Have no conscience. But outward, to protect the little woman at your back. Supposed to be you and her against the world. But you're too weak to go after the real evil. You find the very one you're supposed to protect, the weakest, and most helpless, and empty your vileness on her. Damned abomination."

I drop the Bic, grab Josiah's collar and drag him. Bonk his head on the door jamb and drop him to the gravel. He cusses and moans and laughs. "You know what I always wanted to know?"

I grab the firecracker from his hand. Pry his mouth open and shove it in. Undo my belt and wrap it around his head with the fuse stuck out his mouth. The latch doesn't line with a hole so I twist it under and over thrice.

Yank it tight.

"This what you want to know?" I say.

Josiah nods.

Look for the Bic. Ruth got it in her hand. We lock eyes and make the love of hate and anger.

Woman flicks the Bic. Holds flame to fuse.

Josiah smiles and belly laughs through his nose, and I wish it was fear but it ain't. Sparks follow the fuse into his mouth. I jump forward, pull Ruth back, back, fast as we can without turning away because we have to see the evil die.

In a red boom flash, the top part of Josiah disappears.

Blood and parts spatter the Suburban and Ruth and me. We walk to the body while red and gray soup rains like a plague from Exodus.

I got Ruth's hand in mine and the grit she showed... the desperation for justice... I squeeze her hand. She turns into me, buries her head in my shoulder and sobs.

I feel good about this killing.

Real damn good.

Chapter 47

Sophia Ellen Whitcombe made her peace in absolute darkness. She hadn't consumed any calories in days. After a period of profound hunger, her stomach felt satisfied on nothing. Her body switched to fat-burning. One of the side effects was a mental acuity unlike any she'd experienced in her short life.

She was *clear.*

Sometimes, she thought, no matter what we do to save ourselves, it is not enough. Sometimes evil is more prepared. Sometimes dark forces join and overwhelm us, even when we tell ourselves we are ready for the worst. Short of expecting trickery and deception out of every living being, there was no way to guard against it.

Sophia slept a lot. She was in a grave. When enough time passed that she was sure he'd left her for good, she resigned herself to a wasting, starving, death by dehydration. Yet each time she awoke she was happy for it. When panic overtook her, Sophia reminded herself that whatever was next, was next.

Even if death was a big nothing, it would be peaceful. A lot of people had already gone there. She wasn't as alone as she felt, and it was a blessing to have time to really think about things.

Alone in a pit, beaten, starving, she focused on being grateful. It helped.

More time with the people she loved wouldn't make the love more profound. The value was the love, not the time.

In church people said God was love, but it never made sense until now. She believed, but with little enthusiasm. She couldn't fathom God being good, while also being all powerful. Not if he let her rot in the basement of a house. Still, she made her peace. You don't have to agree to get along.

She moved little. Breathed little. Slept fitfully and dreamed of sunshine. She wanted to live, but each hour, less.

Sophia didn't know that in 1986, a man named Horace Leathers lost his job as sheriff of Polk County, Tennessee. She didn't know his shame and need to atone for failing to solve three murders drove him to the Saint Louis Police homicide section.

Nor did she know that those three interconnected cases haunted him afterward.

He knew he'd made mistakes that left justice unserved and lives in danger. He served St. Louis with distinction, partly because the three unsolveds informed his worldview. The evil of man. The personal failings of Horace Leathers. His burdens made him relentless. A better cop, at a price he wouldn't have chosen to pay.

Over the years, he followed the movements of his only suspect for the three cases. He knew Josiah Swain attended the University of North Carolina at Asheville. Knew that, after taking a degree in criminal justice, Josiah joined the Gleason police department.

October 2008 marked Detective Horace Wycliff Leathers' sixty-seventh birthday. It wasn't easy to walk away from the carnage of being a homicide detective. The obligation was strong. Yet his soul couldn't take any more.

Before putting his career to pasture, he felt a calling to take another look at Josiah Swain.

Leathers said he was celebrating retirement by visiting a town he'd always wanted to see, but despite its easy proximity, never had. Asheville, North Carolina. He wanted to see how the mega-rich lived at the Biltmore Estate. Wanted to stay at the Grove Park Inn. Walk the same halls as the stars of yesteryear.

It was a lie.

Horace Wycliff Leathers stayed at a Motel 6 on Interstate 40 between Asheville and Gleason. He went to Asheville because he wanted another stab at putting Josiah Swain behind bars.

In the morning, he walked a hundred yards to the BP gas station and bought a newspaper. He found a front-page story about the frantic search for Sophia Ellen Whitcombe, a teen missing for six days. She'd vanished on her walk home from school, in Asheville.

The reporter stated the police were working many lines of investigation but could provide no details.

It meant they didn't have anything.

The one lead they might have, they dismissed. A college student with a history of activism said he saw a girl climb into the back seat of a Gleason police car. The witness claimed this occurred on what was most likely the girl's route walking home from school. His description of the girl matched what they knew.

After his account hit the internet, Asheville and Gleason police held a joint press conference. They were still sifting through all the information received from the public. They'd received a lot of conflicting reports. The witness who stated he saw the girl get into a police car had an anti-police history they couldn't ignore. They had a lot of information they couldn't share at this point. Currently their best theory connected the missing girl with the poisoning incident in Gleason. Thoughts and prayers were requested not only for Sophia, but also the other victims. The murdered Gleason residents, FBI agents, and Gleason police.

Last, because two police officers, a young mother, and her children were also kidnapped, police retained hope Sophia was alive.

Leathers reread the article. He tried to conceive how Sophia participated in a shootout several days after she vanished.

The incoherent logic suggested police were struggling to build a working theory. They thought it would be easier to view the cases as connected.

Retired detective Leathers sat in the hotel room chair. He wondered at the synchronicity of the moment.

Had he come to Asheville for a purpose larger than what he'd thought?

Leathers scanned the paper for the names of the missing cops. They were not mentioned. He went to the hotel lobby and looked for the prior day's paper but didn't find one lying around. Finally, he asked at the desk. The attendant hadn't finished the crossword puzzle and had hung onto a copy.

Leathers searched it. He found a story naming Josiah Swain and Leroy Dupont as the missing Gleason police officers.

Josiah Swain.

Leathers thought of the possibilities.

- Swain and the girl were somehow involved. She was a part of the firefight and was kidnapped by this Baer fellow.
- Swain abducted the girl, took her someplace and murdered her. Then was abducted himself.
- Swain kidnapped the girl, took her someplace and kept her. Then was abducted.
- Someone else kidnapped the girl. The activist witness was trying to provoke enmity against the police.

The first option was too convoluted to embrace without significant evidence.

The second—the girl was already dead—seemed most likely.

The third was possible.

The fourth was possible.

Looking at it from another point of view, only one option meant that Leathers could do something about it. If Josiah Swain had taken the girl and she was still alive, then Leathers might find her. Remote, but possible.

Leathers thought it through.

If the witness was correct that it was a Gleason cop, and Josiah Swain was the cop, then he either killed her or stashed her somewhere. Killers evolve. It could be either. But if it was the latter, the girl could be out there somewhere, awaiting a killer who might never return because he had himself been abducted.

Leathers shook his head. If he didn't want this girl's death on his conscience, he had to put himself into Josiah's mind. If the girl was dead, the murder scene and body dump could be anywhere. But he was working from the premise the girl was alive, and if that was the case, she had to be somewhere Josiah felt safe.

Property.

Leathers returned to his room. In fifteen minutes, he showered and dressed. He tucked a Ruger in the small of his back and departed for the courthouse. He wanted to know Josiah Swain's safe places.

At the courthouse, he left his pistol in a locked gun box under the seat of his Ram truck. Inside, he searched the records and found Josiah Swain's home address. He could have used the phone book, but he wanted to learn if Swain had any other properties.

He didn't.

Leathers wrote down Swain's address and, after returning to his truck, consulted a road map. On the drive, he tuned the radio to an AM station, turning up the volume to overcome road noise. At the top of the nine o'clock hour, a female announcer said, *"The latest development in the case of the missing high school girl, Sophia*

Whitcombe. Another witness has come forward pointing at the Gleason police. More after the weather."

Leathers slammed his fist to the dash. He pulled into a gas station and waited for the story to return. After learning he should expect thunderstorms in the late afternoon, the newsreader continued.

"This is an Eyewitness News Four exclusive. Another witness has come forward in the case of missing sixteen-year-old Asheville high school student Sophia Whitcombe. The witness claims she was driving west on Interstate 40 when she noticed a police car in her rearview mirror. She said she worried she was speeding, so she slowed down. But instead of pulling her over, the police car passed her at a high rate of speed. The witness says she saw a young girl in the back of the car with a quote 'terrified look on her face.' Close quote. The witness notified Gleason police three days ago by telephone, and no one called her back. That's when she called Eyewitness News Four. Gleason police have not yet responded to this witness's claims. If she is correct, it means police have been searching for the missing girl in the wrong county. Next, how many lives does your fuzzy feline friend truly have? We asked the experts."

Leathers turned the radio down and studied his map while his truck engine idled. Interstate 40 led west out of Asheville and into the mountains.

Leathers looked up.

Should he continue to Josiah's house in Gleason, or try to track down something unknown, west?

It made sense that if Josiah Swain had taken the girl, he'd taken others. You don't learn to murder at thirteen years of age and retire at sixteen. If he was a repeat killer—and another big if—IF he didn't kill his victims immediately, he'd want to remove them from their surroundings. Both to make discovery less likely and to increase the ease of body disposal.

Leathers knew there were a lot of other ways it could have played out, but in one sense he was lucky. None of them mattered. The only way he could influence the outcome was if it had played out the way he thought. He would play the hunch like it was a fact. Returning his attention to the map, Leathers found the faint lines demarking counties. He searched west, within Jackson and Haywood for a symbol signifying a courthouse. He couldn't drive there and look for a big building because he didn't know which towns were the county seats.

Leathers pulled his cell phone from his jacket pocket and dialed 411 for information.

"City?"

"Yeah, I don't know. I need the locations and phone numbers for let's see... Haywood County register of deeds, and, uh, Jackson County register of deeds. That's all. Yes, North Carolina. Uh-huh. Uh-huh. Thank you. Say that again. What? A little louder. Okay, and the other. Uh-huh. Got it. Thank you. Good. No, goodbye."

Leathers took the first onramp to Interstate 40.

In a half hour, he drove into Waynesville and found the courthouse.

Forty-five minutes later he ascertained no Swain was in the index at the Haywood County register of deeds.

Leathers knew to keep his nose to the scent and not bother with sour moods. Haywood County was adjacent Buncombe County, where Josiah lived. He could have found a hiding place farther west. Leathers consulted his map and continued as planned to Jackson County.

He drove into Sylva and located the administrative building housing the sheriff, recorder of deeds, and tax office. Parking was plentiful, and the autumn chill put pep in his step. He found his way to the recorder of deeds. The woman behind the desk took his request, led him to the index books and a table where he could sit. He searched for Swain, and his gaze landed on a property listing.

A tingle climbed his spine. The trail was neither hot nor cold— it wasn't about proximity in time. The trail was *accurate*. He'd followed a hunch and found a fact.

He'd expected to find nothing, to return to Saint Louis after a few days of making no headway. Now he felt jazzed. His mind started firing, and he was thinking several steps ahead of himself. He walked away and realized he hadn't recorded the address. Returning to write it down, he decided to ask for help finding it.

The attendant at the desk was on the phone and avoided looking at him. Leathers said, "I need to know where this address is. It's time sensitive. Very time sensitive."

She looked at the paper. Pressed the headset mouthpiece to her shoulder. "Honey, hop back on Seventy-four headed west and, at a town called Bryson City, turn left on Twenty-eight. Bryson City's a town not a city." She averted her eyes, spoke into the phone. "Hold on a minute, Suzie, I got to help this man." She covered the mouthpiece with her hand. "After that you'll have to watch the numbers. We good?" She turned away from Leathers. "So listen, she was all up in *red paint*, and I said, 'I ain't going in there ... *hale* no.'"

Horace Wycliff Leathers pushed through the door.

The address numbers jumped in increments of five. When he passed a house without a number but in the right sequence, he figured he had the right place. Leathers drove another quarter mile, found a driveway he could turn around in, and sat for a few minutes.

The house had appeared unlivable. The roof was wavy, with extensive storm damage and missing shingles. The paint was peeling most everywhere. A window was out. The likelihood of anyone except a squatter living in the house was tiny.

Josiah Swain was missing; but it was not unknown for killers to work in pairs. Caution dictated Leathers approach the house on his guard. He drove back. Pulled into the driveway and sat with his window down and the engine off. Any other time, this is where he'd call backup. Operating on his own, he had no one to call.

His engine ticked. He exited the Ram truck. Closed the door by pressing it until it latched. Leathers drew his Ruger and doublechecked to ensure brass was in the pipe.

He imagined this being the death place of a girl, or many girls. They suffered at the hands of a monster he should have put in jail. Even if a miracle happened and he found Sophia, there were likely plenty of other horror stories borne of his failings. Other girls who had died because of Leathers' hubris and incompetence. His bad luck.

He looked at the rotten paint and wanted to throw up.

Leathers prepared himself to find a dead girl.

He studied the terrain, the unmowed grass turned gold and dry. The bowed porch. The sagging garage—oddly built like a barn with a sliding door but abutting the house. He hadn't seen anything like that since visiting Maine.

At the porch, Leathers stopped at steps made from giant sandstones resting on top of one another. He studied the crumbling mortar, then looked at a board—weathered and curling at the end. A half inch proud of the rest of the porch.

Leathers let out a long breath. Turned. Behind, the autumn leaves on hillside trees blazed orange and yellow.

He stepped off the sandstone steps and to the side, pushed away tufts of grass. He looked up under the porch.

"You slimy prick."

He saw plastic explosive, wired to a pressure switch. Step on the raised porch board, depress the switch, and die.

In the context of Josiah as serial killer, the explosive meant he was in the end stages. Killers often pass through phases, beginning with the excitement of daring to flaunt social rules they find beneath them. They don't think about getting caught or having a long career as a killer. They're impressed they have the balls to follow their personal evil wherever it leads them. Mature killers become obsessed with escape. They get good at leaving little trace. And late stage killers realize they can't continue forever. The mistakes accumulate, and they begin planning their demise. They decide to go on their own terms.

Planting a bomb on a porch where anybody might come along and step on it was an endgame action. There's no way to remain hidden after the bomb goes off. No plausible explanation for wiring your porch with plastic explosive. No way of blaming someone else.

Leathers assumed there would be more bombs.

Reason to be careful... but also to hurry. The plastic explosive meant Josiah wanted to defend the house. The odds of finding the girl had increased.

He could telephone Sylva police to come get her. But after a week of confinement, the extra twenty or thirty minutes could be the difference between life and death. And if he only called for support, why bother? If she was in the house, he wanted her out.

Now.

Leathers scanned the rest of the underside of the porch and saw no other devices.

He could navigate around this one, but maybe there was a better way. Leathers returned to his truck and retrieved a flashlight. He walked to the barn-like garage and, dragging his boot toes forward on the dirt, hoping to root up a mislaid mine, entered the barn. He turned on the light and examined the threshold of the entrance to the house.

Leathers wiped his brow and was surprised by the sweat.

He examined the door jamb, pressed it in several places, lightly at first, then with force. Satisfied it wasn't rigged, he looked through the window with his flashlight. He took in the floor, the kitchen area, and the downstairs entrance. The door was padlocked.

He saw the missing girl's picture in his mind and imagined her gasping her last breath while he sought his courage.

Leathers stepped backward, raised a booted foot and drove it through the door.

The dry-rotted wood crashed open. Leathers toppled forward. The explosion he feared didn't happen. He landed on his knees, inside, and balanced himself without setting off anything.

Drawing his Ruger, he stood at a ninety-degree angle to the padlock, and fired. It bounced but remained locked. He fired again and again. His ears rang. The padlock bottom fell from the top and he dropped the twisted metal from the holes.

The doorknob was ajar. It hadn't been latched, just held closed by the lock.

Leathers shined his light into the gap. No wires. Standing aside, he pulled the door. No resistance. With an aperture of an inch, he shined his flashlight inside. He pulled open the door.

He reached for the light switch and stopped. Rigging a switch was easy. He'd use his flashlight instead.

Step by step, he lowered himself into the cool, damp darkness. After six steps, he hunched so he could shine his light around the basement.

He saw the floodlights. The orange extension cord. An upside-down bucket. A sheet of plywood covered in blocks.

"Oh Lord!"

Leathers bounded down the steps. Raced forward and rested his flashlight on the foundation. He threw cement blocks left and right.

"Sophia, I got you! Hang in there."

He threw another block and another, mashing his fingers in the holes and bloodying the tips. Where was the next bomb?

Leathers didn't care.

With most of the blocks removed, he stood at the edge of the plywood and lifted. Those remaining toppled. He threw the sheet of plywood.

The girl was still, on her stomach, head twisted to the side. Her eyes closed, she had a smile on her face. The next thing he saw was her elbows.

They were dirty.

Horace Leathers lowered himself into the pit. Moved the girl sideways, took her in his arms, and sobbed.

Chapter 48

Sophia Ellen Whitcombe floated. She heard God approach, footsteps like concrete thunder. He lifted her, cradled her, and rained tears on her face.

She was home.

Sophia awoke.

Chapter 49

Can't leave two dead Gleason police officers on the road. Got to control when they're found, so I can make some distance. I drag Josiah to the Suburban.

Stinky Joe marks Josiah's death with ceremony: he leaps from the vehicle and takes a squat.

A car rolls by but the Chevy blocks view of the headless body. I wave. The driver waves back.

Ruth walks the perimeter of the gravel lot while I situate the bodies in the seats. Afterward, I wipe off as much blood as I can. Realize I haven't even looked at the clothes Mae bought for me, stowed by the gold. And I haven't had my cheeseburger yet. With a slosh of liquor in me, my appetite brightens, and my brain is strong.

I want to see the clothes. See what I got available for phase two.

Pop the latch and under a coat and fedora is a blue pinstripe in a hanging case. Plus a bag with a straight razor and a set of electric shears. I blink. Remember being twenty-something, selling life insurance to the folks and using their red to close the sale. Last I wore a suit.

I wash off with a cup of water and all I get is smeared. Stinky Joe comes back from an errand.

You hungry? Maybe we oughtta enjoy those cheeseburgers.

"Hungry? I'm liable to fall through my asshole and hang myself."

I eat a cold cheeseburger and give one to Stinky Joe. Fetch another bag and unwrap Joe a second helping.

I eat the fries.

It's finally what you wanted.

"What, going west? This isn't west."

Soon. You got to have patience.

"Soon. Eat up."

I scruff his head.

Ruth returns from her soul-searching walk. Her face wears the consequence of a life's big and tiny evils. Every one with a mark. Evening sun brings a glow, just the same.

"There's still hope," Ruth says. "Josiah was a liar. A killer. We need to call the police so they know it was him. They can search his house. They might find Sophia yet."

I reach her a cold french fry. She takes it.

"Cookeville's twenty minutes," I say. "Use a payphone?"

She nods. "But I'll have to say who I am, or they won't believe anything."

I offer her the paper container. "Better have another fry."

"You won't stop me?"

"They'll shut down this highway and every road for a hundred miles. And if you mislead them at all, you'll be part of what I did. They'll search houses. Bring in helicopters with night vision and thermo vision and all that Star Wars stuff. They'll hound me until I drop or turn myself in. I won't have a chance."

"The girl—"

I hold up my hand. "Five minutes ago, I thought all this cussed craziness finally gave us a chance. I saw you and me heading west. But things is rarely what they're not. And that girl's in a hole."

She holds my look. I offer a hand and she steps to me. Plant one on her lips.

What's losing her one more time?

* 302 *

"Let's get you to a payphone."

We drive with windows down to spread the stink of fresh dead men. Boys messed their drawers.

Ruth and Stinky Joe sit in the second seat; shotgun seat's soaked in blood.

I see the Cookeville sign and Ruth says, "It's top of the hour. See what's on the news."

I press the button.

"…miraculous luck is all I can say.' That was retired Saint Louis homicide detective Cliff Leathers, who earlier today found Sophia Whitcombe alive. The Asheville teen is recovering from her nine-day ordeal at the hospital, but she's in good care, as both of her parents are doctors. Next up: How many children died this summer in swimming pool accidents? Get the facts you nee—"

I turn off the radio. See Ruth's eyes in the rearview, washed clean with happy tears.

Get a room, you two, would ya?

Ruth looks at Stinky Joe. To me.

"You could use a bath," Ruth says.

Make a man sport a chub. "So could you."

From the Author

Thank you for reading **THE MUNDANE WORK OF VENGEANCE**. I hope you enjoyed it. The story continues in a series of fast-paced literary noir thrillers that take Baer Creighton (and you) to the American Southwest.

Book 3:   *PRETTY LIKE AN UGLY GIRL*

Luke Graves turned the family butcher business into an empire by cutting fat off the ledger as well as he cut meat off the bone.

He also learned many men sold beef, but few sold girls and boys. Demand was high—especially for the ones with brown skin—and supply, small.

Ten years later the family business included three sons and a distribution chain that delivered kids for any purpose throughout the western United States.

One evening, returning to Williams, Arizona from a pickup in Sierra Vista, the tire blows out. A chavo bolts the truck and runs for the plain. Cephus Graves takes him down with a deer rifle, then fires at a stray pit bull that catches his eye.

In the woods two hundred yards away, Baer Creighton looks up from his fire. He has a nose for evil men and he's found a clan of them. But he's met his match in Luke Graves.

Baer bleeds in Pretty Like an Ugly Girl.

Everyone bleeds.

Book 4: THE OUTLAW STINKY JOE (April 2019)

Stinky Joe survives the wild Flagstaff winter alone.

But with first melt, he succumbs to warm broth and sleeping pills, placed at the doorstep of a scheming prostitute at the vortex of a politician looking for an issue, a money-launderer wielding leverage, and his 83 year old meth-dealing target.

Stinky Joe learned as a pup: don't ever bite a man. He'll beat you near death. But cornered in a bath tub by a pothead with a gun, Joe goes outlaw.

Within hours the best and worst of Flagstaff are mobile. Sheriff's deputies, the meth dealer and his tracking dog, news crews, and Baer Creighton—with the FBI after him, seeking vengeance for yet another agent down.

Joe has survived the wild, but civilized man is a different kind of devil.

Wounded, hunted, and holed up, there's no way out for **The Outlaw Stinky Joe**.

GRAB TWO FREE BOOKS FOR YOUR GRIT LIT LIBRARY

Building a relationship with my readers is the very best thing about writing. If you enjoyed this book and would like to know about upcoming releases of Baer Creighton, Solomon Bull, or Angus Hardgrave books, join my email list. You'll get maybe two or three emails a year. I hate spam. Won't ever do it. If you get an email from me, it'll be worth reading.

Join the email list and you'll get a free download of **SOMETIMES BONE**.

You can find the signup sheet here:
http://www.claytonlindemuth.com/emaillist/

If you like to jaw with other grit lit readers, get book recommendations for awesome authors, ask me questions, or get an occasional advance review copy of a new release, then join my Facebook group, the **RED MEAT LIT STREET TEAM**. Once in the group, scroll through the recent posts, and you'll find a link to download a free copy of **STRONG AT THE BROKEN PLACES**.

You can find the join link here:
https://www.facebook.com/groups/855812391254215

ABOUT THE AUTHOR

Hello! I appreciate you reading my books—more than you can know. If you've read this far, you and I are fellow travelers. I suspect you sense something is not quite right with the world. It's not as good as it's supposed to be. We human beings aren't as good as our ideals. Yet, we prize and want to fight for them.

I do my absolute best to write stories that portray the human situation with brutal transparency, but also I strive to tell stories that are not as bleak as the human condition sometimes seems. There's no limit to the darkness. Light is rare. But it exists, and I hope when you complete one of my novels, you find your values validated.

I'm grateful you're out there. Thank you.

Remember, light wins in the end.

Made in the USA
Coppell, TX
27 November 2019

11999546R00185